I0779473

ISBN: 979-8-218-47280-1

This novel was created thanks to the use of open source programs. LibreOffice was used to write the novel, GIMP was used to create the cover, and both accept donations. Fancy fonts were found on DaFont.com, searching under the "100% Free" option: DSnet Stamped, Ebba Font, FairydustB, Gotica Bastard, Mechanical Fun, and Nadall.

DarknessOpera.com

I've done my best.

The rest is up to you.

CHAPTER ONE

Death and the Maiden

They're the exceptional ones, those whose livelihood comes from corpses, coffins, and other thanatotic delights.

Rudella considers herself *highly* exceptional. And why not? She owns a funeral home. But we're jumping far ahead of the hearse. Let's start at the beginning, or rather, at the more interesting beginning. When she was a Goth, Korean girl living in Conyers, Georgia.

If you're curious: "Rudella" goes "rue-DELL-ah".

As you can imagine, not many Asians set up camp in the Peach State. The (un)subtleties as to why suited Rudella. She was, and is, naturally interior; in location and temperament. A little air-conditioning didn't hurt, either. Neither did her piles of books and movies. Unless one fell on her, of course. Books came from the library on Green Street, where everyone knew her name, and mail-order catalogs. Movies came from her parents' rental shop: Rewind or Die. That wasn't a cheap pop for nostalgia, by the by.

Her parents knew the kind of world that was waiting to wreck their daughter with its horrors, so they loved her being an indoor cat. As long as she exercised. They were willing to raise a geek, not a statistic. Thus, everywhere she went, she went on rollerblades. Like running with rockets. Speaking of horrors, that was the genre she gravitated to, on page and screen. As you've so far seen, misery didn't pull her to the macabre. She fell into those violent delights and ends by herself. She liked the boobs, too.

Morbid curiosity captivated Rudella in her teenage years and, once a week, she got to hang out in a morgue. Attendants are a notoriously lonesome bunch, so she was welcome once they knew she wasn't going to... do things to the corpses. Months passed before they cracked and told her corpse cops didn't exist.

It was a wicked sort of fun for Rudella, at first. The taboo nature of it all. She started off staring at the lifelessness, sometimes for an hour. The stillness intrigued her even two decades later. Where do you think she touched her first corpse? The head? The leg? Someplace indecent? Of the bits she could've touched under supervision, she did the awkward thing and chose the wrist, checking for an obviously absent pulse. It felt like raw chicken before her mother rubbed it down with gochujang and mayonnaise.

Then the crush turned into a like.

She ditched her high school graduation ceremony; she didn't want to be paraded in front of people who didn't give a fuck about her for four years. "High school sucks" twas ever thus. Her bargain with her parents was that she'd take a photo with them and her diploma in front of Pit and Twig High's sign. Her parting gift was phlegmy team spirit.

During the congratulatory dinner, she broke the news to her parents that she wanted to be a mortician. They were fine since all those horrors took her to handling dead bodies instead of making them. She then broke the news to her parents that the school she wanted to go to was near Chicago. They were fine. Eventually.

The hardest part of leaving was saying goodbye to the family cat; Mur-Mur couldn't know she wasn't gone for good. She couldn't take Mur-Mur, either. Inspiration struck, and Rudella left one of her favorite shirts, with her scent, for the lonesome cat to sniff and sleep on. She also recorded herself to a tape her parents could play whenever Mur-Mur turned wistful. Both worked.

Life went on, with all its undulations, 'til Rudella met a waitress who'd change everything.

Separating stubbornness and strength through an odyssey of pain is a fool's errand.

Under tasteless circumstances, Piri would be called a cyclops because she was born missing an eye. Her mother blamed the devil instead of her smoking, taking her frustrations out on her daughter instead of taking her daughter into her arms. Her father couldn't do anything about it; a drunk driver made sure of that. The modern Polyphemus suffered acutely at "home" until what passed for her quinceañera, when she ran away and never looked back. Neither did her mother.

If you're curious, "Piri" goes "PEE-ree".

Everyone starts off as pieces in a void, waiting for circumstances to pull them into their true selves. No one is a fait accompli since constantly losing parts of yourself and (re)gaining others is the human condition. Or rather, should be. Piri is one of the fortunate ones, unless you know her circumstances.

While finding ways to survive in the gutters of Chicago's south side, she thought she could rely on those who looked like her. She could, as long as she acted like they wanted her to. It wasn't a question of manners; she was always grateful and respectful. She quickly found her way out of house and home, through either her hosts' boot or her own, when she found that people wanted you to be an individual as long as it aligned with their beliefs. So she decided to align with no one but herself.

The life of a teenage runaway can be crippling in its bleakness. You've heard the stories. Piri's written herself into more than a few of them. Suicide never crossed her mind, but she knew she needed as extreme a coping mechanism if she was going to survive. There were little things that helped, like her headset radio. The medley of pop music that B96 offered was her only addiction. She was shattered when it focused on rap because she craved variety. A frantic flick of the dial took her to Q101, which was for rock what B96 was for pop, and she was pleased. Especially when Dance Factory popped up on 99.9 nightly.

But being a musicophile wasn't an extreme occurrence, no matter how much she loved Aqua and System of a Down. She had to make her heart bleeding or calcified. Nightmares of her mother reminded her of what a stone heart was (in)capable of, so she chose compassion. This extremity created an agony debt that she unknowingly forced her subconscious to pay, even now.

Finding out about squatter's rights was one of the best things that happened to Piri during her vagabondage. The long and short of it's that if a building's not occupied, a homeless person can live there. She was 26 when she found out, but better late than never. She chose a place in Hegewisch, a factory town, which ended up being a genius move since it's also a transportation hub.

Having conquered two levels of Maslow's hierarchy of needs in one fell swoop, the racks in the nearby Goodwill in Lansing enticed her with style as well as function. Her figure was at the mercy of others' generosity, but she managed to develop a Punk patchwork she could appreciate. Started designing her eye patches, too.

Maslow brought other needs to Piri's attention. Having a roof over her head meant she could cross things off her years-long to-do list. Being homeless meant the company she occasionally kept was addicts and their dealers. Dealers had a hard time keeping molly because it was in demand. A place where it was in high demand was raves. Piri wanted fuck-all to do with molly, but she was dying to go to raves. Thanks to the company she kept, she knew where and when the best ones were.

And they were glorious. She was introduced to the likes of Dougal & Gammer, Infected Mushroom, and what passed for her first girlfriend. Piri wasn't as ready for her as she thought she was, due to her agony debts. It took a while to get over her, but she did. By then, she was a renter and a waitress.

Life went on, with all its undulations, 'til Piri met a mortuary assistant who'd change everything.

The concept of dinner before a movie along with overpriced, underserved munchies at the concession stand were absurd to Rudella.

Thus, her tummy was particularly rumbly after "Tusk" ended. She was at a Schererville AMC, which meant that the Round the Clock on Lincoln Hwy. was a 30-second drive away. But she didn't feel like dealing with the crowds. Watching a man turn another man into a walrus made her withdrawn and introspective. Driving north on Indianapolis Blvd. that early-Autumn eve, she passed Highland's Round the Clock.

If she believed in fate, she would've gone there since two appearances wouldn't have been a coincidence. She's a rational beast, so she parked her Honda Civic in the Lake Stop lot.

Piri loved working the night shift for two reasons: she's a night owl, and she rarely had to deal with children. There's the stream of nocturnal weirdos, sure, but against the life she lived, their eccentricities ran dry. You can't win a game of Crazy Chicken against someone who did anything to survive. This night was tame. Mostly. She sensed a bit of tension from a group of her regulars.

She was in the bathroom when they came in, so they weren't on her dance card. Because of that, she only knew what she picked up in passing. Something about not acknowledging a girlfriend's presence and not caring if she died. Said girlfriend left the diner crying, and her fella tossed a glass of water in Silent Treatment's face before joining her.

The first thing Rudella noticed was Piri's gloves, fingerless and lace. A striking sight in most places, but definitely in this Indiana eatery. Piri told Rudella, after they made love for the first time, that's how she noticed her. She basically greeted people with one of eight stock jokes about her eye patch, so she was pleasantly startled when Rudella's attention was on her hands.

Piri also revealed, in the afterglow, that she started wearing those gloves because she broke out into hives her first night waitressing. But here, they're strangers with that and much, much, much, much more ahead of them.

Piri's attention was split twixt Rudella and the drama of her regulars, until Rudella remarked on the laced hand gripping the coffee pot. She'd hear their story the next time the group was in, so she focused on earning her tip. Besides, they weren't her table that night. In mortuary college, Rudella picked up the peculiar habit of dipping fries in creamy soups. To Piri's surprise, even if it's cream of potato.

The night was average, so Piri was able check in with small talk. She hated it since it rarely led to meaningful conversation, which she adored, but she learned that customers were like cacti. A little water went a long way. Rudella also hated small talk; something they sensed in each other.

Though it wasn't Christmastime, they got into the stop-start rhythm of their disdain for "Rudolph the Red-Nosed Reindeer", pride of Chicago. The town gave him shit for being different until it benefited them. The two closed out agreeing that fair-weather friends were the worst. Piri was bummed that Rudella left, but liked watching her leave.

A few nights later, Rudella came back to a slightly packed house. Piri's her waitress, but she was having a pistachio situation. The wife of an elderly couple was having a fit because her ice cream wasn't what she asked. Piri prided herself on her ability to take orders. Plus, it's hard to mishear "pistachio ice cream". None of this mattered to the wife. The husband was a broken man long before he sat down.

Piri chose to be compassionate to the world, but the service industry taught her that compassion was on a spectrum. She decided to handle the nag in a Bugs Bunny sort of way, setting up a series of logic traps that ended with the couple leaving. Tipless, but satiating Piri's server sadism was worth more than what they would've left.

She knew the rest of her shift would be a series of similarities, so she told Rudella when she's working again and sent her off with a cherry Dum-Dum.

Rudella came back the night she was told, and knew that getting there later meant business was slower meant that they could have meaningful conversation. She'd pay for it at work, but being somber and being sleepy looked similar to the layman. Piri appreciated the rationale, though she secretly worried that Rudella wouldn't show up.

After a while, Piri addressed the elephant in the booth and asked why Rudella hadn't asked about her eye patch. Rudella figured everyone did, so she wasn't unless Piri brought it up. Piri asked what'd be a good Halloween costume for her, daring her to resist the obvious Sexy Pirate. Success. May at the end of "May". Piri was piqued; Rudella told her that May gouged out her lazy eye, then gave it to the doll she made out of human body parts.

Rudella liked to let people know what they're in for with her as soon as possible. Her philosophy was that if they wouldn't get along, it was better to rip the bandage off instead of tug it. Piri said that she'd look for "May" the next day.

A month's worth of coffee and soup-dipped fries later, Rudella received a gift from Piri as she paid her bill. Rudella didn't have many women friends because she tended to get lost in the fantasy of being in a relationship with them. Because of that, she put a lot of effort into trying to view the waitress through a platonic lens.

Then a crush turned into a like.

Piri took whatever opportunities presented themselves. Her philosophy was that you missed 100% of the chances you didn't take. Rudella seemed like a chance worth taking, so she made her a mix CD. As you can imagine, a fan of Aqua and System of a Down had the capacity to make a chaotic setlist. Because her main influence was radio, there was no rhyme or reason in the songs she chose.

Rudella picked a cardinal direction and aimlessly drove through all 79:43 of "Lake Stop Hot Shot". Alexandra Stan's "Mr. Saxobeat" was one of many surprises, and she latched onto Unwound's "Terminus". Rudella repaid the effort her next visit by giving Piri "Skullomania". Since she grew up with albums, Rudella's setlist had a flow. Myrath's "Braving the Seas" rocked her down to her gel insoles.

Life went on, with all its undulations, 'til Rudella and Piri met a photographer who'd change everything.

Rudella and Piri wish to inform you, dear reader, that they represent no one but themselves.

They neither belong to any group nor want to belong.

Whatever good or bad Rudella and Piri do is a reflection of Rudella and Piri.

They have no interest in your politics.

They'll disappoint you. A lot.

They don't have to like what you like.

They don't have to like who you like.

They want neither fame nor acclaim for being who they are.

They get that you might see yourself in them, but that doesn't mean you can hate them for not making your choices.

They don't owe you anything.

They don't make pop culture references to impress you. They live in the real world, and the real world has video games and Tori Amos.

And, most importantly, **they're fiction.**

If these things aren't to your liking, do the adult thing and stop reading now. They won't get offended. There's plenty out there with you in mind. Don't waste your time with an obviously bad fit.

If you're sticking around, welcome to the freakshow.

CHAPTER TWO

Dreamland Overture

As feelings for her new favorite waitress grew amorous, Rudella knew she had emotional baggage to burn.

Unlike Piri, who wrapped her problems in blankets of compassion and placed them out of sight. Although Piri's lived the much harder life, Rudella's pain was no less important. Comparing emotional wounds was a butter-eating contest: no matter what anyone said or thought, **NO ONE** won.

Since Rudella was willing to even address her issues, it's only fair we focused on her. She didn't know how she was going to address them, but that was fine. Her subconscious needed the merest crack of the door to flood her dreams with the choices and changes she wanted to make. This wasn't oneiromancy, however. Dreams are conversations with the psyche, not with the future.

This also wasn't one dream, but a string of introvertive pearls made over many nights, and not often consecutive.

Fireflies or Stars

On the carpeted road of a swamp, Rudella brushed her hands over a wheat field rustling in the nighttime breeze.

The carpet looked familiar, but the memory eluded her. Literally, though that concept in dreams could be wobbly. Fireflies caught in the wind's swoon avoided her touch, and these glowing skydrops held memories they'd rather not share. Rudella didn't understand their secret, however; she only knew they were pretty.

Her bare feet shuffled across the damp wool as she looked for purpose in the fog. Like their moth cousins' predilection for the flame, she was drawn to the fireflies' light. But they knew she wasn't ready for them, otherwise they wouldn't exist.

Stalks of wheat cracked and squished underfoot as her grabby intentions grew stronger. Still the skydrops evaded her to protect her. One almost failed, sailing through her fingers a wing-flap before she would regret it.

Although Rudella wanted to conquer her problems, she also *didn't* want to. As we all do for certain troubles. She was lucky in that they were things she could ultimately handle herself. Piri would've turned vegetative if she attempted even this much.

That didn't mean Rudella was as ready as she thought as she continued her pursuit.

The Mortician and her fireflies were confused in the torrent of wind-borne leaves from the weeping willows, causing false victories and narrow escapes. Determination fueled both sides in the chaos. To collect. To object. Eventually, with a scream and a flash, one failed.

Rudella forgot the woman's name. If this was a dream she'd remember in the waking, she would laugh at the fact she held in her heart a nameless fiend. Or maybe she made space for better pain. College weekends were for house parties, whether or not you knew the owners. Rudella was content being a homebody in Conyers; her Chicagoland friends wouldn't let her. She wasn't against going places, she just wasn't an adventurer. But who could turn down a morticians' party?

She remembered being led, hand in hand, as if under a strobing moonbeam. Beyond it, grinding bodies and candy lights. The steps from where the two began to the living room grew longer in fondness; despite what happened after that night, the moment was magic and precious for Rudella.

When they finally claimed their space, Rudella could only look down. At their feet. At the carpet. Her dance partner lifted her chin so they could see eye to eye. Rudella didn't remember anything about her face, just the golden drapes that framed it. Her dance partner placed Rudella's hands on her hips and closed the gap between them. She could still feel the knit fabric of her dress, and the thong underneath. It didn't turn sexual, but that didn't bother Rudella. Her dance partner whispered to her she was glad she met her. Dance, little tin goddess.

The come-down happened a few days later. Rudella and her dance partner flirted textually, until she received a call one afternoon. Her partner's fella tore up their dance card and made it clear getting another one would be grievous.

She spent years being hurt, but it wasn't until facing the moment that she didn't know who to blame. The fella was protecting his lady from all threats, but perhaps her dance partner had reason to wander. Then Rudella had a most poignant thought: it was one fucking night in college... get over it, bitch.

Back in the impossible swamp, Rudella took her advice and felt euphoric. She needlessly carried the burden of that disappointment for almost half her life. The relief of it gone was immense, and pathetic. Dealing with the second part was at the other end of her journey. Like how she felt she wasted her life holding on to them because they were fleeting. At this end, she was a beast of burden eager to shrug off its torments.

Instead of chasing another firefly, she held out a warm hand and waited. One landed, and she conquered it. Another did, and she conquered it. Three truths became clear after the landings became routine: the victories were shallow, pleasing, and repetitious. Flashes of the same happy moments and disappointments. Her attention turned to the velvet sky, and the stars peering through the fabric. If something as fleeting as fireflies could make her feel good, the power and fury of stars could affect her in ways that would make her useless to sadness.

She climbed a weeping willow to its crown, then perched on a branch with an upward gaze. Clever got her this far, then tricky got her in. If she were wise, she'd know that her misplaced confidence was like a child toppling a sandcastle and thinking it could take on a skyscraper. But she felt that Piri was a prize she had to rush to win.

Which was why Rudella pulled down the stars, and the mania they're heir to.

Royally Fucked

Rudella regretted it immediately.

All she could do was watch the sky fall apart. Skydrops far larger than the palm of her hand screeched to the swamp in streaks and promises of pain.

The rumbling was coming.

Foolishness she harbored about being able to handle what she put away escaped her as the velvet disappeared. She tried to leap off the tree, but she was frozen. She tried to turn away, and she was frozen.

The rumbling was closer.

She tried shouting at the descending terrors to stop, and the futility was mocked by the cacophony. Tears. So many tears.

The rumbling was.

When it had its way with Rudella and the land, she couldn't see. Or move. She also felt safe. A manufactured safety. Whatever waited for her outside of wherever she was, it was crueler than all the waking world. But she was the one who beckoned it. Dragged it from where she told it to stay for the rest of her life. Because she didn't want to be disobeyed while she and Piri became whatever they'll become.

The bubble burst around her, and she was surrounded by snow she didn't feel. Many of the stars that fell didn't make it, instead staying slivers of memories too ashamed of her newfound strength. Others were more defiant. They delighted in standing tall and burrowing deep. Towering gravestones bound in kohl ivy and emerald roses, each a tumorous monument to assured agony she had to overcome.

It was only when Rudella approached a gravestone that the snow made its presence felt. As long as she kept her distance, it was as comforting as a warm bed after a hard day. But when, step by step, she made her intention clear, the snow was as frigid as denial to a starving child. Still she ventured, forcing herself to not look down to find out if frostbite had claimed her.

She couldn't read the monument when she, at last, reached its summit. However, she knew who it was meant for.

Exhausted, she could only fall through the impossible foliage, into thoughts of Talullah.

Bait and Ditch

Before she gave up her pleated skirts for pencil skirts and her armwarmers for sweaters, when she wore glasses for the look and not to see, Rudella found herself at another house party. She learned her lesson from when she played Follow the Leader, but life is an unending test (sadly, with no definite answers). Nursing her Spirytus and Apple Pucker, she was about to participate in one of her biggest lessons in love. Unwillingly, since people never have a choice over who they fall for.

She was usually a "complete package" kinda gal, but Talullah's hair and breasts caught Rudella's attention behind her beer goggles. She had never seen a festival of colors before; a particularly grand feat with a pixie cut. As for her breasts... It was more like Rudella noticed Talullah wore an "Invader Zim" t-shirt, which was slightly stretched due to her ample quantity. A problem with being a Zim fan was that the caffeinated cartoon was infinitely quotable, but only at a **massive** decibel level. It's like trying to half-ass a song by Björk or Prince at karaoke: you gotta commit, squeals and all, or sit the fuck down. Talullah knew this, hence the tee. Rudella forgot this, thanks to Spirytus. Luckily, the former thought the latter was charming when she exclaimed a quote. Nothing breaks the ice like screaming about bacon in soap.

Rudella and Talullah chatted routinely on the phone after the party, about everything and nothing. Then a crush turned into a like. Rudella thought of asking her out, but that was quite the commitment. Along with the typical threat of a wounded heart, Talullah lived in Rockford. A two-hour drive northwest, on a good day, from Indiana's border to Wisconsin's. Rudella loved fantasy and those Fast and Furious flicks, so she didn't mind the idea of long journeys and cars. But that'd be a drive through Chicago. More importantly, Chicago traffic, which only had worse days and shit days. The joy of ending her vehicular suffering in Talullah's arms was worth it, so Rudella asked her out. They would date the following Saturday afternoon.

Loaded up on Dream Theater albums, Rudella made the bumper-to-bumper journey in her Civic and best fishnets. She picked the Progressive Metal band since they kept her focused and mellow, a great combo on this worse day. When she finally arrived at the park Talullah told her to, she almost proved herself wrong. They wandered and talked and swooned, and Talullah suggested they go back to her house. In her living room, with desire between them, she made another suggestion. Rudella took a knife, and hacked at her left foot until it was a mess of blood and dedication. The more you suffer, the more it shows you really care. Right?

Days passed, and Rudella mutilated and humiliated herself through them for Talullah. One night, Talullah cradled what was left of Rudella, head and arm and torso, while they waited on her porch. Her remains were hung from the awning like lanterns of mangled flesh. Rudella asked if she could finally have a kiss. Talullah stares at her. Rudella, crying, asked again. Talullah remained still. Rudella, angry, asked again. Stone. Rudella plunged her only hand into her own chest, her ribs breaking with

each enraged, hopeful tug until she ripped out her beating,
artery-tethered heart.

"IS THIS WHAT YOU WANT?!"

Talullah's attention drifted to the street with a warm smile.
Rudella's Friend had taken the bait. Talullah excitedly ran to them,
the two kissing passionately under the streetlight. Rudella's Friend
thanked Rudella for getting them together before disappearing
into the night with a new paramour.

Rudella could only fade away.

With My Skin Define

The first thing Rudella noticed was that she wasn't cold
anymore.

What was left of her. Next was the flora bound to the
grave. Wilted. Feeble. Desolate. Save for a final bloom. She
thought of whispers regarding Talullah and her Friend she was too
self-loathing to acknowledge. Talullah left Rudella with much
anguish, but she was at least spared the shame of having a
clown college drop-out's fingers inside her. The chuckle that
escaped her choked the rose; its dry petals tickled her face as a
fond farewell.

Rudella felt there was another grievance to vanquish, so she couldn't bathe in her schadenfreude for long. There was the dilemma of her severed limbs, and her heart in the palm of her hand. Careful as she was, she couldn't avoid cutting herself on shards of broken bone as she put her organ right where it belongs. How would she seal the wound, though? Fumiko Hayashi said that she loved the pathetic tenacity of human beings who carried on living in the infinite vastness of the universe. She would have an affection for Rudella as she reached for ivy, though Rudella wouldn't consider herself pathetic. Not with what she was psyching herself up to do.

Her maimed ends screamed almost as loud as she did with each desperate, fruitless grasp at ivy. She sometimes took breaks to cry, partially burying her face in snow. From pain, from frustration. When she finally grabbed her prize, it was almost by accident. So much so that she almost let go. She didn't have enough strength to pull, so she rolled away, letting gravity do most of the work and hoping she didn't lose her heart in the process. The ivy gave, then snapped. She chewed off a stretch around a foot long, then chewed either end to as fine a point as she could muster. By then, she screamed herself hoarse, so the sounds she made as she onehandedly pierced and bound her flesh shut were cracking gales through broken windows. Her scattered limbs anxiously waited for their turn.

Her sinewed deed done, Rudella encouraged her arms and legs to do what they're meant to, finding ambition in thoughts of Piri. It was when she noticed how stained the snow was with her blood that she heard something in the air. A voice and melody that she couldn't place, yet their intentions were clear. To lure. To shame. Lure, so she could find her next gravestone. Shame, since she knew who waited for her. It was a syren's song, and this song's for suffering.

Rudella used the memorial of Talullah for support. Standing on freshly-stitched legs was a chore. Walking on them more so, her limbs slid at their wounds, but she had to learn quickly. The song made intrusive demands. It also brought up thoughts of Brigitte. Rudella did with her something she thought she never had in herself: she stole her from a friend. The still-there shame flowed from the song, through her body, and she could move with ease. Move she did, with ivy stretching and the wet clapping of her wounds, while blood from where she lain spread outward to snow below and above.

Shame gave way to hatred, and Rudella's wounds sealed completely to make her a fully-formed, patchwork woman. Her hatred was aimed at herself because, after she and Brigitte were over, she finally realized the terrible thing she did. Not over the act itself, but because she didn't care that she hurt people. Hatred opened its doors to acceptance and her rationalization that her infliction was no different than what she received, and her act was simply a symptom of the universe. Then she hummed along with the song.

Crimson smothered all traces of white from the dreamscape, and Rudella wrapped herself in a blanket of cruelty as she thought about why she broke up with Brigitte. They were together for a few months, already traded I-love-yous. Happy, a life of wonder ahead of them. One day, Brigitte was about to take a shower and called Rudella in the bathroom. She couldn't remember what the conversation was about, but her following thought was clear, years later. As Brigitte readied the water, Rudella looked at her and knew she could do better. The fallout was quick as a shutting door, messy like mascara-stained tears, and over like a blocked number.

From Brigitte's ruin to the ruin of herself. The syren was a red-crowned statue of Rudella, it's song from a dilapidated speaker at its feet. The statue, posed as not to tell if it's hiding or waiting, was marble and onyx. The minerals steadily pushed for majority; you may have made her mistake by assuming their conflict involved morality.

The blanket of cruelty became a new skin for Rudella. It protected her from and caused her pain, and would make Joel-Peter Witkin salivate. She didn't feel cold... or anything. Not even that her name was hers.

She chose to be "Disease", then went into herself.

CHAPTER THREE

My Alcoholic Friend

As important as Piri's first day at Lake Stop was, that night pushed it further; when she was tempted by her vagabond life.

Like many life-changing choices, it grew out of surprise and disappointment. She worked an evening shift; luckily, a slow shift. Her vagabond life forced her to masterfully read people, so she had few beginners' problems with customers. Apart from pirate jokes and the usual, varying levels of entitlement occasionally thrown at the Front-of-House staff. Those customers never threatened her with knives or guns or worse, so handling them was like playing with a box of pups that tipped terribly.

Speaking of tips, being what customers wanted her to be would routinely lead to nice ones, but she also knew that jealousy would corrode her work relationships. Because of that, she wasted no time in getting friendly with her co-workers. Not friends; she couldn't be everyone's friend. Nor did she want to. The friendliness led to respect; too many people underrated that which was key to any relationship. The friendliness couldn't be obsequious; fawning would be certain death for respect, and patience.

Piri discovered Lake Stop through amusing circumstances. After settling into her squatter life in Hegewisch, she panhandled enough money for clothes and had enough clothes to need a laundromat. After figuring out her neighbors' schedules, she knew when to leave and return without getting noticed. She tested her theory a few times in low-risk circumstances since science is a constantly revised hypothesis. Satisfied, she hopped on a Pace bus with her sack of dirty vêtements and pocket full of quarters.

A few spin cycles later, Piri met Theda and bonded over episodes of "Maury". They didn't have a choice: the trash talk show was the only thing on the laundromat's crappy TV. No matter the time, no matter the day. Never a rerun, either, which annoyed Theda because she was in an episode (as an audience member) and Piri didn't believe her. Not that Piri would've missed her: Theda had Champagne tastes, with beer money.

If you're wondering, "Theda" goes "THEE-dah".

A problem that claimed Piri at the start of her squatter life was an unconscious desire to latch onto people. Her vagabond life taught her to trust no one, which protected her from death or worse countless times. It also gave her no one to talk to about anything that didn't involve food, water, or shelter. She was a loner by nurture, aching for companionship. Not sex, though she'd soon find a way to deal with that baggage. Nothing would please her more during this time than having someone to talk to about everything and nothing. Making up for a lifetime of lacking. All of this to say that Theda helped her achieve a great need, at a great cost.

After waxing nonsensical enough times, Theda invited Piri to her apartment atop a store. It was a quick bus ride from her Hegewisch squat to the Calumet City end of Burnham Avenue, which was splendid. Piri stopped by one afternoon with a bag of double dark chocolate Milano cookies and chocolate hazelnut Pirouettes. If she was gonna be real friends, she was gonna start off right. Theda was <u>very</u> appreciative. After giving her crap about being bougie.

Essentially one room with a kitchen and a bedroom attached, Theda's apartment wasn't much. The kind of place you moved to in your 20s 'til better came along, and were still there in your 60s. Theda's around Piri's age, so that epiphany was decades away.

The last time they spoke, they got on the subject of wrestling. Mainly how Theda was a fan and Piri never saw a match. Theda, as a fan of late-'90s/early-aughts WWE, couldn't let that stand. Which was why Piri's introduction, starting with Stone Cold Steve Austin and The Rock's first Wrestlemania match, went into the night. After a lifetime of bottling so many things inside, the joy of watching two guys having a slobberknocker of a match for over a half-hour and living through their violence was indescribable. When it was over, she went to the bathroom and bawled into a towel; a few of her agony debts, suddenly and in vain, struggled to be paid.

What Piri didn't notice when she came back, and should have kept her walking to the front door, was that Theda didn't ask her if she was ok.

The Rub

Hanging out with Theda was also part of Piri's long reintegration into society, and it wasn't something as simple or terrifying as pretending to be her.

Each person has a specific morality that, as long as they honor it, keeps them from picking up habits they shouldn't. Piri's vagabond life complicated her morality, but she managed to stay Neutral Good. Which means she does the right thing regardless of what the law says.

Many nights at Theda's were spent with a press-on nail sitting on an armrest while she popped open cans of Old Style. After spending nearly two decades seeing people drink themselves to death or worse, Piri **never** drank. With Theda, she tried being around people who did drink without being (obviously) disgusted. Theda had Manzanita Sol for anyone who didn't want beer, because only sick fucks said no to apple soda, so Piri was placated.

Another part of the long rehabilitation was tailoring a person suit. Piri didn't know how fucked-up she was, but she knew she was. Because of that, she knew she had to present at least a semblance of normalcy or else she wouldn't be allowed to do anything. No one wanted to be around a hot mess. So she spent her time with an unaware Theda trying out quirks and traits until she made "Piri". This "Piri" would be the first of many until she tailored the perfect fit. No one wanted to be around a hot mess in a bad suit.

One visit, somewhere between DeBarge's "Rhythm of the Night" and Deniece Williams' "Let's Hear It for the Boy", Piri rolled cigarettes in Theda's kitchen. Piri **never** talked about her vagabond life, but she did mention that she rolled cigarettes when she was stressed. She didn't smoke, she just liked the distraction of creation and repetition. Theda did smoke, and asked if she wanted to make a few bucks rolling a pack or two. Piri did, so she did. Their conversations were notoriously random; this one led to Theda admitting that she was raped more than once, with neither fear nor shame. Piri was a secret member of that terrible club because she hadn't learned to hobble its power over her like Theda did. Partially because she didn't know she could. The hard, unpredictable road that would lead her to that goal was paved that night.

Theda finally had enough money from her casino gig to put a down payment on a car, which is why she and Piri were at a dealership one day. Leasing was the greatest invention for Champagne tastes and beer money, and Theda's credit score was music to the salesman's ears. When Piri later looked up why credit scores exist, she was annoyed; she could spend her life never late paying a bill, but that wouldn't mean shit if she only paid cash. Fiscal responsibility only mattered if it was on plastic. She also went down a dark hole about why debt was good for the financial system because of defaults and interest rates... but that wasn't why Piri was with Theda that day. As Theda and the salesman geeked-out over transmissions and heated seats, Piri looked at all things shiny and chrome, and was utterly uninterested. Not in cars, but the desire to stay in fashion. So much time and energy and money (interest rates!) were wasted on a concept created to be fleeting. She'd never let herself be shackled to haute couture or the status quo.

Theda vroom'd out of the lot with Piri in her gently-used, blue, Mazda RX-8, with Teena Marie's "Stargirl" album pumped through the speakers. "Lovergirl" took them to the nearest Auto Zone, where she bought a bit of safety and aroma. After taking the pedal-to-wheel version of The Club on and off 'til it became second nature, she hung a coconut air freshener on a vent. The album, like their destination, was put on random as they went cruising north on Burnham, watching buildings turn to cornfields, 'til Theda had to turn left or right. She hadn't been to Indiana in a while, so she went left.

As she got close to Indianapolis Blvd., Theda's tummy started to rumbly. Piri pointed to the Round the Clock on the right, but Theda didn't want lemon rice soup. She turned left on Indianapolis since the strip's packed with eateries, then proceeded to shoot down each of Piri's suggestions. As they were about to pass another Round the Clock, Piri pointed out that two in one trip had to be fate. Theda wasn't having any of that, then she saw Lake Stop and pulled in.

Still riding the new car high, Theda offered to buy Piri lunch and ordered a perch for herself. Piri didn't want to abuse the privilege, so she played it safe with a grilled cheese sandwich. As they enjoyed themselves, Piri knew that she wanted more of this for herself. Being able to go wherever she wanted and do whatever she wanted on a whim, not having to worry about money. Sure, on the surface, it sounded like her vagabond life, but having weather-controlled four walls and a roof and a car was never a possibility in those days.

Then Piri noticed the Help Wanted sign and wondered how quickly she could make "Piri".

Piri gave up on calling Theda after her fifth try.

She was at the nearby gas station because she didn't want her new boss to think there was already something wrong with her. She already broke out in hives on her hands. Miserable thoughts buzzed around her head like the fluorescent bulbs above her. Superstitious ones told her Theda not answering was a sign that her plan to be a better person was wrong. Paranoid ones told her getting a taxi would give the game away to her "neighbors". Morbid ones told her staying in one spot for too long would invite those who came with knives. Absurd ones told her to walk home since buses didn't run that late. Morbid ones told her those who came with knives wouldn't follow her. Paranoid ones told her she could still sneak into her squat if she was careful. Superstitious ones told her the ten-mile walk was better than thirteen. Buzzing was left to the fluorescents as she walked to Ridge Road with misguided determination.

Absurd thoughts told Piri she could be home in four hours, at the most. She read that humans walk, on average, three miles an hour. With ten miles ahead of her, four hours made sense. But there was no accounting for stamina. Yes, she was healthy. Yes, she wore gym shoes with gel insoles. Yes, she had a worthwhile goal. All of those meant nothing since she was near the end of her day, after spending a chunk of it on her feet. Her expectations with time would be a series of diminishing returns. Still, she headed east, passing Kennedy Avenue and Downtown Highland.

Paranoid thoughts drew her attention to a house atop a grassy incline. There was nothing particularly unique about the house; it was one in a row, save for it being empty with its lights on. It was too nice to be a squat, unless the person wanted to get arrested in a hurry. She couldn't think of a reason why an empty house would have its lights on. Except it being a murder house. She had seen many crime scenes and kinds of death, and what they had in common, aside from tragedy, was that she felt them before she saw them. Intuition was very important to those who could only depend on themselves, and a vagabond life sharpened that blade acutely. The knife edge of danger told her that house had secrets it wouldn't share. Or rather, she wouldn't want it to share.

Morbid thoughts told Piri to do very bad things to each driver who didn't offer to give her a ride. Not to her squat; just three or four miles to knock them off her journey. She was easy to spot in her fireman's coat, with reflector strips irradiating neon under their passing headlights. The driver in the Taurus, she wanted all their tires to burst so the car could go into a sparking spin-out into a gas station. Pump Five. The driver in the Camero, she wanted their car to remember it was an Autobot, but was bad at transforming, so it tried repeatedly with the sack of guts and bones still behind the wheel. The driver in the Hummer, the car she hated the most, she wanted to have a nervous breakdown, pull over, cut the interior to shreds with the key, eat

all the pieces from pedal to muffler, and die of reverse-dysentery.
She never saw a biker with sidecars, but she had something
vicious ready.

Superstitious thoughts taunted Piri with notions of choices
that were "good" and "bad". If the next light stayed green when
she got to it, she would make it home ok. If the stars didn't come
out from behind the clouds, she wouldn't make it home ok. If the
raccoon saw her when it crossed the street, she'd make it home.
If the next building she passed was a bike shop, she wouldn't
make it home. If the next street started with an "h", she'd be
homebound. If a passing car played 4 Strings' "Take Me Away",
she wouldn't be. And on. And on.

When the bad weather began having its say, hours after
Indianapolis Blvd. and now in Illinois, Piri's phone rang. Her sole
contact aglow. In a relative moment of clarity, she only had two
thoughts: disappointment and desperation. Theda sounded
drunk, asking if she could get a ride to her place. She showed off
her new car to friends at a bar in Downtown Highland, and now
they're post-gaming at her apartment with "Head of the Family".
Piri asked if she took Ridge Rd., and Theda barked something
about taking I-80 West. Piri asked if she remembered anything she
was supposed to do. Theda thought about it, then laughed her
way through no. Piri hung up, deleted her sole contact, turned off
her phone, and cried about her fucked-up life.

As she sat curled in a storefront's doorway, Piri was depressive about what she should do. It was easy to get to Hegewisch from Highland: west on Ridge Rd., then north on Torrence Ave. The problem was there was a lot of Ridge Rd., and even more Torrence Ave. She could practically touch the latter from her stoop... but there were so many steps left to take. Her feet were already aching. It was too late, or early, for buses. Her paranoia about a ride to her squat was still vibrant. If she went south, she could escape everything. A forest reserve was a mile down the road. Another mile or two, a huge, abandoned bar. Perfect places to restart her vagabondage. She always stayed clean to make a few bucks from blood donations, so she wouldn't have to worry about money when what she had ran out. She mastered poverty, anyway.

But she knew where that road ended, and she knew that wasn't where she wanted to be.

Disaster Must Be Earthed

Whenever Piri recalled that night, the Torrence stretch always had a touch of amnesia.

She remembered turning onto the street, but her next thought was being a few houses away from her squat under the morning sun. The stinging pain in her feet and the stiffness in her legs made only the shortest steps possible. Exhaustion made her eyes burn to be let close. Those things were vivid years later, yet she never could remember how she got there.

Despite being at the end of her interstate odyssey, she still had to obey everyone's schedules. In seventeen minutes, she could pass out on her air mattress. The sole thread to her sanity was knowing she didn't have to go back to work for two days. A thread she held onto as if her life depended on it for seventeen minutes. When the time passed, she swung from that thread into a slumber that lasted almost a day.

Piri's first thought was that she could've had a taxi drop her off a block away. Her second thought involved jumping into a TARDIS and smacking herself with it at the gas station. Her third and fourth thoughts involved the strongest Icy Hot product she could find and fingerless gloves to hide her hives. All of this to distract herself from the dull pain from her toes to her hips, and see how badly the damage of being on her feet for around 12 hours straight was. When she finally did and saw it wasn't nearly as bad as she imagined, she wanted to give Dr. Scholl's a blowjob.

When it was time for work, she walked a bit like Frankenstein's monster, but she had an apron full of Icy Hot Pro patches and dark tights to hide them under. She took her clearheaded advice about taxis for a few days, then one of the girls at work mentioned the Erie Lackawanna Trail that went from Hegewisch to Highland and beyond. Pedal power could get her to work in an hour.

Thus Piri's first paycheck went to a ten-speed she found at the Lansing Goodwill, and called it "Hardstyle".

CHAPTER FOUR

Tablesetting

An interruption: Rudella and Piri's tale is disinterested in "Will they?"/"Won't they?" tension.

We know they will, otherwise why waste your time? Because of that, their tale has the freedom of leaping around like a laser-baited cat. It's a very demanding presentation. Luckily, it only makes two demands. One is that you pay attention. Don't worry, the gals play fair. The other is that you stick with it.

Unconventionality offers fruitful rewards.

Periods of Adjustment

Before her spit dried on her high school's pride, Rudella was on an Amtrak from Georgia to Illinois to do some deathly learnin'.

Her research told her that the Vrehas Institute in Lansing was the best fit for her. And for her parents' wallet. She didn't get a scholarship, but she didn't have to worry about much else since they didn't want a job to distract her from studying. Their supportive dollars only stretched so far, so she had to settle for an ok apartment and car.

If you're curious, "Vrehas" goes "VREE-hahs".

She didn't need a roommate, which was something she'd still be grateful for over a decade later. There wasn't space for anyone else, anyway. The living room took up most of the floor plan, with a nook for a kitchen and the bathroom essentially a bedroom closet. Her white Honda Civic was easy on gas and as reliable as clock chimes. She would've preferred it in black, but beggars and bitches.

Gratitude for not ending up in a "Single White Female" spin-off aside, Rudella had never been alone until her first night in her ok apartment. She had always been solitary, but at least one of her parents was always home with her. There was no one to bother her, or help her. No one to cook for her, or make her clean. No one to worry about her, or be disappointed in her. No one to annoy her, or love her.

She suddenly realized this night was a peek into what her life would be after her parents died, then stared at the sky through her second-story window 'til morning turned the black into blue.

Although Rudella had a Honda, her rollerblade habit was hard to kick. She spent the next day wheeling around her part of Lansing, surprised by how much it felt like Conyers, then finding out what it's like to get to Vrehas from her place. After finding the library, of course. If she showed up a year or two earlier, she would've met some Ridge Rats. Skateboarders and such who hung around the Downtown Lansing strip on Ridge Road. Not that the Goth recluse would've had much to say to them. Anywho, because of her habit, she stayed slim with toned legs, which meant she could eat anything. That would be put to the test when she saw that Waldo Cooney's sold pizza slices, and was close enough for her 'blades. If she took the long way home, she could burn off at least half a slice. Brilliant!

She didn't account for indigestion from speeding, thus Rudella was in a bad place when she unlaced on the living room floor. Of course, that was when her parents called to check in on her. They wanted nothing to do with North Korea when they left, so they got a speech coach to help them lose their accents. Because their teacher was a nice Italian gal from Long Island, they sounded kind of like Michelle Pfeiffer in "Married to the Mob" (becoming their favorite American movie, naturally). They also never taught Rudella to speak Korean, apart from the bits she learned by osmosis. They wanted to put as much distance twixt them and Kim Il Sung as possible.

They also spoke to their daughter on separate house phones instead of sharing one. Her soldierly father told her that he put money on her debit card to buy furniture so there was more than the bed he bought. Rudella thanked her appa as her mind went into Designer Mode and he reminded her debit, not credit. Her boisterous mother told her that if anyone tried anything with her to grab a brick. Rudella reminded her eomma that Lansing didn't have bricks lying around, then asked if Mur-Mur was ok. Mur-Mur meowed for food.

The convo went on for another half-hour, Rudella's tummy uncomfortably rumbly. She learned a long time ago that cutting them off or hinting that she wanted to hang up would backfire badly or spectacularly. Her situation was desperate, and her flop sweat was fierce, so she had to be rude to her bumonim and get an earful when they called back.

If you're curious, "appa" goes "AHP-pah", "eomma" goes "OWE-mah", and "bumonim" goes "boo-MOE-neem".

After her situation was handled, and got that earful, Rudella called her bank and checked her balance. These were flipphone days, and browsing the net on her Razr was aggravating. It was still in the afternoon, so she had plenty of time to find a furniture store. An aggravating search later showed her a Value City ten minutes away. She then remembered the Goodwill three minutes away. Also, since she didn't plan on having people over, she didn't need things like a dinner table. So much money saved.

As she drove north on Torrence Avenue to get started, she saw a Best Buy. A Best Buy full of movies to buy when she was done with responsibility. So much money spent.

Two weeks later, Rudella parked her car in the Vrehas lot for the first time. Nothing about it screamed, or even whispered, it's a college for the death-inclined. If anything, a passerby would think it's a stationary store. If they fancied stationary.

Rudella was in her short skirt, long jacket phase. With hair almost as long. A damn fine find at Goodwill was the leather messenger bag slung over her shoulder. Made her kinda feel like Indiana Jones. Would she be Illinois Jones, or Georgia Jones? Perhaps Transylvania Jones, being of the morbid persuasion? Not that it mattered on this late-August day. A Perfect Circle's "Pet" shut off as her car did, and she took her first step into Vrehas and the rest of her life.

Vrehas was a humble mortician college; Rudella was one of ten in her class. Each student had their own desk and rolling chair. The room's walls were covered with posters and photos that ranged from bad puns to crime scenes. There were also figurines big and small that acted as anatomy lessons. The stereo on the teacher's desk that looked like it came from the 1920's played Camille Saint-Saëns' "Danse Macabre". On the blackboard, elegantly written in red chalk: "Everyone Dies". Vrehas was perfect.

Introductions and introverts, even if the room's full of them, went together like boiled piss and vinegar. The only solace Rudella took was that she didn't go first. When it was her turn, she stammered her way through her intro with her Conyers accent. Not because she was nervous; days could pass twixt her sentences, so she didn't have the best conversation skills.

Though Rudella got through her name and where she was from, she still had to explain why she wanted to be a mortician, with the added pressure of explaining why she chose a place as out of the way as Lansing from Conyers. She told her morgue story and her cadaver fascination, then that she chose funeral homes over body farms because she wanted to comfort people instead of fill science journals. Body farms were still cool, though. As for why she chose Mordor over Rivendell, she explained that she always liked Chicago but wanted to be near instead of be there. Vrehas was the best place for the money she had, and South Suburban College being 15 minutes away to get her state-required credit hours didn't hurt.

Torturous as it was, the sharing showed her class they could be unapologetic about their thanatophilia, and did so in a variety of intriguing ways 'til graduation. But these were the early days, and she had an English class to get to that was 15 minutes away.

A month of death-borne scholarship followed and Rudella had, among other things, a new haircut to show for it. Her drapes were caught in her car door, which only needed to happen once for her to do something about it. To make sure it could never happen again, she rocked a bob. Short enough to be cured of her paranoia, long enough to have style potential.

Which parent took the coiffure news the hardest? Her appa, funnily enough. Sure, her eomma spent ages and dollars on shampoo, conditioner, and combs... but Rudella always had long hair. There were many points in her life where he thought, with military conviction, she was still his little girl. Even when she moved. When he saw a pic of the new her on his phone, it finally hit him like a dummy round that his ttal was growing up.

If you're curious, "ttal" goes "tahl".

A Fate Worse Than Destiny

In which Rudella discovered having similar tastes, no matter how rare, might not be enough for tolerance.

One Autumn afternoon, Rudella sat in the spacious SSC
lobby with a tuna sandwich. She skipped lunch to make it in time
for a class, and was making things right before she went home.
She loved tuna, but found out eating too much led to something
silly like mercury poisoning, so she didn't eat it often. She thought
of how lucky Mur-Mur was to eat it, wet or dry, whenever she
pleased. Then she thought of Mur-Mur's breath and wished she
didn't.

Rudella never had much interest in the people around
her. However, she knew that being a mortician meant she had to
not only start, but play catch-up. She essentially threw herself out
the window and figured out how to survive on the way down with
the scholarly choices she made. Along with all the deathly
business, her field of study at SSC was Sociology. Those weren't
enough, though. She had to make friends and even at Vrehas,
introverts tended to hang out by being alone together. Would it
be fair to say that she was (un)consciously prowling for potentials
in the lobby? Perhaps.

The first thing Rudella noticed was the mini backpack;
Luna, the black cat with the crescent mark from "Sailor Moon".
Or rather, Luna's head. To say Rudella was a fan of anime was an
understatement. She's the sole reason her appa's video rental
store had an anime section. "Sailor Moon" was one of her firsts
and couldn't get enough of its magical girls smiting evil in the
name of love and justice. She was always the one introducing
people to anime, so to have found a woman in the wild dressed

like a schoolgirl and Sporty Spice wearing Luna's head on her back filled her with awe and wonder. And fear since she knew she **had** to say hello.

The most she could muster was that Luna was a mumbled affirmation, which was enough for Honbria. Like many, she thought Rudella was Japanese. Or Chinese. Sometimes even Hawaiian. Not that it bothered her. She didn't want to belong to any group, but she did enjoy conversation.

If you're curious, "Honbria" goes "HOHN-bree-ah".

After being quietly disappointed, Honbria asked Rudella who her favorite Sailor Scout was. Rudella said the bookish Sailor Mercury was her girl 'til the brooding Sailor Saturn stole her heart. Honbria claimed the tomboyish Sailor Jupiter, which explained the Sporty Spice. She then asked if Rudella wanted to walk to Andy's Hot Dogs. It was on the corner and cheese fries were calling her name. Yes. Yes, she did.

What was soon apparent to Rudella, and those around them, was Honbria was as excitable as she wasn't. Like one was a double espresso and the other chamomile tea. Rudella was no less enthusiastic, however. She finally had someone to talk to about anime who wasn't in a chat room or on a message board. The clerk even accommodated her request for a dipping cup of pickles (a habit she's had since she was wee [normally with a peppermint stick]).

They ranted and raved and carried on about discovering "Sailor Moon" in the early-90's, finding out about Saturday Anime movies on Sci-Fi Channel in the mid-90's (Rudella loved the hard sci-fi of "Gall Force: Eternal Story", Honbria loved the fantasy of "Tenchi Muyo! in Love", and they met in the middle for the space fantasy of "Iria: Zeiram the Animation"), and getting stupid-excited when Toonami was unleashed in the late-90's.

If the convo was sex, Rudella would've been multi-orgasmic.

Somewhere around "Gall Force", Honbria got a text from her boyfriend asking if she'd be ready later, quashing Rudella's romantic whimsies. Honbria remembered the text in the middle of the Toonami wave and had to end things there. She then asked if Rudella could drop her off at her house; it was a quick drive to South Holland, near Aurelio's Pizza. No problem. They traded numbers, Honbria thanked the clerk for putting up with them, and the two otaku left.

If you're curious, "Tenchi Muyo" goes "TEHN-chee MOO-yoe", "Iria" goes "EAR-ee-ah", "Zeiram" goes "ZAY-rahm", and "otaku" goes "owe-TAH-koo".

Rudella's social experiment of sorts was a success. In the months since Andy's pickles, she and Honbria became great friends. Life at Vrehas was also swell, with the class having "Six

Feet Under" watch parties while they waited for the fourth season. How could almost-morticians be anything less than ginormous fans of a show about their inevitable livelihood?

The Honbria fun never got in the way of Rudella's studies, though. She loved what would eventually be her job too much, and her bumonim would kill her with disappointment if she did anything less than her best. Honbria had less of a plan, taking random classes 'til a trade jumped out at her. They didn't hang out at Andy's after Rudella found out that Honbria lived close to a Checkers. She thought they were only in Georgia, so she made time and space for either a Big Buford or tenders and a Coke whenever she could (and double-time to rollerblade those calories away). Honbria soon learned that she called every drink a Coke.

Their adventures took them far beyond SoHo and Lansing, too. Things got serious between Honbria and her boyfriend, so she moved in with him to his house in Griffith, Indiana. It was only 20 minutes away from Rudella's apartment, so it wasn't a problem for her. She and the boyfriend weren't close, Rudella wasn't suddenly a social butterfly, but they did bond enough over "A Clockwork Orange" to be cool.

Most of the two's time together took place in Bourbonnais, a 50-minute drive south of Lansing. Chicago's a metropolis, industrial mountain range and all, but there's a sheer drop-off in urbanity southward. Buildings, buildings, CORN.

Rudella laughed long and hard the first time she witnessed it because the switch was so absurd. It also kind of reminded her of the drive from Conyers to Atlanta.

Honbria's mother lived in Bourbonnais after retiring, and made her daughter visit twice a month since she was paying for whatever she was up to in college. There wasn't much to do in town except be with her mother, so she checked to see if any anime fans were around. They were, and they hung out for a year before Rudella joined.

They made a rotating set of basements their clubhouse. Honbria's mother wasn't gonna put up with their shenanigans, so it was never hers. Rudella didn't say much 'til someone asked her what her favorite series was, then she stammered a rant about "Witch Hunter Robin". A choice befitting someone who found comfort in the Black. She also humble-bragged about Rewind or Die; how she introduced the folks back home to the gender-fluid, martial arts antics of "Ranma ½", the sci-fi monster brutality of "Guyver: Bio-Booster Armor", and the wartime Red Riding Hood in "Jin-Roh" among other anime. She knew she was being tested, and showed no quarter. They celebrated by watching something that should be on every anime fan's shelf: "Otaku no Video".

If you're curious, "Ranma" goes "RAHN-mah" and "Jin-Roh" goes "JEEN-roe".

Honbria drove initially, then traded with Rudella 'til the latter took over completely. The former's rationale was the Honda Civic was much better on gas than the Ford Taurus. Rudella didn't mind; the destination was worth the journey. Metal became the soundtrack of the road, and the timid Bourbonnais Banshees perked up when the Civic arrived with Anthrax's "Gung Ho" blaring. Not because she knew the band, but because she also liked metal. Japanese metal, in particular. X Japan, Sex Machineguns, and visual kei bands like Malice Mizer and Psycho le Cému. Visual kei bands were bands who felt how a band looked is as much an art form as what they played. The J-Rock Gal spent a night introducing Rudella to them on YouTube while the others played the quirky "Gitaroo-Man" on the PlayStation 2.

If the convo was sex, Rudella would've been multi-orgasmic.

If you're curious, "kei" goes "kay" and "Cému" goes "SAY-moo".

Rudella was grateful for Honbria and her friendship, even with the odd favors she asked for. She didn't need as much coaxing to talk, and she had plenty of friends to talk anime with. Doing most of the driving was a damn fine way for her to quickly learn the land. When she moved to Lansing, if her destination wasn't near Ridge Rd. or 159th St., she was as lost as a drunk bassist in a drum factory. Since Honbria, she could go 15 miles in any direction, plus Bourbonnais, with her eyes closed. One slice of happiness still evaded her, though.

None of the Bourbonnais Banshees was of sapphic persuasion. Rudella was sure some of them probably wanted to experiment and she could have a particular kind of fun with that, but that's all it would be. There was also the strong chance of resentment or repulsion when her playmate had enough. Essentially, don't shit where you eat. Answering bi-curious questions was as far as she wanted to go with them. Not that she was any sort of expert. Yes, she loved women, but she hadn't found any to love her back.

Rudella lived in Chicago's backyard, but she couldn't find many options for introverted women under 21 to meet and greet. She tried dating chat rooms, but the women there only wanted to fuck. And more than a few weren't really women, if you know what I mean (and I think you do). All of them thought she was cute (and Chinese), so she at least got some surface-level satisfaction.

When Honbria heard about Rudella's irony of it being easier for her to find lust than love, she said run with it. Her theory, that her boyfriend agreed with, was that dates were investments in blowjobs. Spend money on food and fun conversations all you want but, at some point, the other person expected your head in their crotch. Rudella denied it, thought about it, then agreed.

Honbria pointed out that there were lots of women who wanted to save her lots of money, so she should take advantage of the privilege. Her boyfriend added to watch out for crabs.

A few nights later, Rudella found her head in a crotch from Homewood. It was a strange experience because it was her first. Her partner in lust took the lead, enjoying her breasts and warming her fingers 'til Rudella came, then told her to go down. Rudella was proud that she got her hot and bothered so fast… but she wasn't expecting how humid it was down there. It wasn't a problem, she just wasn't prepared for a taste of Georgia Summers while she, y'know, tasted. Then she wondered if all women were like that. Then she wondered if she was like that. She didn't notice when she diddled her skittle, but she had other things on her mind besides her dew point. As she licked and fingered and sweated, she felt a wave of pity for every woman who'd go down on her. Not enough to tell them not to. She wasn't altruistic. She'd simply be a little kinder after they came up for air. Speaking of coming, her partner in lust did in all her twitchy glory and was ready for her slightly pitying taste of Georgia Summers.

After a while, Rudella decided she was done with flings. What worked for one woman didn't work for another, some went all night, others were one and done, some were stiff as a board, other fucked like their ass was on fire, and on and on. Putting as much effort into orgasms as she did into graduating wasn't a good deal for her. She'd rather find one woman and figure her out through their relationship. Since there weren't many options for introverted women under 21, she settled again for the hopeless romantic life. There was a gal she met, in her plaid skirt phase, but that came to a disastrous conclusion.

After one of her classes, Rudella was surprised to find Honbria waiting. Her boyfriend just broke up with her, and she had a day to get her stuff out of his house. Rudella thought they'd grow old together somewhere in the loop twixt quarrel and reconciliation. When Rudella asked why they broke up, Honbria stayed mum. Rudella wasn't close enough to her ex to ask him, so it would stay an unsolved mystery.

Despite being part of the Banshees, the J-Rock Gal lived a half-hour west of Rudella, in Evergreen Park, so she was recruited to help with the sudden move. Honbria's ex was cordial, but he made no effort to hide that he wanted Honbria gone double-quick. He was obviously hurt, but there was something else in his eyes that Rudella couldn't figure out. Regret? Acceptance? Despair? Relief? Honbria's Taurus went to pasture two months ago, so her livelihood was split twixt the Civic and the Saab. The convoy then headed to her annoyed mother's house, unloading their wares into the basement.

Rudella got a warm bit of thanks, the J-Rock Gal got the same plus fifty dollars, and cracks started to form in a foundation built on favors.

Keeping tally of who does what in twixt friends makes it a web of bartering instead of a friendship. But all involved should have a feeling of equality. As Rudella sat in her car, ready for yet another Bourbonnais trip, she thought about what Honbria's done for her.

Introducing Rudella to the Bourbonnais Banshees was fantastic... but she was one desperate search away that would've led her to an anime convention an hour north if she never saw that mini backpack. Anime Central would've introduced her to hundreds of otaku over a weekend in May. She could've created the Lansing... Lamias from that batch, and still leveled-up her driving and social skills. It could've been a mutual appreciation society instead of the one-sided thing she had with Honbria.

When Rudella checked her driver side mirror, she saw the same look on her face Honbria's ex had when he kicked her out of her life.

CHAPTER FIVE

Freighthoppin'

Once upon a time, among the gutter and grime, Piri tore her tether to normalcy and decency.

This wasn't a story of how she came of age, because no one did. Personal growth didn't stop because you're old enough for porn or Jäegerbombs, or because you tried to find yourself in Bali. This also wasn't a story waiting for change in a cup at the end. Charity was fashion; understanding was flesh.

A year from when she took up her vagabondage, the man-made disaster of the Towers falling occurred. The world was anxious and the United States was traumatized. Piri was indifferent: she could be killed anytime for far less than pissing off zealots, and strangers would walk past her corpse without a second thought.

The knock-on effect for a traumatized country that believed it was invincible was it becoming protective with extreme prejudice. The United States was full of fear, unknowing how to handle an emotion it never felt before. There was also anger. Since the executioners fell with the Towers and their master was an ocean away, panicked Americans felt they had to punish innocent people who even resembled the villains.

Many pieces of shit took advantage since angry people were easily led. Even now.

The threat of further danger put all manner of travel under a spastic magnifying glass. Years later, Piri could still vividly remember the eerie days of plane-less skies, though it was the lens' focus on another mode of travel that collapsed her world. It was always tricky to get on and stay on a freight train, but the Patriot Act made fools of anyone who tried. If they weren't sent to a black site first.

Freighthoppin' was Piri's favorite way to get around, before terrorists ruined it. Besides being free, she loved it because she could easily tour not only Chicago, but also Illinois. Or beyond, if her fancy was tickled. Freight cars came in a variety of shapes and sizes, but none lent itself to comfort. Which was why she kept a pillow in her knapsack; otherwise, her fancy would need to be tickled by a jackhammer to get through the callouses.

Sometimes she read, but most of the time, she watched the slow parade of nature pass her by. Outside of civilization, the Midwest was lush with trees, crops, and water. Particularly gorgeous when Autumn leaves started to fall. Of course, Illinois was the prettiest. She didn't care for paintings or photography, but if she decided to take up either, she'd only work from September to November in the Prairie State.

As for what she'd read, that depended on dumpsters. When a book didn't sell, a store could tear off the cover and mail it to the publisher for a refund. The catch was the store couldn't sell the book, essentially destining them for the dumpster. They *should* have gone to the recycle bin, but that's beside the point.

Books didn't sell for many a reason, and not all of them had to do with quality. Because of all that, Piri had quite the rotating library in her knapsack. One book that lingered was Victor Hugo's "The Man Who Laughs". The story of a disfigured person who lived in a corrupt world couldn't have been more tailor-made for her, although it was almost 200 years old. Hugo must've had a TARDIS.

A favorite pastime of Piri's was crashing birthday parties. Mostly for food, but also people-watching and discovering Dance Dance Revolution (3rd Mix). In a big enough shindig, she could get away with being a friend of a friend (of a friend). She was homeless, but that didn't mean she looked a mess. Not all of them did, despite what many thought.

If she took a bath in a sink, and happened to have a Ziploc bag of decent clothes and a bottle of Dolly Girl in her knapsack, she could pass for your average teenager. The deal-sealer was the Jackie O shades she found on a Hyde Park bench.

Trendy, and conveniently hid her… singular vision. Her long, wavy hair could only do so much.

Otherwise, she wore her Crustpunk armor: frayed denim, safety pins, and a general fuck-you attitude. Perfect for repelling most fuckin' people she didn't want to be fuckin' bothered with, in the first fuckin' place.

During a typical day of wanderlust, listening to Supertramp's "The Logical Song" on her pocket radio, Piri waited in the bush. She learned that near a railroad crossing was a perfect place to get caught, but a mile or so away by some trees?

Hoppers and gondolas were her faves because they were open-topped; easier to get into than trouble. From the ground, however, you couldn't see if they were full. Drowning in coal dust or getting impaled by a rusty bit of track wasn't Piri's idea of a good time. Her solution: tossing a rock and hoping for the sweet, sweet echo of nothing inside.

After hearing that pleasing sound, she hopped in the hopper. It wasn't as empty as she thought.

Freighthoppin' existed before Piri was even a zygote, so surprise wasn't part of the equation when she saw the man at the other end. Ditto if he told her to get out. Too many people drew attention, and finders keepers. But he kept to himself, so she did the same. She swapped her radio for her pillow and a torn-cover about rock formations. She was already tired after a day of panhandling, so she didn't need to read long before she passed out.

The slow lurch and clang of the cars stopping woke her. Wherever they were headed, they were there. She couldn't get a sense of where she was. Or when, apart from it still being daytime. The man was standing over her, jerking off and mumbling to himself.

When she took up her vagabondage, she gave herself two unbreakable rules: stay clean, don't get pregnant. The pervert was satisfied with self-indulgence, so she didn't worry about her second rule. The threat of STDs, however, flared with each stroke.

It'd be ok if he came in her hair. She could cut her hair.

She slowly reached for his busy hand, dread quickening her breath. Taking his hand, she could at least guide him away from her face. If she moved as fast as she wanted to, the pervert might've turned rapist. Or worse.

When her flesh finally touched his, coupled with the sound of her breathing, he released faster than she could react. Almost. Instinct made her flinch. And scream.

What neither noticed during their tension experience were footsteps of a guard crunching on gravel. But *he* noticed *her* scream.

He rushed up the outside ladder and saw a shocked man with his pants down, standing over a frightened minor.

In an instant, she went from lucky to clever and she continued screaming, adding that the man kidnapped her and was trying to rape her.

The pervert knew he was fucked and tried getting away, but the best he could do was break his leg after climbing over the metal wall. While the guard and others handled the pervert, Piri scrambled to find where he came. She'd have to get a new pillow.

Another log on the agony debt fire.

Luxury and Power

More important than why Piri became homeless was why she *stayed* homeless when there were ways to do better.

The obvious place would be a youth shelter, but Piri loved getting older since she'd be further from annoying kids. Since she couldn't punt the nation's brats to the moon, she'd dump them in Nebraska. It'd be like boarding school except with amber waves of grain. The anklebiters would be safe since the state was flat like week-old RC Cola, so they couldn't fall off anything. And the crotchlings would only be locked in 'til they were emotionally mature enough to know the difference between a debate and an attack. More than a few would be stuck 'til their 20's.

Piri would have to admit she had been abused before going into a domestic abuse shelter, so that was out.

She sometimes went to your run-of-the-mill homeless shelter since it had free pads (the threat of toxic shock was enough to avoid tampons), and she could occasionally take a decent shower or get a decent meal. However, the sometimes were rare. The shelter didn't allow people to stay so it could keep a steady rotation of those in need, but that wasn't why she didn't make her visits routine. Even though she slept rough, she was in denial that she was homeless. Being a regular would be admitting otherwise.

Her holding onto vagabondage was why getting transitional housing and getting on the royal road to normalcy and decency wasn't going to happen, either.

An emergency shelter was for people suddenly thrust into homelessness, through nature or nurture. It was fine for Piri during her first month, but guilt was the push that made her move. Plus, newcomers were understandably in terrible places mentally, and she had a low threshold for others' pain.

See how she felt about traditional housing to know why she didn't do permanent supportive housing.

She'd need a family to be in a family shelter.

A faith-based shelter offered help with a comma, not a period.

Where did Piri lay her head after the towers fell? Chicago being a metropolis meant there were empty buildings big and small to take a chance with. Dilapidation could kill, as could hands. And her bark was worse than her bite. Groups were protection from fiends, but also bait for cops. The right-sized group in a far away building would be ideal. Which was how Piri found herself in a no-look shelter with a gang of four.

Everyone had a story. No one wanted to hear it. No one wanted to share it. Knowing too much about someone could make you the wrong kind of sympathetic, or make you an accomplice after the fact.

Perdita and Tegan were twins who looked like they backpacked across America too many times. The former had to be right, while the latter tried to be right. They hated "The Shining" as much as you'd think they did.

Streetwise was from parts unknown, with an unplaceable accent. She said her name once but no one understood it, so they gave her a nickname. She dressed loudly, with holes patched with clothes that fell apart, and had a gambler's mentality.

A fellow Crustpunk, Ilyse, was the ostensible leader, but don't call her a queen bee. She'd punch you in the throat before or after telling you they just get fat and lay eggs all day. Like you can figure, she was an overcompensating kind of tough. She had to be to survive.

If you're curious, "Perdita" goes "per-DEE-tah", "Tegan" goes "TEE-gan", and "Ilyse" goes "ill-EES".

Each had a part to play on the decrepit stage (the building they hijacked was a black box theatre). Piri was the youngest, so it was easiest for her to guilt restaurants and bakeries for food they'd throw away. Perdita and Tegan panhandled and found things to sell. Streetwise was the gal who knew a guy and could get them things, if the barter was good enough. Ilyse fucked anyone up who tried to fuck with them. And **no one** brought anyone new.

It took a month since the Towers fell, but they settled into their new lives. They didn't kid themselves: it wouldn't last. However, they were going to stretch that taffy until planned obsolescence had its say.

Streetwise got someone to do a line tap, so they had electricity as long as they didn't use a noticeable amount. Which was why, in these cooler months, they had a power strip filled with cords to electric blankets on the tiny stage that ended up being their bedroom.

The barter was that Perdita was "elected" to have morning convos with the someone for a week, after losing a game of Seven-Card Stud against Streetwise and Ilyse. She thought it was boring as shit 'til the someone broke down why hippies sucked.

They preached about peace and love, yet they only helped themselves. Then they had the fucking nerve to sell their "altruism" through the same companies they "rebelled" against when age made them gray and desperate.

When Tegan heard the rant, she asked if that meant she couldn't do shrooms anymore. To which Perdita replied that hippies ruined the world, but she'd be damned if she let them ruin her fun.

Another night, Piri brought back a bag of stale rolls, which
was fine (I guess), and half a bottle of ALAGA syrup, which made
her royalty for a few days. Not at all an overreaction. If you
thought you liked syrup and never had ALAGA, you never liked
syrup.

Anywho, ALAGA was reason enough to party. When
every day was shit, any distraction was welcome and convivial as
fuck. A blank CD could hold 80 minutes of music, at the most.
Unless you turned it into a data CD. Then you had 700 megabytes
to play with. A three-minute song at 128kbps was 3 megabytes.
With the power of Napster, and a CD player that could play data
CDs, a distraction could last past dawn.

Ilyse was the DJ, so there was a lot of Plasmatics (check
out "Mistress of Taboo"), Sleater-Kinney (and "Dig Me Out"), Mo-
Dettes (ditto their killer cover of Rolling Stones' "Paint It, Black"),
The Slits (and "Shoplifting"), and Neo Boys ("Empty My Head",
too) on random.

Piri found a pair of shitty, tiny speakers during one of her…
book trips, saving everyone the grief of passing headphones
around. Which worked out for her since, while the others partied,
she sat in a dressing room and read a torn-cover about the
history of Independence Day. King Missile's "Detachable Penis"
snuck on Q101 and her pocket radio, ending just in time for her to
switch to B96's DJ Mixdown.

Perdita stumbled in to check on the candlelit Piri. Or rather, was sent by Tegan to make sure Piri didn't mess with her psilocybin garden on a bit of birch. Perdita told her sister she didn't have to worry, and again she was right about something.

Piri said she hoped no one thought she was a snob; she just didn't think she should drink 'til she was 21, and they were passing around a bottle of Monte Alban Silver. Perdita giggled at the idea of obeying such an arbitrary law in their shameless lives, but she respected Piri and promised to send word down.

Before Perdita left to rejoin the distraction, Piri asked what it was like to be on shrooms. Perdita told the story of Tegan's first trip, and how she saw an octopus in a toilet while the ceiling laughed at her.

Piri pointed out that it wasn't Perdita's story, and Perdita said that she didn't have one. Tegan crumbled her shrooms and mixed them with yogurt to make them go down better, but Perdita ate hers raw, like nature intended.

Just because one had to be right all the time didn't mean they *were*, and Perdita threw up before the magic happened. Her drunken parting advice: always use yogurt, and never trust a big butt and a smile.

Once upon a December, Piri rode a CTA train to the CTA bus to another CTA bus that would take her a few blocks away from the theatre. In her knapsack, dinner for everyone by way of the ends of meats and cheeses from a deli. A great deal, and all she had to do was scrub a few toilets. The less you knew about said toilets, the better.

The car she was in was oddly barren for being almost dusk; as deep into the day as Ilyse wanted everyone back. Due to the dangers that lurked past sunset. Piri was making good time despite the briskness of a winter day. There was a couple at one end, and a woman across from her.

The woman took a note from her purse and gave it to Piri. It said that she shouldn't worry, that what was about to happen was normal, and to make sure no one hurt her. Before Piri could ask anything, the woman convulsed on the floor.

The couple ran to the next car, mumbling something about al-Qaeda. The woman was kind enough to warn strangers about her epileptic seizures, but her note didn't say anything about epilepsy. Because of this, Piri was lost in the randomness of what took seventy seconds, frightened for the woman and for herself.

Another log for the agony debt fire.

Back onstage, Tegan sniffed a cup of yogurt, and it passed the fresh test. Her Psilocybe caeruplipes (blue-foot shrooms, to their friends) were finally ripe and ready. Ilyse wanted to give them a try but never had shrooms before, so Tegan's co-pilot on the magic carpet would get a stem with her yogurt. A cap, the most potent part of the blue-foot, went to Tegan.

Piri was fine with watching them trip, so that's what she did. After rolling a cigarette for Perdita and Streetwise (Tegan taught her; Perdita corrected her), who were having a smoke break in the alley. The twin wouldn't join them for all the money in the Powerball, but the migrant would when she was done.

Parents told their kids they should tell teachers when they're bullied at school. That teachers would protect them. What parents didn't tell, because they didn't know, was that school boards had other plans.

Bullies had parents, too, and apples fell close. With crooked lawyers and their bullshit in tailored suits. Whether or not the bully was proven as such, lawsuits were black marks. Thus, in an exercise of casual dissonance, it was in the school board's best interest to do nothing.

It wasn't like the bullied kid would shoot up their class. They might simply run away, stuffing their frustration and pain into their fists and saving those weaker than them from becoming them.

75

What happened when they took a psychotropic?

CHAPTER SIX

Otaku Life and Death Routines

When you're 21, you're no fun. Nobody likes you when you're 23. Let's see how the Georgian import fared at 24.

Rudella triumphed over the educational system with her mortuary science and sociology degrees, and not a speck of student debt. Apprenticeship and being a mortuary assistant didn't make the money flood, so she still drove her Honda. Still lived in her ok apartment, too.

Because the area was lousy with forest preserves, seeing deer in the building's backyard was common. Some Spring days, she saw fawns lying by themselves. Their mothers did that when they're too young to keep up while they foraged, and left them forever if a human touched them.

In the years since Honbria, her effect on Rudella lingered. To protect herself from leeches who deluded with their big personalities, she created a big personality to cancel them out. Destructive interference, for those who want to impress their nearest and dearest. It was exhausting, but she played a bigger version of herself instead of making up someone, so she didn't bump into a crisis existential.

Graduation led to apprenticeship, which brought Rudella to Sunset Shores Funeral Home and life as a mortuary assistant. It was also in the south suburbs, which saved her a ton of grief. She wanted fuck-all to do with Chicagoland north of Pilsen and Bronzeville, the neighborhoods at the edge of insanity.

Rudella went to Anime Central, in Rosemont, the year after she left Honbria behind. Rosemont, like most places in Chicagoland, was simple to get to. Rosemont, like most places in Chicagoland north of Pilsen and Bronzeville, was aggravating to get to. Streets, highways, and byways were equally convenient and miserable. The road to Rosemont was also the road to O'Hare, one of the busiest airports in the world. Then there was the added insult of paid parking. All of this to say that Rudella, a hardcore fan of easy traveling, hated going past Pilsen and Bronzeville more than when her underwire popped.

That first ACen was great and terrible for Rudella. Great because Shinichi Watanabe, the creator of one of her favorite anime, was there. You wouldn't expect a devout of the morbid to love something as manic as "Excel Saga", but she couldn't get enough of its craziness and bobbleheading to other anime.

She was also introduced to what would be a new favorite anime, "R.O.D the TV", since some of the creative team and a voice actress were there to show it off. An action series about three sisters who could control paper hired to protect an author was quirky enough to make her curious, then she was caught in its honey trap. The composer, Taku Iwasaki, had "Witch Hunter Robin" on his CV, so she double-gushed about that. She'd triple-gush about him working on "Soul Eater", a fun series that takes place at the Death Weapon Meister Academy, but it didn't exist yet. She was also able to form her Lansing Lamias, destroying her need to visit the Bourbonnais Banshees. She didn't hate the latter; they were more Honbria's friends than hers, and she was bound to see Honbria again if she stuck with them.

If you're curious, "Shinichi Watanabe" goes "shee-NEE-chee wah-tah-NAH-beh" and "Taku Iwasaki" goes "TAH-koo ee-wah-SAH-kee".

There was also terribleness at the Hyatt Regency O'Hare. Apart from the drive. The Japan fetishists were loud and proud, which wouldn't have been a problem if most of them didn't think Rudella was Japanese. For one, they kept asking her questions in Nihongo. At best, she could only butcher the language with the bits she picked up from watching subtitles all her life. The lady fetishists had a strange habit of wanting to touch her hair; she found the nicest way to show them her eomma's teachings. She was fine with being a bitch, but she was no one's pet.

The early days at Sunset Shores were an intense learning experience for Rudella. She was well-versed in death, but understood little about dying. Vrehas taught her plenty, but there's a difference between knowing the path and walking the path. Everything she knew had an academic sheen she had to dull with experience. The grieving didn't care about how long rigor mortis took to unsettle, they wanted to know why their loved one had to die.

The funeral home was modest and comforting, with the requisite funeral director and embalmer. It also had people Rudella didn't expect to see in anything less than a funeral mansion. Like a death doula, a funeral celebrant, and a gravestone conservator. A death doula helped the dying and their loved ones get through Those Final Moments (a birth doula did the reverse for expectant mothers). A funeral celebrant arranged funerals for the lapsed and irreligious. A gravestone conservator kept graves looking spiffy.

Having ensnared her dream job, Rudella was clothed with appropriate enthusiasm in her long dress phase, inspired by the titular character of "Witch Hunter Robin". The folks of Sunset Shores thought she should go simpler, but also that she should be allowed her harmless eccentricities. Especially when it obviously made her so happy, though none understood how much of that was her mask. They also took bets on her sticking with all those layers during Summer.

In that apprenticed year, there were many lessons learned. As a proper employee, there were many more. Of the ones that formed Rudella's core as a mortician, there were few. She forgot that being one was a job, and there were lots of mundane cogs in that well-oiled machine. She didn't forget that death waited for no one, but the funeral director made sure he was the only mortician there who shared the same hours as emergency professionals.

Another core lesson was Rudella attending her first living funeral. She was confused by the concept, too. Instead of gathering friends and family after someone died to mourn, a living funeral gathered friends and family before someone died to celebrate. Their life, not their death. She was fascinated by the party for the moribund because she assumed that all American funerals were draped in tragedy. Seeing people enjoy themselves at an event with "funeral" in the header that didn't involve dancing on graves showed her there was more than one way to move on, and it was as healthy as misery. Still, she felt more comfortable among tears.

Yet another core lesson involved Rudella's first baby funeral. She never wanted kids, her endometriosis helped confirm that, but the cataclysmic nature of a dead infant wasn't beyond her. She lingered through the service as silent support, for reasons obvious and not. She had a hard time swapping "died" for "passed". She felt that the sooner one accepted death, the better, and that "passed" softened an inevitable blow.

She would be thanked and chided by families for her choice of comfort, which she settled on it as she silently supported the family of the one in the tiny coffin.

Beyond the Grave

One overcast afternoon, the kind Rudella preferred, she and the puckish gravestone conservator worked their magic on a granite slab.

In her years with Sunset Shores, she learned how to be a help to everyone, even getting a certificate for the jobs that needed it. Her bumonim's favorite overachiever, thanks to her bumonim's one ton of pressure. Helping the conservator only required steady hands and patience, and it didn't hurt getting to hang out in graveyards all day. He also made it a point to be the first person to buy her a drink when she turned 21. She'd always remember sitting at the bar with him at Benchwarmers, throwing back a Mike's Hard Lemonade, George Thorogood's spin on John Lee Hooker's cover of Amos Milburn's "One Bourbon, One Shot, One Beer" on the jukebox.

By now, she swapped her Robinesque look for the functional elegance of Re-l from "Ergo Proxy", a recent anime whose cerebral darkness she wrapped herself in. The character's blue eyeshadow became red on the Georgian import. All with a little help from Goodwill.

If you're curious, "Re-I" goes "REE-ehl".

As Rudella carefully scraped moss from granite, she enjoyed her new bangs and how they didn't get in the way. The conservator, brushing dust off the other side, asked how many vegans did it take to screw in a light bulb. She was clueless, and he said that it didn't matter, they're better than you. They chuckled at the elitism (it's not vegans they have a problem with, it's the snobbery [can't expect people to team-up with assholes, kids]), then she asked how his wife felt about his new obsession.

A while ago, it was her turn to drive, which meant her tunes came out the speakers. He made it clear their first trip that he wasn't a fan of heavy metal, so she set out to find one song to prove him wrong. After many, many, many, many failed attempts, she won him over with Lacuna Coil's melancholy "Senzafine".

He tried to return the favor with Creedence Clearwater Revival, but she was already a fan, thanks to her bumonim. One loved Peter Gabriel, the other loved Phil Collins, but they met in the middle with CCR, for some reason. "Tombstone Shadow" was obviously one of her favorite songs, but she also loved "Before You Accuse Me", "It Came Out of the Sky", and their cover of Marvin Gaye's cover of Gladys Knight and the Pips' "I Heard It

Through the Grapevine". He then threatened to take her to a karaoke bar to hear her sing any of them, or Gabriel's "Sledgehammer". She agreed, on the condition that he sang Mötley Crüe's "Live Wire" in all its falsetto glory. Silence.

As they finished up, they ranted about how modern revenge stories are stupid. The stories forgot the most important rule: if revenge was what you sought, dig two graves. Instead, they treated the act as a prize for the tormented, not a further punishment. Suddenly, Rudella was warned not to take revenge for this, and smelled a particularly rank fart before she can ask for what. While she tried in vain to get the stink out of her nose, she saw an oasis in the distance.

Rudella didn't care much for comics 'til a few months ago. Cinema and anime scratched her entertainment itches plenty. More than that, she didn't want to deal with the decades of history that Batman, the X-Men, et. al. brought with them. She had some time to kill while waiting for the funeral director to settle burial affairs, so she went inside a nearby comic shop. She saw walls of the usual superheroics, but she also saw one wall of indie comics. Compared to the likes of DC and Marvel, they were essentially made yesterday. Some literally were. She found a new itch to scratch.

The first book she bought was the first volume of "Dogwitch". It was discounted, but those five bucks paid for something that ended up being worth more to her than a Pagani

Zonda. She didn't know comics could tell stories like a witch living in a forest with a porcelain doll and stuffed dog, with the three making magic fetish videos. Violet Grimm was Rudella's kind of fucked-up; the following two graphic novels confirmed that. She even took to wearing the same B&W-striped thigh highs, which introduced her to garter belts since they kept sliding down, and a button with Violet's icon, a radiation symbol with a pentagram in the center.

If you're curious, "Senzafine" goes "sehn-zah-FEEN" and "Pagani Zonda" goes "pah-GAH-nee ZONE-dah".

"Dogwitch" led to "Dawn", about the goddess of birth and rebirth, with the god of death as her lover. "Dawn" led to "Witchblade", about a lady detective who's chosen to wear a magic gauntlet, and the fiends who wanted to take it from her. "Witchblade" led to "Kabuki", about a lady assassin in a Future Japan who decided to get out of the game, then had to figure out what it means to be human. "Kabuki" led to "Hack/Slash", about a woman who traveled with a brute in the US to kill monsters, with a B-movie flair. And on and on.

Back in the graveyard, Rudella asked the conservator if she could take a break to check out the comic shop across the street, reminding him that she earned it for putting up with his swamp ass. He gave her the ok, and asked to get him a Jones Soda, if they have any. That's how she discovered Papercuts Comics, and where she met Raissa.

If you're curious, "Raissa" goes "RICE-ah".

Four Color World

Part of the fun of wandering into a new comic shop was discovering books stocked with the whimsy of the owner and their customers.

Part of the pain was dealing with the elitist prick(s) who put all their worth into their love of comics, lashing out with **extreme prejudice** towards anyone who even mildly disagreed with them. It's not wrong to love comics, or anything, but molding your life around one love made everyone's opinions a potential threat.

Fun and pain were always on Rudella's mind before she entered a new comic shop. Luckily, Papercuts would only be fun, despite it looking like your average bookstore. With gaming tables in the back.

A book that was on her list for a while was "Johnny the Homicidal Maniac", and there it was. A little farther, "The Crow". A skip away, "Ghost World". She could only laugh at the fact that three B&W books she'd been desperate to find were right there. Dinner for a few nights would be Hot Pockets, but she'd made mistakes that cost more than that. So, with a pep in her Doc Marten'd step, she took the nihilistic, the sorrowful, and the caustic to the counter.

Raissa was a no-nonsense Rockabilly with Goodwill sensibilities, and a husky voice that was shades of Kathleen Turner. She loved comics; so much so that she did the insane thing for a woman and jockeyed the register for Papercuts. Being a lady geek meant the fella geeks wanted to either belittle her or fuck her. She didn't mind awkward geeks. As long as she treated them respectfully and reminded them to speak up, they respected her and spoke up. The ones who felt they had something to prove were the horndogs. To them, she acted like a Wobbuffet: all counterattacks. If she started something, she'd be a slut. If she corrected someone who tried to correct her about Kelley Jones not drawing interiors during Batman's Knightfall arc (he only did the covers), she'd be a smart slut. The adjective's what was important, as far as she was concerned.

Raissa never saw a peppy Goth before, slightly smelling of grass, but that's who approached her at the till. As she rung Rudella up and appreciated her taste, she understood why. She was also amazed by her Dogwitch button. She thought she was the only weirdo who knew about that series. They geeked-out about it for a few minutes, then the peppy, grassy Goth left with a promise to come back soon.

Rudella was so elated, she forgot to check for Jones Soda. They didn't have any, but they did have BAWLS. She was so tickled by the idea of giving the conservator BAWLS that she bought it. She'd regret it on the way back to Sunset Shores, though: it was basically fizzy caffeine. And there was traffic.

It was while Rudella read "The Crow" on her couch, Russian Circles' second album spinning in her stereo, that her bumonim made their weekly call. Forty minutes of nothing in particular ended in four words of devastation: her cat was dead. It wasn't a surprise, she was almost 15. But it still hurt. A lot. The blade in her heart was twisted when they told their wrecked ttal they threw Mur-Mur in the garbage. Then they hung up. When, at the witching hour, she ended her weeping psychopathic fantasies, she swore she'd never get a cat again.

She decided also to give her best friend some semblance of a proper end. She printed her favorite picture, Mur-Mur grabbing a toilet paper roll with her front paws and kicking it with her back, and burned it in effigy.

Papercuts became Rudella's new haunt, because of its selection and certain members of its staff. Raissa worked there all the time, so it didn't matter which day she stopped in. Well… Raissa made it a point to not work on Magic the Gathering or Heroclix days. When Rudella told her why she didn't bother with mainstream books, the gauntlet was thrown. It was the summer of "Dark Knight", but Raissa didn't want to start with such a low-hung fruit. Eventually, she had to since Rudella didn't care for anything on the higher branches.

First, Raissa brought up Tim Burton's Batman films. To everyone's surprise, the Goth was a huge fan and "Batman Returns" being the best Batman film was the hill she'd die on.

Then, Raissa went in for the kill and brought up the Elseworlds line, alternate retellings of DC characters; specifically the Batman and Dracula trilogy. To everyone's surprise, the Goth was a huge fan and Vampire Batman being the coolest Batman was the hill she'd die on.

The fruit was plucked, puréed, and spread like jelly.

As the months went on, Raissa continued her education of Rudella. Rudella visited other members of the Batfamily by way of the film noir-tinged, Brubaker/Pfeifer "Catwoman" runs. She was a big fan of Pete Woods' take of Darwyn Cooke's Catsuit redesign. From there, the all-women team book of James Bond proportions that was "Birds of Prey". Neither series had a Madonna/whore complex. Nor did they have an agenda outside of entertaining the reader. Nor were they male stories in female skin or gender agnostic; they would only work if the characters were women.

"Birds of Prey" stood out to Rudella because the team was led by a woman in a wheelchair, and she couldn't think of anything that had a handicapped person in a position of power. She was bummed when that was changed for nostalgia reasons.

Rudella complained one visit about most comics being chaste, and Raissa introduced her to the works of Milo Manara and Guido Crepax. "Click" and an adaptation of Pauline Réage's "Story of O", respectively. Rudella was very interested, then asked if Raissa was worried parents would complain about the store having erotica. Raissa replied, with some vulgarity, that worry often gave small things a big shadow. Plus, the books were on a shelf behind the counter. Which took them to talk of people willfully being homogenized and not taking chances. Rudella dusted off her Sociology degree by bringing up the fact that no civilization thrived by being monocultured, and that even Nazis teamed up with Japan. Raissa warned her to not say the N-word so close to the Jack Kirby comics.

During another visit, Rudella asked something that'd been nagging at her for a while. Papercuts had overhead speakers that were at the mercy of whoever worked the register. Some of the Raissa times had a foreign-sounding band Rudella liked, but couldn't figure out who they were. All she knew is the singer sometimes shouted "PARTY!", so it became the PARTY! band to her. Raissa said she was enjoying the Gypsy Punk stylings of Gogol Bordello, and that the "PARTY!" song was "Suddenly... (I Miss Carpaty)". Rudella was sated.

If you're curious, "Gogol" goes "GOE-gole".

It was when Raissa told Rudella she had cute boobs that things changed for the better. Raissa wasn't into her, she was saving herself for Lee Ving, and recognition of her cute boobs by women (straight, gay, or otherwise) was a leitmotif in Rudella's life. The nickels and pennies of it all was that Raissa followed up with admitting her boobs were lopsided. It was a slow day, so no one else was around to hear. She then pulled a bra insert from under her halter top, shook the chicken cutlet in Rudella's face with a cackle, and put it back. After some adjusting. Hard to find a better way of saying they're best friends now.

Papercuts, like most comic shops, bought old comics. You'd think that all geeks knew how to take care of their floppies (heh), but you'd be surprised. And not every comic in the "new release" section sold out. Because of these things, shops had to occasionally... adapt their inventory. Proper care for a floppy was to bag and board them, so they didn't get dirty or flop, then put them in a long box for easy storage. This took a long time, so the staff had to name the first line-up of Chris Claremont's X-Men to find out who the lucky one was. Which is how Raissa got stuck bagging and boarding (she mistakenly named Gambit, then blamed the animated series), and how Rudella got stuck helping as a best friendly favor.

Under the condition that they watched the Phantasm series while they did it. Because, of course, the assistant mortician knew about the one horror series involving morticians.

Bagging and boarding's easy: cardboard sheet went into plastic bag, floppy went between them, sealed bag with tape or a tuck, repeat. It's also, as you could imagine, tedious. Especially with the stacks in need on the gaming tables. Rudella loved the Phantasm series, and she could recite each movie by heart. Raissa wasn't interested in them, although she did like the atmospheric mortician horror of "Dead & Buried", but they kept Rudella's hands busy. So, after the first ten minutes, their conversations got increasingly random.

Rudella complained about girl problems, like why she broke up with her recent girlfriend after seeing her in the shower. Raissa didn't care who someone fucked, but she didn't wanna hear about the rainbow life if she didn't have to. She was curious, though, about why people like Rudella use "LGBT". A sore spot for Rudella, but not why you think. She didn't think she needed an adjective because she loved women because she felt it "othered" her. As far as she was concerned, she and Raissa were the same and shouldn't be adjective'd just because one preferred labia to testicles. She also didn't hang her identity on her preference. Her example was that it was like reminding people she had a liver. Everybody had one and knew it was important, so it was more than a little silly to focus on it.

A half-hour of randomness led them to how terrible the internet is. At least, for one of them. Raissa wasn't a Luddite, but she used it for emails and not much else. Rudella prescribed the internet's viciousness to anonymity making assholes out of everyone. When she was done, it was Raissa's turn to make an odd analogy. She said that the internet's basically a cave full of angry puppies, with a hole in the ceiling. You stuck your head in, and the echoing barks could make you go mad. But the puppies couldn't hurt you. And if you left the cave, you wouldn't know they were there.

Raissa made the mistake of paying attention to "Phantasm" only near the end. Rudella said that the movie could've been called "Ambiguity", to give you an idea of the Rockabilly's quandary. The most she could put together was that it maybe had to do with aliens, but Rudella wasn't offering any help. Partially because she couldn't. That reminded Raissa of her pyramid theory, to which Rudella rolled her eyes at the start of. Raissa knew why, and promised it wasn't about aliens. Her theory was that they were skyscrapers of the Before Common Era. That they came to a peak since it was easier to build upward with the tools they had. Rudella played devil's advocate and pointed out that pyramids weren't just in Egypt. Raissa retorted by pointing out that if you put a bunch of toddlers in separate rooms with blocks, some were bound to build pyramids.

As "Phantasm II" glowed onscreen and their convo resumed its randomness, Raissa brought up the surge of comic book movies since the dawn of the millennium. Then she got distracted by someone making a quad-barreled shotgun. Then she went on about how although it's cool to see adaptations, she never wanted them. She wanted great comic stories, and she was worried that companies would focus on adaptations instead of their source material once the money dump trucks started pulling in. She had another worry that was more existential; comics would start mining from its past more than usual for those nostalgia bucks until they were just relaunches and sequels. Someone told her that longevity wasn't a privilege and that you still had to adapt, and she wanted to pin that to every comic editor's wall.

At then end of "Phantasm II", as someone melted from embalming fluid mixed with acid, Raissa asked if the fluid was yellow. Whenever people found out what Rudella did, they either freaked out or leaned in. The ones who leaned in tended to ask the same bland questions about ghosts, smells, and zombie shelters. You could imagine the amount of confetti and streamers fluttering in her head after getting a decent question. She rambled about how formaldehyde's pink so the decedent's flesh looked healthy, but she had to shine a red light on them during the service for when it wasn't enough. She added that the new car smell was part-formaldehyde, and it was wise to press the "outside air" button and use it for a few minutes on a hot day or else you'd be poisoned. She went to ramble about how replacement hips and such were sent to recycleries, if families didn't want them. She then rambled about how caskets exploded if they were sealed too tight due to the gas built up from the rot. She also added a warning about grapefruit juice and how it could kill because it has furanocoumarins, which intensified some drugs' effect on people to a dangerous degree. Oh, and sometimes teeth popped like corn in the cremator. When she was finally done, she was buzzing like a vibrator after a Shakira concert. And she was hungry.

One burrito-as-big-as-your-face later, the ladies got back to work and "Phantasm III". Somewhere towards the middle, Raissa told Rudella to take off her mask. Rudella feigned ignorance, but Raissa reminded her that she had a career involving superheroes, so she knew all about false identities. She saw it slip in a big way with the formaldehyde, but she noticed it happen a few times as she's known her. Raissa explained that most of the time, Rudella acted like a caricature of Goths. She didn't think Rudella was a poser, but it was obvious with the slips that there was more to her than her packaging.

Rudella wiped away a tear, not knowing if it meant joy or sorrow, then told her about Honbria.

CHAPTER SEVEN

As Fears Go By

Once upon a time again, the discarded girl tried to get through this thing called "life".

The man-made disaster fresh in everyone's mind was the levees failing New Orleans as Katrina held her sway. Most people made the mistake of thinking the hurricane was the sole cause of the catastrophic damage.

The Category 5's path veered northeast of Louisiana after making landfall. Plus, Katrina's sisters, Rita and Wilma, arrived months later and were far more powerful, yet their fallout was much less severe. Rita and Wilma, combined, caused 172 deaths and $40,900,000,000 worth of damage along their path; their older sister caused 1,392 deaths and $125,000,000,000 worth of damage along hers.

How did man fuck New Orleans?

It began with a boom.

In 1965, Hurricane Betsy visited New Orleans. When the Category 4 arrived, there was a boom at the levees; the Ninth

Wards, the closest to them, drowned. The levees were rebuilt, but not strong enough to handle another Betsy. Promises were made, promises were broken, and Katrina arrived 40 years later with another boom.

Worse than the broken promises was the ineptitude. The levees broke, in the first place, because the Army Corps wanted to save a few bucks. Around $100,000,000 was saved by planting the levees' metal sheets almost five meters shallower than they should have been.

The government was molasses in helping New Orleans once Katrina had her way; what should have taken hours took weeks, and even then... If you wanted to piss off someone from NOLA, say "FEMA". Or any insurance company. Even a whisper would tempt a slap or two.

The media chose ratings over integrity and compassion, reporting miseries without double-checking their sources, causing needless harm.

It was something Piri learned to do well, unfortunately. "No", whether whimpered or bellowed, wasn't a word rapists understood. Fighting back got her broken, beaten, and scarred, so she stopped doing that after the fourth time. And it wasn't only men: cruelty was genderqueer. She could at least take what little solace there was in knowing she stayed clean and didn't get pregnant, though it was always a burden.

Rape crisis centers had pills to stop STDs and pregnancies before they started. She stopped bothering with rape kits; justice ignored homeless women, especially ones who weren't blonde and pathetic.

More logs for the agony debt fire.

However, the panic from her assault 50 seconds old convinced her that she needed a Plan B pill. Now. There wasn't ever a point in her life where she wanted to be a mother. Among many other reasons, the idea of a skeleton growing inside her freaked her out. Plus, being a homeless parent was as irresponsible as someone could be. She pulled up her pants behind a Walgreens, so she didn't have to go far to steal.

A side-effect of Plan B not working was vomiting two hours after taking it, which was why she was in a gas station bathroom with a can of Arizona Tea. The bathroom didn't have a blue light, which meant addicts didn't use it (the light made it hard to see veins), which meant people would forget she's in there.

In all the times she took the pill, she never threw up. But just because something hasn't happened didn't mean it wouldn't happen.

As Piri waited, her mind was cacophonous with thoughts of STDs. She could get to the closest crisis center blindfolded, but her luck could've also run out.

Her rapist was a drug dealer. He might've gotten high on his supply. If he dealt heroine, he used needles. Maybe dirty needles.

He might've gotten HIV. Which could turn into AIDS.

She might have AIDS.

She might have AIDS.

She sounded crazy to herself. Syphilis made people crazy. She didn't know how to spell it and she might have it. Or herpes. She thought about checking for telltale bumps. Was that itching the start?

She might have AIDS.

She might have AIDS.

What's left of her life might be ruined. At least she didn't puke.

She traded the bathroom for a bus kiosk as she thought about what to do next. She still had her tea, but the can was something to hold as a comfort.

She might have AIDS.

She didn't dwell on her rapists much, and had the nightmares to prove it. This one hit differently, though. She didn't know why, and two equal truths presented themselves to her.

He had to pay. She wasn't able to send him the bill.

She knew how to survive, not how to hurt. Or worse. And she wanted worse. More than a fat kid wanted their bully alone with an alibi, she wanted worse.

Like lightning from an azure sky, she remembered reading about informants, then took a bus to the nearest police station.

The nerves weren't just because she hadn't been to a crisis center yet. Revenge, *true* revenge, had a rule most people have forgotten about thanks to the last few years of pop culture.

If you wanted revenge, you dug two graves. You didn't get out alive. Metaphorically, or otherwise.

For Piri to do what she was about to, she had to accept that, at best, she'd become more dead inside. But her rapist had to pay, and the suavely dressed detective walking into the interrogation room with her partner could send the bill.

Despite evidence to the contrary, Detective Terentia still believed in the purity of justice. Less than half of all serious crimes were reported, around 11% of those ended in an arrest, and around 2% of *those* ended in a conviction. Then there was the other, corrupt side of the coin with the likes of Joseph Miedzianowski, Richard Zuley, Jon Burge, and Ronald Watts. But she was a good cop who wanted to protect and serve, and hoped the nervous Crustpunk had worthwhile info.

If you're curious, "Terentia" goes "teh-REHN-tee-ah".

Before asking what Piri knew, as her partner stood in the corner, Terentia put a folder in front of her and told her it had what happened to informants. Piri could only get a few pages into the thick folder full of murder.

Terentia then told her about whosarat.com, a site criminals used to keep tabs on the snitches who needed stitches. The detective wanted Piri to know what being an informant would cost. She also told her what being an informant would pay. Piri would be Third World rich.

Piri told Terentia what she knew about her rapist, which was a lot. Even among the homeless, people didn't notice her much. Or rather, because of her defect, didn't want to notice her much. Because of that, she got to overhear many a great and scandalous thing from lurkers of the demimonde.

Her rapist was one of the bigger drug-dealing players, and loved showing it. However, massive as Piri's info dump was, it wasn't anything Terentia didn't have on him. The detective even had DNA evidence from various crime scenes. But he was too clever to be brought in.

When Terentia finished laying everything out, Piri let out a laugh that was, to put it mildly, disturbing. Terentia thought it was in defeat and was about to console Piri when she asked if the detective only needed his DNA to arrest him. Terentia said yes, and Piri's ugly laughter picked up again.

After winding down and wiping away tears, she admitted she had a fresh sample between her legs.

Pros and Cons

The first thing Piri did with the burner phone Terentia gave her was throw it away before anyone saw her with it.

She had a feeling that cops bought their burners in bulk, and that one of the quickest ways to get on whosarat.com was being spotted with one. She memorized Terentia's number, so it was just a matter of buying a phone that didn't scream "informant" and explaining why in a voicemail. She also kept it turned off most of the time, checking it only at the end of the day. The more controlled the situation in which she could do her job, the better.

Her phone's background was the Venus de Milo, the ultimate disability success story.

One night, huddled somewhere in Garfield Park, Piri received something from Terentia. Garfield Park was one of her favorite places on the West Side, full of flora and architecture, so her mood was all the more joyous. She held onto her phone as if it just offered to save her life. Which, in a way, it did.

The gift was a picture message: her rapist's mugshot.

She rocked back and forth like her body was fanning away her stress, and bit her lip to muffle her laugh from potential passerbys. It was a high she'd be glad to chase.

Piri figured the best way to be an informant was to not hunt for info. Better to grab a foam noodle and wade in the pool of disillusionment 'til info floated past her. People were suspicious of the shark, not the goldfish. Also helped to not be greedy. Flooding Terentia with info would either make her question validity or draw too much attention. Besides, Piri was paid by the week, not commission.

She and her knapsack tended to hang around weed dealers. To no one's surprise, they were the most chill. Plus, she thought it was stupid the law treated THC worse than alcohol. Most of the lives ruined by weed were by possession, whereas booze ruined by misadventure. Not to mention the ruin that was caused by what passed for cigarettes after the additives had their say. Did you know you could grow tobacco, for personal use, in Illinois?

Along with waiting to accidentally hear news about any of the harder drugs, she liked finding out where and when the next underground rave was. She dressed the Crustpunk as a matter of safety, not taste. Studs, pins, and spikes scared most people, which made her harder to hurt.

However, she was a frustrated raver, at heart.

She'd love nothing more than to go into an abandoned warehouse packed with party people, bright lights, and Happy Hardcore 'til they died, and let go of her troubles and pain for one night. But she knew what she was. Or rather, assumed what others thought of her. So she spent those nights on warehouse lawns, lousy with longing.

Oddly, some of her best info came from couch-surfing. She was friendly enough with a few people in shitty apartments to enjoy occasional nights with four decrepit walls and a leaky roof.

She had the chance to burn new data CDs for her knapsack, too. Some paid their rent by being stash houses, and some of *those* whittled down their student debt with what was left over. College degrees were the new junk bonds.

Piri waited two or three weeks before telling Terentia about a stash house crash pad; enough time for other people to get blamed.

Around this time, Chicago was slowly tearing down its public housing projects. Mid-20th century monuments to the failure of good intentions, the projects were supposed to be a refuge for low-income families, but became hives of infamy.

There were good people there; however, gangs made the loudest noise and had the perfect salve to distract those who felt forgotten. Living in places like the Ida B. Wells Homes, Loomis Courts, the Cabrini-Greens Homes, and Stateway Gardens made feeling forgotten part of life.

Terentia hoped that Piri could get any insight into either place, to which Piri swiftly replied with a cackle and an R-rated negative.

Terentia expressed her frustration with people keeping quiet about criminals they could help stop. Piri sighed disappointingly at the detective's selective memory and brought up the police's code of silence. The detective was speechless.

The smattering of drug busts Piri led Terentia to over a few months helped, for the most part. There was one instance where the dealer's lawyer said that Terentia had to reveal her source.

Any good cop could tell you there were two glaring problems with doing that. The obvious one: the informant would get on whosarat.com. The existential one: informants, confidential and potential, would never trust them.

Terentia didn't give Piri up. The judge demanded to know who her source was, or she'd be held in contempt.

Terentia kept Piri to herself, even as she was handcuffed.

She had to spend a month in jail, but she didn't have anything to worry about. News got around fast inside, and convicts protected her from anyone who tried to start any shit.

To them, all cops were bastards... but she was <u>their</u> bastard.

In a group survival situation, the first person to die was the know-it-all. The arrogance of their knowledge left them blind to glaring mistakes. The last person standing was the paranoiac because they were too afraid to do dangerous things.

Piri the Paranoiac adapted to informant life well. As well as someone in her position could. With half a decade of agony debts yet to be paid.

What did Piri do with her money? That's what Terentia thought as the two rode on Lake Michigan. It was her informant's birthday, and she offhandedly mentioned once she'd always been curious about the structures she saw in the distance on the beach.

They were riding in a rented motorboat, Piri in her Jackie O disguise, towards one of the curiosities, also known as a water crib.

From the coast, you couldn't tell what they were. Maybe boulders, but they looked constructed. Maybe buildings, but they didn't make sense being so distant.

Water cribs were created to save Chicagoans from the Industrial Revolution. Factories dumped waste into the same Lake Michigan where people got their drinking water (for a centuries-long case of literally shitting where you ate, check out the history of the River Thames).

It was discovered that if you went far enough from the sludge, water was untouched. That's where water cribs came in; pumps that flowed the safe water through underground tunnels inland. Two miles away, at first, then four miles because "moderation" wasn't on the industrial docket.

Terentia took Piri to the William E. Dever Crib, north of Navy Pier and resembling peppermint candy. Or rather, as close as they could get. It was still in use, and the fear of "9/11 II: Electric Boogaloo" put it under heavy surveillance.

Piri didn't mind, though. It would've been groovy to go inside, but she already had a better view than most. Then she looked landward.

Anyone could see Chicago from the north, south, above, or west. Sharing the same view as the sunrise, however, was the privilege of the few. Even in the stark light of day, Piri found the sight beautiful. While she was enchanted, Terentia saw what not even her mother had.

Piri with the delight of a child.

What did Piri do with her money? How did she do it? Answering the second question first, Terentia set up a P.O. Box for Piri since she didn't have a home to mail her checks to. The P.O. Box also helped keep them from meeting until it was necessary. Or for a birthday present.

Terentia also helped Piri get a state ID. When Piri picked up her check, she took a bus to another part of Chicago, always different, and cashed it at a store. Then she put the money on a card and hid it where no one would look. The card didn't have a limit, so she didn't need multiples.

As for the first question… not much. She still had no intention of rejoining society. You might point to her rapes as a reason to stop living rough, but a woman could get raped walking her dog. Or doing her job. Or saying "no". Or saying "yes". Her Third World wealth simply accumulated, and she used only what she needed.

After getting dropped ashore, the birthday girl made her way to an arcade in Crestwood and spent an hour working up a sweat with DDR Extreme. She ended her Standard run with Creamy's bubbly "I Do I Do I Do", Sharon's poppy "I'm in the Mood for Dancing", and NW260's intense "Drop Out".

She treated herself to a small pepperoni pizza, and a large Sierra Mist, in the restaurant area while the feeling came back to her legs. Some guys tried to join her, and stormed off with slander when she made them leave. To fuck with them, she shared this silly truth: there's no manly way to eat a hot dog or an ice cream cone. Then she saw them in the golf course agonizing over a polish sausage with cries of no-homo.

From Hollywood Park to a motel. Still in her Jackie O disguise, with an AIDS-free bill of health, Piri waited for a knock on her door. You'd be surprised at the quality of affordable escorts, if you searched long enough.

Being homeless didn't stop her from being horny, but vagabondage made her bring a particular set of baggage to the bedroom. As for the escort, Piri could pick someone up as she was, and has, but she was too mentally exhausted to put up the effort.

She had a thing for long, wavy hair thanks to Dina from "Salute Your Shorts", and the escort on the other side of the door didn't disappoint. The escort wore a tube top and sarong skirt, and was brave enough for polka dots.

Piri paid her, and made a connect-the-dots joke she got a kick out of. The escort sat on the bed, then loosened Piri up with a convo about nothing.

Piri stood quiet for a few seconds, making the escort curious and nervous.

Piri took off her shades, tucked her hair behind her ears, and waited for a reaction.

The escort offered her a hand, then drew her close. Kneeling, Piri's gaze became focused, and yearning.

With a quivering voice, she asked if she was pretty. As she gently caressed Piri's tears away, the escort told her she was beautiful.

Piri hid her face in the escort's lap and asked again. Again, the escort said she was beautiful, repeating it with a tender whisper as she stroked Piri's short hair as if she were a wounded pet.

Piri softly wept as the escort continued her simple motion. Her life had been spent being called all manner of variation of "one-eyed spic bitch", all three she had no choice in. Even though she paid for it, being called something nice was one of the best presents she could get.

To repay her kindness, Piri spread the escort's legs and told her to lie down. She did as she was told.

Piri kissed her thighs in a way that sensually tickled. A welcomed warmth and scent came from above.

When she pulled aside the lace, Piri smirked at how wet and bare the escort was. It didn't take long to discover what she liked, or make her shudder blissfully.

The escort, remembering why she was there, sat up and traded places with Piri as she trailed her tongue on her neck, with soft bites that made her shiver.

Trauma had an unfortunate habit of reminding you it existed in dastardly ways. Which was why, as the escort worked her way down to make Piri feel at least as good as she felt moments ago, Piri vomited on the stucco wall.

The escort jumped back, managing somehow to stay clean.

Piri, drenched in tears and mucus and shame, apologized over and over and over and over.

Unsure of what to make out of what just happened, the escort left before it happened again.

She must have been curled under the warm shower for a half-hour before rational thought finally returned to Piri. She didn't want to think about how to clean up her mess, though. That was a tomorrow problem.

Instead, she thought about how she could apologize properly to the escort. Her mind went to other escorts.

Then to prostitution.

Then to sex trafficking.

Then she came up with a proposition for Terentia.

CHAPTER EIGHT

A Betrayal

A year from the night of comics and confessions, Rudella strapped the burden of nihilism to her back.

One of the Lansing Lamias, the playful Delora, was a fan of Industrial music and dressed equal parts maiden and rivet queen. The genre was on Rudella's radar, having found comfort in the black and still in her Re-I phase (with grown-out bangs), but like any genre worth a damn, the entry points were overwhelming. After a night of anime at her apartment, Rudella heard a few bars of something enticing as Delora drove away. Rudella texted her about it the next day, and Delora told her it was Nine Inch Nails' "Pilgrimage". A not-obvious choice from an obvious entry point, but Rudella walked through the Industrial gates, just the same.

If you're curious, "Delora" goes "deh-LOE-rah".

Turned out, Chicago was a fantastic place for the rust and grind set. Wax Trax Records, the font from which many aural perversions and agony flowed, set up shop in the Windy City. The problem for Rudella was much of it was north of Pilsen and Bronzeville. Delora lived a few minutes from her, in Lynwood, so she made her a deal: they'd take one car and swap when they were close to the Line of Aggravation.

Rudella's world opened up considerably once she didn't have to suffer the shitty traffic and parking that came with Downtown and the North Side. Sure, she was still in the car, but there's a massive difference between being a driver and a passenger. Nightlife was splendid, and she wouldn't have found local bands like I:Scintilla (give "Scin" a listen), Angelspit ("Skinny Little Bitch", too), and Ministry (ditto the Update Mix of "Jesus Built My Hotrod"), or followed the dark club trail of Scary Lady Sarah any other way. She missed out on the glory days of Neo Nightclub, but it's memorialized in "The Company", a film about life in Chicago's Joffrey Ballet.

Plus, Industrial girls loved making out with a mortician.

If you want to know about the alt life she missed out on, read Leor Galil's "Neo: Where Misfits Fit In" and "The Saga of Punkin' Donuts" Chicago Reader articles.

The zenith of Rudella's time with Delora was when Nine Inch Nails came into town with their NIN | JA tour. Despite her recent urban nightlife choices, Rudella wasn't a concert gal. However, Trent Reznor said that it was his last tour, and she wasn't going to pass the chance to see him live. Even in the nosebleeds. On the right flank. Jane's Addiction didn't make it, so Tom Morello's band, Street Sweeper Social Club, was the opener. It was his birthday and to celebrate, he drunk-played a guitar solo with his teeth. Then the sun set, and Nine Inch Nails erupted on the stage.

One of Rudella's favorite NIN songs was their cover of Gary Numan's "Metal"; they played it early, so she could enjoy the rest of the show without that "Will they?! Will they?!" tension and properly lost her shit when they unleashed the "Wish"/"Survivalism"/"Mr. Self Destruct" combo. Reznor even joked about making out with a mustached guy in the front row.

If the concert was sex, Rudella would've been multi-orgasmic.

The nadir of Rudella's time with Delora was a month later. It was a typical day of death and music 'til she got home. She didn't bother to go inside her apartment when she saw the door open. Too many horror movies warned her about what could happen. When the police arrived, she followed them inside. She expected chaos and disarray; she got something far more mundane and disappointing.

Her furniture was in its usual place, her drawers were uniformly closed. But her shelves were utterly empty. Years of building, curating, and loving books, movies, and music that were as much a part of her as her fingers. Insurance would replace them; she made it a point to photograph everything. It was the fact that the thievery could've only happened by someone she knew.

When Delora didn't answer her phone, Rudella was suspicious. When Delora's roommate said she was gone, Rudella was desolate. She never thought someone she shared so much of her life with would want to destroy the gift of her friendship in such a way. But the bare shelves were clear proof.

A tender part of herself died that night, and she closed herself off from the Lamias, and Raissa, for a long time.

Sunflowers in the Blistered Earth

Friends don't let friends drive drunk, marry for money, or leave their pity parties neverending.

Raissa finally got Rudella to crack. Only if Raissa came to her. Only if Raissa went to a bar she chose. Only if Raissa paid for her first drink. Only if Raissa promised not to ask if there was anything she could do. After agreeing to those terms, Raissa met

Rudella on a slow Thursday night at Shannon's, leaving her white knight syndrome at her basement apartment in Country Club Hills.

The first thing that caught Raissa's attention was the helicopter. Rudella told her that's how she'd find the bar, but she thought she was joking. There it was; with an Ace of Spades on its nose and metal soldiers on approach. The next thing was the hangar behind the helicopter. Before she could wonder why, she saw the airstrip behind the hangar. Shannon's, and its liquor, among it all. Raissa needed a moment to take in the absurdity before going inside. Then she remembered a bag in the front seat of her (leased) yellow-checkered MINI Cooper.

Rudella recently discovered David Bowie through two cover albums: the thoroughly Goth "2. Contamination" and the fabulously femme "Spiders From Venus". Most Bowie cover album thought he only existed in the '70s, but those two spanned decades. Because of Bowie, Rudella was in her Thin White Duchess phase, with black slacks and vest over a cuffed white blouse. She also rocked black lipstick and a spiked collar when Raissa found her in a booth nursing a cup of coffee. Raissa was still the Rockabilly, in a poodle skirt and leopard print shirt. Both fashions were thanks to the good folks at ebay.

Shannon's was, for some cruel reason, a bar on the second floor. There were stairs as well as an elevator, so the architect had a certain amount of pity. The place looked like a backwards L with a stubby base. Said stubby base had booths, a

TV, and large windows overlooking the baffling hangar and airstrip. The entrance sat at the edge of the base like Humpty Dumpty. The body had the bar-bar in the middle, a TV behind them, tables beyond them, and a dartboard up top. Across from the bar-bar was a jukebox in the wall, bathrooms (poor bartenders...), and more tables.

Since it's connected to the internet, the jukebox could play whatever you could think of. The bartenders, Marla, tall and bubbly, and Natasha, short and worldly, liked a lot of music, and tuned-out what they didn't. One or two Metal songs were fine, but they had to warn Rudella more than once that a whole DragonForce album was too much, for sanity's sake. Though she would've loved to hear "Heartbreak Armageddon" that night. Which was why, as Raissa sat across from Rudella, the Darkwave antics of She Wants Revenge were in the middle of their second album.

Years later, in a big instance of small worlds, a friend of Rudella's would have a costume party wedding... and the bride's mother would be Natasha.

Raissa asked Rudella what smelled like coconut. Rudella admitted she always snuck some Atole Tradicional Coco into her caffeine fixes, never drinking what's left at the bottom. Her demeanor was cold, due to the nihilism, yet connected, due to the friendship. Raissa asked how Rudella found out about this place. Rudella said that she and her mortician friends discovered it a few years ago, adding that it had 1/2-off Wednesdays. Perfect for broke college students.

Working behind the counter for as long as she had, Raissa knew how to read people. She knew Rudella wanted to talk, otherwise she wouldn't be there. She also knew Rudella would leave if she wasn't warmed up, otherwise she wouldn't be asking the bland questions neither of them would bother with. But Rudella didn't look like she was gonna rabbit, even with caffeine for help.

Raissa asked about the new pin next to the Dogwitch one, and Rudella told her that it's Sgt. Frog. An anime about an alien frog who wanted to take over the world; it's as daffy as it sounded, and sounded a little like "Invader Zim". Raissa hid a smirk since she had proof that despite Rudella's malaise, she was the same Goth chick layer cake.

Natasha stopped by, introduced herself to Raissa, and asked what the twosome were having. Rudella said a Blue Motherfucker on Raissa's tab, to which Natasha rolled her eyes and let out a "here we go" sigh. Rudella assuaged Natasha by telling her it was her only drink tonight. Raissa wanted to know what the fuck a Blue Motherfucker was, and Natasha told her it's basically a Long Island Iced Tea with Blue Curacao. Raissa gave Rudella the evil eye, while Natasha gave Raissa a sympathetic pat on the shoulder. Raissa thanked her, then ordered something far less fuckity-uppity: a Bee's Knees.

Spying the bag Raissa brought, Rudella asked what's inside. Raissa didn't bother hiding her smirk this time: Rudella was reaching out. Then she revealed the mystery and gave it to Rudella. The first volume of Alan Moore's "Swamp Thing" run. A.K.A., the last book Rudella was supposed to pick up before the break-in. Raissa said that it was gonna collect dust in Rudella's reserve box, so she bought it for her.

Rudella hesitated to take the graphic novel; it would be the first time she touched anything geeky since Delora's disappointment. She told Raissa as much. Raissa reminded her that she wasn't Delora, and to take the damn book before she did. Rudella's eyes went soft, then did what she was told.

Raissa asked if Rudella wanted the bag, then asked why she never saw her with a purse. Rudella thanked her for the book, and bag, then said that she made sure every dress, skirt, and pair of pants she owned had real pockets, even if she had to sew them in. Continuing, as Natasha came back with their drinks, she said that people who had purses made sure to fill them, and she didn't need the grief.

After putting the Blue Motherfucker and Bee's Knees right where they belonged, Natasha told Raissa she's glad Rudella's girlfriend was here to cheer her up. Raissa choked on her drink while Rudella told Natasha that Raissa was saving herself for Lee Ving. Raissa also choked because Natasha took care of their drinks, if you know what I mean (and I think you do). Natasha asked who was Lee Ving, and Marla incredulously repeated the question from the bar-bar. Raissa and Marla tag-teamed facts about Lee and his punk band, Fear. Natasa left, having had enough, and the fan club high-fived each other from across the room.

Rudella, after enjoying a sip, told Raissa that, from what she and Marla said, Lee was gonna pound her harder than the Long Grove Bridge if they got together. To which Raissa said that she'd just sleep in a tower whenever he was horny. Rudella was baffled, then Raissa realized she never told Rudella she was asexual. It was Rudella's time to choke on her drink, which burned with a high-proof fury.

Whenever a straight person found out about Rudella's sapphic tendencies, they were obnoxiously inquisitive. She swore she'd never be like that to anyone. But she didn't think she'd meet someone who wanted nothing to do with sex and wasn't raped or molested.

No, Raissa never got horny. No, Raissa wasn't lying. No, Raissa never had an orgasm. No, Raissa never wanted an orgasm. No, Raissa wasn't lying. No, Raissa didn't dress the way she did to be sexy. No, Raissa never had erotic fantasies. Yes, Raissa had morning dew (HA!), but that had to do with norepinephrine and not wet dreams (aw, man…). No, Raissa wasn't lying.

Since the ice was broken in a big, bad way, Raissa decided to finally ask Rudella a question that'd been nagging her since that first day at Papercuts: Where was she from? Raissa couldn't pin down Rudella's accent beyond "Southern". She didn't ask before since she figured it was a leitmotif in Rudella's life (it was), but after being asked in a medley of ways why she didn't fuck…

After another sip, Rudella said she hailed from Conyers, a town east of Atlanta on I-20. Raissa tried <u>REALLY</u> hard to not make a Georgia peach joke; the murder-glare from Rudella meant she was expecting one, too. Successful, Raissa asked what Conyers was like. Rudella told her about the botanical garden and the cherry blossom festival, about Olde Town and the snow-thick pollen, about her "cousin" Calantha and her BFF Mur-Mur, about how awesome Waffle House was and how much college football season sucked, about Hightower Trail and Dinky the Train.

If you're curious, "Calantha" rhymes with "Samantha".

When Natasha checked in on the two, Raissa asked if she knew Rudella was from Georgia. Natasha thought Rudella was from Louisiana, then broke the news to Marla, who said at least it wasn't Texas. Natasha thanked Raissa for pulling back that curtain and asked what she wanted. Loaded fries and another Bee's Knees.

Raissa wondered how bad Hurricane Katrina was down there; Rudella said it wasn't as bad as the Storm of the Century. Raissa took the bait, then Rudella explained how back in '93, Georgia was hit with a ginormous blizzard when it was in the 70s a few days before. Rockdale County only got four inches, but further north was fucked with around three feet. She was only a kid, so she only knew she didn't have to go to school for a while. She had clearer memories of the spillover from the '96 Olympics and how much she hated those people.

When Natasha brought a fresh Bee's Knees, Raissa asked her how she knew Rudella had sapphic tendencies. Natasha told the story of Rudella and a gal she was with telling her about a guy who fell down the stairs, grabbed the railing, looked at them, laughed, then let go. Raissa didn't get why that was a giveaway, then Rudella sighed and said that they shared the same smeared lipstick. Natasha chuckled as she thanked Rudella for not slamming her drink, then rejoined Marla.

Raissa sipped, then asked what else was going on with Rudella's accent. Sometimes she sounded like she was from Brooklyn. Rudella corrected her by saying it was Long Island and told the tale of her North Korean parents learning English from

Michelle Pfeiffer. Another murder-glare warned Raissa to not make a big deal about it. Raissa complied, then wondered why they chose Georgia. Rudella pointed out that no one was going to look for North Korean refugees in Conyers, GA.

In the early days of their friendship, an angry parent complained in Papercuts about how people who read comics didn't care about real-world problems. This got the gears running and made Rudella and Raissa play a long-running game about who was worse: Leopold II of Belgium or Pol Pot. Rudella argued Leopold II, Raissa argued Pol Pot. Whenever there was a lull in their conversation or someone wanted to change the subject, they'd continue the game. When Rudella brought up the Congo Free State, Raissa knew it was time to move on from Georgia. Before she could counter with yet another Khmer Rouge atrocity, Natasha dropped off her fries. Point: Rudella.

Raissa didn't offer to share. Petty Point: Raissa.

If you're curious, "Pol Pot" goes "pole paht" and "Khmer" goes "KAH-muhr".

Rudella was about to pout 'til she was soothed by cellos and crooning in the air. Raissa asked who was singing; Rudella replied that she was gonna play Blaqk Audio's first album but Shannon's didn't need to see what "Between Breaths (An XX Perspective)" did to her, then she thought about Birthday

Massacre but she figured folks needed a Darkwave break despite how much she wanted to hear "Horror Show".

Raissa reminded Rudella that she didn't answer her question, then Marla shouted something about Rasputina's first live album. Rudella asked how the fuck she knew that. Marla said Melora Creager played cello on Nirvana's last tour, and had been following her since then because how could she not follow the cellist who played with Nirvana. Rasputina loved songs about history and satire, which you can get a hint of in "Rats".

Dumbfounded, Raissa asked how much money Rudella put in the jukebox. Rudella deflected with a bladder check and went to the bathroom. Raissa checked her texts with a smile, then wrote a reply and enjoyed her fries.

Suddenly, she felt a wet finger trail her cheek. A quivering voice asked her to teach her to pee.

When Rudella eventually got off the floor, she continued cackling as she rubbed her freshly sore arm.

After sitting/calming down, Rudella brought a handful of hair to her face, then asked Raissa what she knew about dyeing. Raissa tersely replied that she knew enough. Rudella explained how she wanted red hair, but not cartoonishly red. Raissa tersely told her to try henna. It was natural and would make her hair as red as she wanted. Rudella thanked her as a guy approached her. Before he could say anything, she angrily did the international sign for cunnilingus at him. Smurf mouth and all.

An overreaction, but he got the point and went away. Raissa chortled (yes, chortled), then called Rudella a damn fool. Rudella warned her that she'll get her turn soon, then reapplied her lipstick.

Rudella, with her legs on the booth and her back to the window, complained about how cumbersome garter belts were when it came to the bathroom. Raissa wondered why since they on went under panties. She might as well had unlocked the secrets of the universe with how Rudella stared at her with awe. Rudella rushed to the bathroom to fix her year-long mistake then, satisfied, returned to her reclined position with a satisfied butt wiggle.

Raissa wondered aloud why no one complained about Rudella's song choices yet. Rudella told her that anyone could interrupt her since the jukebox allowed you to jump the line. But there would be drama if someone played Carrie Underwood's "Before He Cheats". Raissa had a 'Nam flashback to all the times she suffered it on karaoke nights, finishing her drink to forget it. The two agreed that if the person's such a piece of shit that they'd cheat, leave 'em and make a song about *that*. Like Sophie Tucker's "If Your Kisses Can't Hold the Man You Love".

Raissa glanced at the TV, then asked Rudella if she watched this new show, "Breaking Bad". Rudella scoffed, bringing up how it starred the dad from "Malcolm in the Middle". Raissa tried dissuading her from that line of thought, but Rudella wasn't budging. She was still mourning "The Wire", but "True Blood" helped a lot. Raissa giggled, then told Rudella how could she not love a show about horny vampires down south (heh).

Just as Natasha brought a fresh Bee's Knees, Rudella explained the great AIDS burger moment on the show... but Natasha only heard "AIDS burger" and left as swiftly as she arrived.

Raissa remembered that the guy who made "The Wire" was making a new show, "Treme", and told Rudella. A slice-of-life show about a New Orleans neighborhood... three months after Katrina. Rudella was intrigued, then asked who was in it. Raissa didn't recognize most of the names except John Goodman, Kim Dickens, and Steve Zahn. Rudella had a quite unkind word to say about Steve, and Raissa asked why.

After some tapping on her smartphone, Rudella jealously showed Raissa a scene from "Bandidas", a fun western with Salma Hayek and Penélope Cruz as bank robbers. The presented scene involved Steve tied to a bed while Salma and Penélope, in their lingerie, took turns kissing him to prove a point.

Raissa saw another tab and gave up butchering the name before asking Rudella what it was. Rudella explained how Ankoku Butoh, "dance of darkness", was created in Japan in '59 as a grotesque rebellion against traditional dances. Raissa asked if Korea had something similar; Rudella said she didn't know much about Korea, thanks to her parents. If they didn't want her to know, she didn't bother learning.

If you're curious, "Ankoku Butoh" goes "ahn-KOE-koo BOO-toe".

Rudella's attention flitted across the room, then to Raissa, then to her half-gone blue booze with a cackle. Raissa was confused 'til she saw him. A smuggerfucker of a dude-bro had his sights on her. The air distorted around him, heavy with Axe body spray.

Raissa knew she'd have to be more extreme than Rudella to repel the beast in the popped-collar polo. So she took a deep breath and slow screamed at him, which was what you think it was, never breaking eye contact with her resting bitch face. Her Shepard tone of a warning freaked him out, but not enough to make him and his Ed Hardy trucker hat go away.

'Til she took another deep breath.

CHAPTER NINE

Your Loving Arms

Once upon a time, for the last time, miseries of the street-mad girl caught up with her and she broke a promise.

After living a quarter-century, our next man-made disaster leered at Piri from the mirror. Her agony debts left her bankrupt, mentally and emotionally, forcing her to readjust in a women's shelter. Bedlam was a step too far. She needed empathy, and empathy needed experience. Shelter dwellers were burdened with experience.

Throughout her vagabondage, word of many shelters passed her ears. She shared the good ones and warned of the bad ones. The one she shared the most, Tender Revolution, was where she brought herself to. It wasn't easy because all she had was the name. Women's shelters had victims whose abusers salivated at the chance to find them, so their locations were secret.

Only known to gatekeepers at crisis centers. Piri finally asking for help after years of visits made them practically jump to show her the way. Which was how she met the Shawnee woman who ran Tender Revolution, Gaspara, and collapsed in her arms.

Prohibition started because women didn't want to get beaten by their drunk husbands anymore. There had been the Family Violence Prevention and Services Act, and the Violence Against Women Acts. There had been hundreds of stories, thousands of songs. Yet abuse was still prevalent and relevant in America, and cruelty was genderqueer. So were victims, though Tender Revolution catered to battered, homeless, pimped, and addicted women.

Tender Revolution was a brick triplex, with a massive backyard and respectful neighbors. The inside was sparse, yet serene, and each floor had four bedrooms. The sad nature of victimhood was its abundancy and of sanctuary was its scarcity. Because of these things, and to not feel crowded, there could only be four victims to each floor. No children since helping victims recover was struggle enough. They could stay as long as they needed to, but they were gently reminded that there was always a woman worse off than they were.

The massive backyard helped the victims recover, by either busying themselves or having space to daydream, so they could become survivors. But the switch was neither assured nor lasting. Similar to addiction, victimhood could burrow deep into the mind, or deeper into the genes. Wherever their roads took them, even if it was in a circle, Gaspara helped them along as best she could.

However, her patience wasn't infinite. If a woman became destructive, she was gone without hesitation or forgiveness. Everyone there deserved equal respect; plus, bad behavior was infectious to the susceptible.

Before Gaspara bought what ended up being Tender Revolution, she had a **long** conversation with the landlords of the flanking triplexes. Victims in recovery brought with and unpacked all manner of baggage. Such clamor to the unprepared could bring the police to her door. The victim's abusive nearest and dearest would be notified, and that would be the story of her.

Gaspara, in her uniform of modesty save for her layered pearl necklace, explained all this to the landlords, who explained all this to their tenants, and all agreed to keep the shelter secret and safe. And to let Gaspara be the one who called the cops (but all hoped it'd never get that bad).

Piri had a room to herself on the first floor. It was Gaspara's floor, and the two only had to share it with one other woman. It being ground level meant that if Piri developed any… hazardous tendencies, she didn't have anywhere to fall. And she was in a hazardous state.

Her first night was filled with screams, as was her second. And third. After her fourth, she was rational enough to apologize to everyone for her terrors. They knew that whatever her world was must have been fucking grotesque for her to be there. Being almost irreparable unlocked the doors to Tender Revolution. Besides, Piri wasn't the first woman there to bellow throughout the night. Nor would she be the last.

Piri's apology was one of the rare times she spoke to anyone in those early days. She spent most of her time sitting in the corner, next to her knapsack, where she could easily watch the window and the door. To the point when sores formed where she sat, and her muscles ached from the tension.

Gaspara didn't want any assistants visiting her, lest she'd feel overwhelmed and agitated. She also quickly learned to not block Piri's view when she checked on her, or else she began to shake and cry. She ate and drank very little, and what she had was hard for her to keep down. When she slept, she did it under her bed surrounded by things that were quick to make noise.

A month later, Gaspara was shocked to find Piri, sun-drenched and nude, standing at her window. The sores only discolored Piri's skin, but Gaspara was saddened, just the same. Piri had headphones on, so Gaspara knew she couldn't get her attention with a tap on a shoulder: Piri could've been scared to death, or worse. She could faintly hear what was playing, figured out it was repeating the same song, then got Piri's attention by saying her name, loudly yet gently.

Piri turned to face Gaspara with a tragedy-soaked eye, indifferent to her nudity. She placed an earcup to her temple so she could hear Gaspara and stay committed to what she was listening to. Gaspara, in an attempt to protect their intimacy as well as test the new progression, asked if she could close the door.

A voiced croaked from saying almost nothing but screams for a month, the shattered melophile gave her permission.

After waiting in vain for a negative reaction, Gaspara asked Piri what made her leave the corner. Piri's eye flitted to her covered ear as she brushed it on her shoulder. Gaspara asked if she could listen, and Piri gave a lot of thought. She said it was ok when it restarts, but to give it back when it was over. Gaspara thanked her and waited.

After much hesitation, Piri handed the headphones to Gaspara, then returned to the window. The cord was taut in the space between them, and Gaspara asked if she could take one step closer. Piri shook her head fearfully.

Gaspara stayed, placing the headphones over her black drapes with threads of gray, thanks to age and stress. The song played that she would later find out Piri had been listening to since she arrived: "Just Be", with Tiësto and Kirsty Hawkshaw.

Piri would also confess at the window she was like a boiling pot, and the song scraped the bubbles off the top.

Two days later, Gaspara took Piri to the hospital for what would be her first check-up. That didn't involve rape. Like most people, Piri assumed that she needed insurance or else she'd owe money she'd never have.

Like most people, Piri didn't know hospitals were obligated to pay 100% of the bill to those who qualified because of their nonprofit status. Every hospital in America. Do a web search of the hospital's name and "financial assistance", then follow their instructions to a healthier life. If you qualified. If you didn't, you could ask for an itemized bill and have a chance of talking them down into not charging you anything.

Another bit of nonprofit trivia: the NFL league office, until 2015, had a 501(c)(6) certification. That ended because people saw its commissioner, Roger Goodell, made $44,200,000 in 2012 (14% of what the league made that year) and, quite rightly, called shenanigans. Because of the certification loss, the league office didn't have to report how much commissioners made. Funny that.

Piri was healthier than she thought, yet still had a few problems modern medicine had to fix. She stayed clean, and didn't get pregnant. One problem, however, wasn't the bill.

A few days later, she was mentally well enough to venture into the living room and spend most of her time watching movies. A nearby mom-and-pop video store went out of business recently, and gave their stock to Tender Revolution.

Every night, while others slept, you could depend on her watching either "In the Cut" or "Boxing Helena". One was a gorgeous erotic thriller about a woman who fell for a shady cop as a serial killer entered her life, and the other was a gorgeous erotic thriller about a man who mutilated a woman as he put her on a pedestal.

If you asked Piri, and Gaspara asked plenty, she couldn't tell you why she watched them so often.

Two weeks after that, she stepped into the massive backyard. She sat by herself in the patchwork gazebo of wrought iron and anodized steel, stacked on so many tires. Some of the dwellers had the radio on while they tended to the garden; the BP oil spill was the latest man-made disaster, and the world's birthday present to Hitler.

Piri's eye traced leaves and loops of the iron, patterns of the rainbowed steel, until a Spring breeze drifted her, at last, into a screamless slumber.

Whispers in the Sexercise Lounge

Then she came up with a proposition for Terentia.

The day after Piri's birthday, she texted Terentia the non-emergency code for them to meet. The day after *that*, they met in their usual place. Terentia's father had an empty store for lease, and she promised to keep it looking spiffy for potentials. Which meant she had the only key. Well, she and Piri.

When they were settled, Piri told Terentia she wanted to focus on cracking sex trafficking. Terentia was surprised; partially because of the proposition, partially because she didn't think of it first. She asked why now, and Piri explained her motel thought process while leaving out the messy bits. She concluded that she wanted to do her part in keeping women from being stolen, Shangri-La to Bumblefuck.

Terentia reminded her that men were also trafficked. Piri semantically added hunks with cunts and chicks with dicks, which got a startled chuckle from Terentia. Political correctness was the purview of those who knew when their next meal was. Terentia added that most trafficking happened in homes, by people the victims thought would always protect them. Piri reminded her that there were still plenty of traffickers beyond the gauze of domesticity.

World War III already happened. It was just a sequel with a different title: The Cold War. World War IV was still in progress, though it seemed the War on Drugs could only end in a Pyrrhic victory. World War V was the latest, but the War on Terror had echoes of Vietnam. Because it didn't have "war" in the title, Terentia naïvely thought human trafficking could be stopped with enough effort. Despite it being the oldest war by millennia.

You'll find out **a lot** more about sex work in five chapters, but you should at least know here there's a difference twixt sex work and sex trafficking. Sex work is consensual. Sex trafficking is, through force, fraud, or coercion, "the recruitment, harboring, transportation, provision, obtaining, patronizing, or soliciting of a person for the purpose of a commercial sex act."

Terentia asked if taking on the task was personal. Piri almost said that it wasn't, then remembered all the pretty women she met during her vagabondage who disappeared. Maybe they went back to reality. Maybe they were killed. Maybe they were snatched. She couldn't help everyone, but she could try helping the third.

How did one break a sex trafficking ring? How did one find a sex trafficking ring? How did one find a sex trafficking ring without getting trafficked and murdered, not necessarily in that order? Terentia had an idea, but it would be tainted by lawful intentions whose stench would get Piri found out, then trafficked and murdered. Not necessarily in that order. Piri figured she'd have to play the long(ish) game, and that's what she did.

Piri knew which greasy spoons Chicago's working girls ate after work, so she started there. She didn't approach them, just showed up a few times. Then, after an early morning shift, a working girl waved her to her table. They knew each other from a party they crashed at Excalibur a few months ago. Piri was there for music, and the pro was there for… table service. They bonded on the corner of Dearborn and Ontario, and occasionally bumped into each other in the demimonde.

After that morning, they frequently bumped into each other. Always at the same booth, with or without work friends. They got a kick out of Piri, and Piri loved their stories. One of the gals even offered her a bump, but she preferred Coca-Cola over cocaine (although they came from the same plant).

Like the dom who had to take quick laughing breaks during what some of her slaves begged her to do.

Or the pro who played Dueling Moans with a couple on the other side of the wall (she celebrated her hard-earned victory with tea and honey).

One time, a gal brought a portable DVD player and everyone watched Lizzie Borden's "Working Girls". Then they watched Ken Russell's "Whore", which was like being at a rock concert. The manager banned movie-watching after that.

Terentia's sole piece of advice was to get close to a foreign prostitute; chances were, she was promised a ring by someone dashing and ended up in one, instead. It took three weeks of idle chatter, but Piri found who she was looking for.

Silencio was a woman without a country, in more ways than one. She was a child of divorce whose parents were Swedish and Italian. She never felt comfortable in either country as custodial visits flung her to and fro. Her only constants were song and cinema; her parents had collections of both.

The majority of her stability came from America, whose place in her heart grew as she felt more alone between two worlds. She wanted to live there more than she wanted to breathe, but chances eluded her.

Until she heard about a show that was like "Eurovision". On "American Idol", everyone had a chance to be a star. She wouldn't end up like Bette Midler in "The Rose" or Jennifer Lopez in "Selena", though. She worked it out.

She'd find out where and when the next round of auditions were, steal the money she needed to fly there and then, then straight up blow Paula Abdul away (oh, oh, oh) weekly on her road to fortune and glory. And adoration. She already had her stage name, conjured to tell the world how she'd leave them after hearing her sing.

Once stateside, she made the apocalyptic mistake of trusting the first smile thrown her way.

Without a lick of hyperbole, suspicion was the difference twixt life and death in all things Silencio. An Escalade with blacked-out mirrors, and terrors within, was never more than 15 feet away. She made the terrors and their bosses a lot of money in her four years of captivity; foreign pussy was the best pussy, and customers loved how her being limp in bed was like fucking a still-warm corpse. Survivalism even convinced her to like it.

But Piri needed to know Silencio, despite the working girl whispers of what the terrors had done. Their brutality, and the efficient quiet in its wake, meant they weren't people to fuck with. But Piri needed to know Silencio.

Panhandling was more a skill than people assumed. It wasn't a matter of standing somewhere and hoping for the best. Not if you wanted to make money. You had to know where to go and who to look for. Piri took pride in her panhandling skills, and a side effect of said skills was being an expert people deducer.

A quick look at Silencio and her two-tone shearling coat and her knock-off Louboutins told Piri that vanity was the window she could slip through.

For the next two weeks, Piri spent her free time at a library reading and re-reading fashion books, and spent her early mornings astounding Silencio and her ego with what she learned. When Silencio asked the obvious question of how could someone who knew so much about haute couture dress like a bum, Piri replied with two words that earned her a sympathetic slice of coconut cream pie: student debt.

The pie earned a collective gasp from the working girl booth.

Life being what happened when you made other plans, Piri got a rather large helping of life at the witching hour, one day. Silencio brooded in her usual seat, which was a shock to Piri. Usually, the Italio-Swede was awash in melancholy. Anger and its children didn't seem to be possible. Yet there they were, as plain on Silencio's face as her focus on Piri as she timidly approached.

She oscillated from English to Italian to Swedish like a pissed-off fan on caffeine, but the gist of Silencio's rant was her pimp brought in a new batch of girls from New Orleans, whom he treated better than he did her. Four years of captivity and hustling fica, and she was about to be tossed aside for a bunch of scared Cajun tikarna.

Two truths came to Piri. One: Silencio was jealous. Two: Silencio just admitted she was trafficked. Piri thought it'd take longer to hear that sweet, sweet news. She played off the trembling in her voice as fear when it was excitement as she asked Silencio to confirm the second truth.

She did. Loudly.

Piri then asked Silencio if the opportunity for revenge came up, would she take it.

She did. Loudly.

Piri got Silencio to calm down, then made her order a double cheeseburger. They had to make it seem to the terrors in the Escalade that things were normal. They also needed time, and double cheeseburgers took a while to make. Hopefully, more time than a taxi needed to park behind the diner.

The black screen of Piri's burner phone taunted them as the two clocks counted down. She went to the bathroom to see if they could climb out the window. Otherwise, they'd have to bolt through the kitchen and hope for the best during the chaos.

After seeing the good news, she opened it as far as it would go, then went back to Silencio and the taunting screen.

The scent of the sizzling meat patties grew perilously stronger as the phone remained woefully static. Then it BURST alive like a fireworks show.

Piri told the driver to expect them out the bathroom window soon, and he went with it as if it was just another night.

Silencio left the table first. Piri watched the Escalade as inconspicuously as she could, then counted to 30. Silencio could get to the cab by 30.

On 28, the chef's bell rung. Piri gripped the table instead of screaming or jumping.

On 30, the waitress brought the timer in a sesame seed bun to an empty table. The terrors in the Escalade waited for a princess who would never come.

Fourteen hours and eleven breaks in an interrogation room later, Terentia and her partner had everything they needed to destroy what was revealed to be the Neon Peach trafficking ring. Throughout all of it, Silencio had the sadistic glee of a pride of lions running a train on a big game hunter. The street-mad girl was wherever she went; staying at the station would've exposed her.

Piri would soon be devastatingly exposed in a way only soldiers and children would know.

145

CHAPTER TEN

Before the World Shuttered

Deep into their love gone long, Rudella and Piri will have a spat that coasts them into silence.

Rudella will make sure she is up and out before Piri. She won't want to go anywhere, but her hearse will need cleaning and the late-February day will make it too cold to get her hands wet. So she'll put her hair in a ponytail, pull on her favorite striped sweater, and drive to a car wash. Eventually.

Around a decade ago, she discovered Miranda Sex Garden in a corseted boxset she found at a Borders. "A Life Less Lived" was three CDs and a DVD worth of a (re)introduction to Goth rock bands big and small, with essays written by, among others, Chicago's dreary queen, Scary Lady Sarah.

Miranda Sex Garden only made four albums before splintering off and doing other things, like Mediæval Bæbes, but Rudella loved every minute they mixed the medieval and the modern in a way no one else did. She didn't listen to their first album much, but "Suspiria" will be on its nth spin in her stereo while she broods on her meandered way to the car wash.

Piri will face the empty space next to her in bed. She will want to apologize with breakfast, but will only have a stray hair on her lover's pillow to serve. She will have stayed up longer than she meant to looking for southern recipes on her phone. The ones she'll think would be perfect either needs things the fridge won't have, or will take too much time. She'll remember she has tenders, then will go to bed knowing she'll make Rudella the best damn microwaved chicken and waffles (and ALAGA) this side of the Mason-Dixon. Then Rudella will prove her wrong.

She'll know Rudella won't want to be bothered when she was in a mood, so Piri won't call her after she eats. Instead, still in one of her Amy Brown faerie tees-turned-pajamas, she will go about her morning. She will be mid-semester of online classes to get her special ed teaching degree. Her way of keeping humanity's flame lit 'til the next generation finds its kindling. Amends to Rudella will never be far from her mind.

The small town they'll chose to live after winning the Little Lotto is a patchwork of nature and industry. One of Rudella's favorite places will be a park with a pond; she'll visit when she was happy, sad, or just because. She will be pensive as she lays at the back of her spotless hearse, Miranda Sex Garden's "Fairytales of Slavery" album played low. Breaking up with Piri will be far from her mind; they will have been through **far** worse. Still, she'll wonder why, even now, Piri will still capable of a mistake like that.

They will have sworn off Valentine's Day ages ago, deciding to declare their love for each other whenever they wanted instead of when the calendar told them. One such declaration will come from Rudella because Piri will be yet another person who wants to be Legolas, Elven Bow King. As a joke, Rudella will buy her a beginner's archery set. Whenever Piri will use it, she'll think of Rudella. As she laces up her armguard this time, she'll want to forget.

The next town over will have an incredible secondhand store Rudella will visit at least twice a month. It will specialize in books, movies, and music, and will have a steady resupply of all three. Rudella will be in constant amazement with what some people dare give up. Books and things Piri will have to pry from her rigor mortis'd hands, or will be bidding battlefields on ebay. All within driving distance, for peanuts. Rudella will find herself there, with echoes of malaise, as she searches the music section for nothing in particular.

Determination, depending on which end of the microscope you look under, was one of Piri's strengths or weaknesses. She couldn't have lived the vagabond life, or had done what she did to leave it, without a bit of obstinacy. As you can imagine, said obstinacy occasionally got her into trouble. Which may or may not be why Rudella will do an Irish exit that morning. However, it'll definitely be why Piri will be surrounded by crumpled paper as she watches a tutorial on her laptop.

Piri is much less discriminating about Dance songs than Rudella is about Metal songs, so she'll be as glad as she's surprised by her compilation album gift, "Stompers Agony". Rudella will say she knows Piri is taking the silence harder than she is, so she gets her something to show they are ok after clearing her head. Then she will notice the crumpled paper around the laptop.

Rudella is a sucker for anything Japanese, yet Piri will want to put effort into her mea culpa. She'll search online 'til she finds a tutorial of making an origami skull. Hard to find anything better for her Japano-thanatophile. She'll be determined to do a good job, which will be fine except she never made even a paper airplane. When she gives Rudella the folded fruit of her labor, she will appreciate her failures as if they were successes.

They will come a long way.

The most suck-ass thing about the lingering drama surrounding COVID-19 will be that it could've been avoided.

If people stay inside early enough for the virus to make itself extinct, humanity will have kicked back with a Strongbow and gloated about it pulling a Neo. Instead, humanity will take every bullet to the face the Coronavirus shoots and shut down the world (more than once). Folks will have learned fuck-all from the influenza pandemic 100 years ago, letting millions die. A man-made disaster, and embarrassment, for the ages.

Some will be justified. You can believe a Christian Scientist or the Amish if they said vaccinations are against their faith. They are so hardcore about being anti-medicine, they'll literally die before taking an aspirin. You can also be extremely suspicious of those who quote the same chapter and verse, yet eat meat on Fridays.

Then there'll be the walking prolapses who'll screamed bloody murder about the evils of vaccines, yet will not admit to getting one or not. At least bigots are true to their convictions. The Americans with Disabilities Act will rightfully protect the impaired from answering the question and revealing their immunocompromised disability. But one will wonder how many of the prolapses have such an issue. Or can spell it.

The Venn diagram of the two groups and those greed-induced tumors on society who took advantage of relief funds will probably make a perfect circlejerk.

All these grievances will be symbolized by doctors forced to wear garbage bags and be called monsters while they save lives.

Because Rudella will run a specialty funeral home, her parlor won't inundated with decedents like other morticians'. Because of *that*, she'll let other homes store their dead in her freezer 'til they'll be needed. The bittersweetness will be they didn't stay long, but idiocy towards the Coronavirus will keep the flow of corpses constant.

Since Piri's courses will be online, and her therapist will be fine with being online, her routine will stay the same during the first lockdown. Except there'll be no place to go when she is done for the day. She'll find the college after a bit of heavy vetting to make sure it was A) accredited, and B) beyond criminal sponsorship. Rudella will allay her doubts about Vrehas by telling her it got most of its donations from an eccentric taxidermist (thanks, Maureen).

While on the subject of higher learning's questionable antics, the College Board is "a non-profit organization that clears a path for all students to own their future through the AP Program, SAT Suite, BigFuture, and more." It's also a signatory of the Student Privacy Pledge, promising not to sell students' info, 'til it was busted for doing so in the late-2010s. It left the Pledge instead of not selling students' info.

Piri's early quarantined downtime will be spent obsessing over the news, then decompressing from the news. A video that'll win her rapt, repeated attention will be Aaron Toney's "Stunt Reaction Challenge (Worldwide Edition)". He and stuntpeople 'round the world will daisy-chain clips of them beating each other up. The inspired will follow 'til the trend reaches its two-peak apex with his ultra-geeky, Rudella-approved "Fight Challenge Round 2", and Zöe Bell's "Boss Bitch Fight Challenge". Piri will sleep good after watching the latter.

But trends are transient, and there will be much more quarantine to go than the two months that passed. Rudella will keep busy with death work and unwinding: feed crows, (re)read books, (re)watch movies and shows, but mostly listen to gloomy or heavy tunes as she stared at a shimmering sculpture.

Piri won't want to fall back on camgirl habits, so she'll be found with her compound bow and arrow in the backyard of their house lovingly called the Lilith Pit. The day after her overzealous return will be a sore one, and her bandaged fingers will be almost useless for a week. When she recovers, she will waste no time picking up the compound bow again. With a little more temperance.

As days go by, her arrows will get closer to the bullseye 'til they hit nothing but red. Then she'll put up photos of annoying people and tear them apart with trick shots. Then she'll make an unknowing Rudella her new moving target with rubber darts. When an annoyed Rudella threatens to shove the darts in an uncomfortable place, Piri will go back to the backyard and settle on blowing out candles with arrowheads.

One day, she'll get a raging case of cabin fever, and tell Rudella as much. Rudella will say there's nowhere to go; the antsy one will say there's everywhere to go. Like Downtown Chicago. Rudella will complain about traffic; the antsy one will remind her that there's none.

Near Lake Calumet, along I-94 West, Rudella will park her meat wagon crooked in the middle of the highway. Piri will wonder aloud why, and her lover will tell her that she's awestruck by how empty the roads were. Piri wins the coin toss, so their convo will be scored by "Secret (Take You Home)" on a Kylie Minogue playlist.

Rudella, taking advantage of the barren situation, will do something she always wanted to. Piri will think she's nuckin' futs for lying on the tarmac, 'til she remembers why they were out. When she joins the deathly one, she will be astounded to be living through another disaster with plane-less skies.

They'll drive past Buckingham Fountain in ten minutes, Rudella laughing in disbelief and glee the whole way. From where we left them, in typical times, the trip will just be getting started at ten minutes.

In another two minutes, they'll be at their first downtown stop: the Michigan-Wacker Historic District, where the Chicago River meets Lake Michigan. Rudella will park crooked in the middle of the Michigan Ave. Bridge, with defiant satisfaction. If she had anything in her bladder, she would've added "pissing on a parking meter" to her list of defiances.

In 2008, Mayor Richard M. Daley sold all of Chicago's meters to, waitforit, Chicago Parking Meters LLC for a billion dollars. They could do whatever they wanted with the 36,000 money machines for 75 years and not share a cent. Prices went up, Chicago fell more into debt, and no one's smart enough to do anything about it.

While Kylie sings "Too Far", Rudella will lean on her hearse and marvel at the towering 1920s architecture surrounding them. Before Piri can join her, she'll bolt to the southern end, flip-flops flip-flopping, and look over the edge.

Piri will wonder what-the-fuck and join the now-pouting Rudella, thinking she looks cool as her trenchcoat rides the lakefront breeze. The bummed one will point downward with an elbow, to the walled-off street across the river. She'll explain that Joker tried to blow up Harvey Dent down there. Piri will ooo and ahh, then say they should check it out. Rudella will grumble something about it not being the same since the walls weren't there in the scene.

Unlike Rudella, Piri could cry at the drop of a hat. Rudella was more likely to either brood or get angry when she was sad. Piri will notice a familiar, sullen quiet from her lover, then joke about tearing down the walls since no one could stop them. Rudella will whisper that she wasn't supposed to be the only one, and Piri will ask what she means.

Rudella's voice will crack as she explains, gripping the railing for support. Dreams were things you woke up from; she and her Vrehas friends had goals. They were going to be the morticians all others desired to be, and they bragged about how nightly. By the fire pit, under electric stars, Deftones in the air. However, goals only worked if you stayed in the race. One by one, her morbid compatriots fell off the track. Because they quit or stopped talking to her. Not even Shannon's survived. Standing on the bridge and the sunny side of success, she'll feel that her years with them were wasted, yet she'll still hold onto them. Especially those nights.

From her phone, the lachrymose Piri will pause Kylie, then search for something. Finding it, she'll turn the stereo up and tap Rudella on her melancholy shoulder. When the Goth turns around, the Punk will tap her phone and toss it onto the hearse's front seat. The latter will offer her hand, the former will take it, and the two will slowly dance as the Purity Ring remix of Deftones' "Knife Prty" echoes off the limestone.

Piri will feel the shift in Rudella's chemistry, and Rudella will show her immense gratitude with a kiss. When she finally comes up for air, she'll admit that finding movie locations isn't why she was downtown. One of her reasons will be two miles away.

It's impossible to overstate the importance of 206 S. Jefferson St. to the world. Comparatively not much as a hearse approached it, but it was a Big Bang of music when it was the Warehouse. After corporate greed killed Disco in the late-'70s (like it killed Metal in the late-'80s), stores were stuck with *a lot* of records. Disco Demolition Night tried its damndest to destroy them, though more than a few of the entitled wreckers cared more about the color of the musicians than their genre. They'd shit guitar picks if they knew Rock and Metal were children of Blues.

When the Warehouse opened, it had Frankie Knuckles on the turntables. Without a lick of hyperbole, he changed everything about Dance music. Remember those Disco albums collecting dust? Some of them were sold at Import Records. Fans of what Frankie unleashed, gay and straight, would go there and ask for Warehouse music, which was shortened to 'House music.

Crate-digging led to discovering hidden gems instead of pulling the usual suspects off the wall. But there was still a finite number to choose from. What was a disc jockey to do? Live mixing, for a start. With two turntables and a mixer, a song could be chopped up, mashed up, sped up, slowed down, and looped in front of a crowd. Common stuff now, but it blew minds at the Warehouse and other clubs.

Then DJs added drum machines. Then they mixed genres. Then they made their own genre called, waitforit, House Music. Then Europe discovered House Music. Then House Music exploded like a fractal. Then House Music and its children took over the world. Thanks to Frankie Knuckles behind the decks at the Warehouse.

Piri will know all that. Rudella will only know that the Warehouse is important to clubheads. She'll also know that Piri will cry like a baby surrounded by happy onions if she went there. Rudella prefers double bass to dropping it, but she won't pass up the chance to let her lover have all the time she needs with 206 S. Jefferson St.

Sure enough, after Rudella parks crooked in the middle of the street, Piri will cheerfully bawl as she approaches the building. House classic Big Sister's "'Round We Go" courtesy of the stereo. She will surmount an unthinkable amount of shit in her life thanks to what Frankie Knuckles started there. She *still* won't want anyone knowing what happened the night of Ilyse's bad trip, though.

Not even you.

At first, Rudella stays by the hearse to let Piri have her moment, but she'll be called over so it could be *their* moment. Piri will bury her face in Rudella's chest, repeating her heartfelt thank-yous to her and Frankie. Rudella will rub her back, comforting her 'til she's done.

Later, Rudella takes a photo that Piri will be embarrassed by and glad of. In the early-'00s, the block was renamed Frankie Knuckles Way. Standing atop the hearse, Piri will pose under the honorary street sign, blazing smile betrayed by a tear-puffed eye.

As Rudella warned, the Warehouse is one stop she will make while the world is barren. Stoplights and speed cameras work whether people were on the road or not, so she will be stuck doing normal time driving north. With the quarantine, however, it will be like coasting through suburbia. So much so that she'll take the winding way to her destination, listening to the Power Metal stylings of Frozen Crown's "Crowned in Frost" album, and admiring the Windy City's beauty while it's not clogged with people.

5800 N. Ravenwood Ave. is home to the largest cemetery in Chicago, Rosehill. Three-hundred fifty acres of Victoriana unbound. Crypts, tombstones, mausoleums, memorials, *and* a nature preserve resides within its borders of limestone and wrought iron since 1859. Everything will wait for Rudella to find her way inside.

Piri will be passed out, exhausted from crying and crossing off a big entry on her bucket list. Which will be fine: Rudella wants to enjoy Rosehill alone, and Piri will call if she needs her.

When Rudella was a kid, one of her main comforts was "Mannequin", an '80s relic about a guy who worked in a department store and found a mannequin that turned into an Egyptian princess when they were alone. Hijinks ensued. The whole movie wasn't her binky. That would be the scene with them playing dress-up while Alisha's "Do You Dream About Me" hyping Lil 'Della up. Whenever her appa didn't see it in Rewind or Die, he knew his ttal was making a mess in the living room.

A bit of preamble to explain why Rudella will spend her time in the empty Rosehill peculiarly. The Symphonic Metal of Ad Infinitum's "Chapter I: Monarchy", a concept album about how Louis XIV was a piece of shit, will play low in a pocket. She'll quasi-dance with herself through the cemetery like no one's watching, bare feet kicking up her long, lace skirt. Whenever she notices a new resting place, she will imagine what the person in their Chicago overcoat is like through her cadaverous shimmy. She will never be there again, so she'll want to enjoy herself.

As she waits under a tree for her second wind, her thoughts will turn to Mary Shelley. Specifically, how she lost her virginity on her mother's grave. Rudella won't want to fuck on a grave. That would be indecent. She also isn't an exhibitionist. However, the idea of fucking in Rosehill will be too delicious to pass up. It will be a ghost town. Even if someone shows up, there'll be over 300 acres to spot Rudella and Piri doing a little shake and fingerpop. If graveyard sex was good enough for the creator of Science-Fiction, it'll be good enough for them.

Piri will be a hard one to wake up but, with an energy drink and a little focused tenderness, she'll come around (in more ways than one).

CHAPTER ELEVEN

What Friends Were For

When inconvenience presented itself was when a friendship showed its quality: tissue-thin or molasses-thick.

It was almost a year since the end of the Mayan calendar, which meant those who wanted the easy-out of an apocalypse were miserable. Hard work and long life with no rewards disappointed the fools who thought they were so important, the world should end before they did. Even tried conjuring another failed apocalypse with scorpion billboards.

The rest of the world was celebratory, which was how Kazenjammer's first album, "Le Pop", filled Rudella's ok apartment, stolen items replenished, as Raissa touched up her henna'd hair. Rudella, in her old Waffle House tee and bike shorts, asked what genre they were. Raissa, in her sailor pants and fuzzy top, could only come up with "fun". That was good enough for Rudella. Raissa added they put a cherry pie recipe in a song, which reminded Rudella of the cookie recipe Tool put in "Die Eier von Satan".

Raissa begged Rudella to let her do something with her hair like her French twist, but Rudella was fine with her bob. Bummed, Raissa asked if the liège waffles were done. Rudella could at least cheer her up with those. If you've never had liège waffles, you've never had waffles. They're fluffy, yet slightly crunchy due to the caramelized sugar; they were as awesome as they sounded (unless you're diabetic). Putting syrup on them was putting a hat on a hat, as Rudella warned Raissa.

If you're curious, "liège" goes "LEE-ehj".

As they enjoyed their waffles and waited for the dye to set, Raissa brought up how "prior knowledge" didn't make sense since all knowledge was hindsight. The second you knew something, it became part of your past. Rudella added "reputation preceded you" was something stupid that smart people said because preceding was a reputation's natural state of being. It'd be like pointing out headlights were in front of a car like it was mindblowing. She started ranting about the redundancies of "I myself", "she herself", et. al., but Raissa cut her off with a waffle bit.

After a good washing and blow-drying, Raissa went on to clip Rudella's ends. The latter wondered aloud who they'd dress up as Halloween next year. That year, they were Daria and Jane (have fun figuring out which was which). Raissa suggested

Michael and Janet Jackson (again, have fun), and Rudella almost high-fived a pair of scissors.

Raissa was finished when the sky was twilight blue. Rudella was in her corset-and-dress phase, so she put on a corset and dress. When she entered that phase, Raissa gave her shit about how much corsets must suck, then it was Rudella's turn for a little education. Corsets were a choice, and didn't give women a slight case of death. They ached if worn too long, but the same could be said about heels. Rudella couldn't eat a lot while wearing a corset, just as she couldn't stop herself from feeling sexy.

Rudella asked what Raissa wanted to do since the night was young and so were they. Raissa thought Rudella had work the next day, but she was off. The Rockabilly asked the Mortician how she kept normal hours when people died all the time. She explained that Sunset Shores had enough people so some could work in the daytime while others could take the graveyard shift. She added the real question was how could she work through endometriosis pain; that was like jamming a chainsaw up her cooter once a month and letting it run for three days.

Since Rudella was free and wasn't dealing with a chainsaw massacre, Raissa asked for a favor. She prefaced it by telling Rudella they'd be riding in her (leased) MINI, and that she'd only have to drive one way, and that she'd repay her kindness by taking care of her comics for a month. Rudella's mind was immediately filled with horrors of Downtown Chicago, but Raissa assured her they wouldn't be going anywhere near there.

They'd be going to Grosse Pointe Woods, Michigan.

Rudella asked where the fuck Grosse Pointe Woods was: around two towns north-ish of Detroit. She asked why the fuck Raissa needed to go there: lost a coin toss. She asked who the fuck's over there: an uncle. She asked why the fuck Raissa didn't go earlier in the day: traffic's a motherbitch 'til sundown. She asked why Raissa needed her to go with:

Because Raissa needed Rudella.

An Unexpected Journey

Spending five hours behind the wheel in an underbust corset wasn't how Rudella imagined her night, but she was a slave to friendship and fashion.

Headed out at seven, she figured it would take around five Metallica albums to get to Grosse Pointe Woods, so she planned accordingly. Raissa didn't mind: the driver was the DJ. She also had a week-long Heavy Metal course forced upon her with "Metal: A Headbanger's Journey", "Global Metal", and "Metal Evolution".

She did wonder why Rudella started with "St. Anger" since even she heard fans hated it. Rudella told her she stopped playing Follow the Leader in kindergarten, and "Shoot Me Again" was one of her favorite songs. She skipped to track seven to show off the song about being better than the shit people gave you: a long-suffering gal at the Papercuts till could relate. Raissa said it was weird none of the songs, so far, had guitar solos since Metal was known for them. From the West, a regretful wail from Kirk Hammett rode the wind. Having proved her point, Rudella skipped back to track three, still practically at the starting line on I-94 E.

Raissa reached for the glove compartment, then changed her mind.

Typical randomness went through their conversation as they rode through Indiana. Like how it was weird everyone's fine with Ancient Romans on stage and screen speaking the Queen's English though Rome's in Italy.

However, the geeks couldn't stay away from comics too long, which led to Raissa complaining about the state of the mainstream. The industry almost cratered in the '90s because companies catered to the speculative market. They spent more effort on variant covers and headlines than on telling good stories. When collectors were bored of bullshit, millions of issues sold became thousand, with nothing but subpar stories to fall back on. And they were doing all of that again. Indie comics were fab, but the industry was held up by the pillars of DC and Marvel.

Rudella's heard variations of her rant since she's known her. Like a good friend, she egged Raissa on with talk of retailer exclusives, holofoil covers, pointless reboots, and the anguish of overly long and convoluted storylines like Spider-Man's Clone Saga. Raissa was positively poached.

Another Raissa bugbear of the four-color world was fans complaining there's too much social commentary between covers. Granted, writers lately used hammers instead of gloves, but they always had eyes on the world around them. One of the first things Superman did was stop a man from beating his wife. Wonder Woman existed to educate boys about womanhood. "Dark Knight Returns", the ultimate Batman tale for many, was steps away from a newspaper. Plus, true believer, Stan Lee was so woke, he was cocaine. 'Nuff said.

The cornfields of Indiana gave way to the forests of Michigan, just in time for a new album and a snack break. Changed time zones, too. While Raissa loaded up on chewables and drinkables, Rudella thought they looked like cartoons in a Norman Rockwell painting. Raissa thought the gas station clerk probably thought they were Satanists, so she quickly got in and out.

But not before something absurd caught her eye.

As Rudella put in the first disc of "Garage Inc.", Metallica's covers album, something small and hard landed in her lap. She laughed at it, then laughed again when Raissa got in. A block bound in brown paper and twine, with a white label stamped "Deer Crack". Complete with a whacked-out deer. Rudella asked if it was real, to which Raissa replied fuck if she knew. She also warned to hurry up, lest the clerk tried exorcising them. Rudella sped back onto I-94 E, fueled by a double album worth of guitar solos and a king-sized Payday.

Again, Raissa reached for the glove compartment. Again, she changed her mind.

It was when she heard the cover of Nick Cave and the Bad Seeds' "Loverman" that she paid attention to the stereo. Metal wasn't her bag, but Rudella wore it well. Most of the covers played were Punk songs, for which she was also bagless. There was a Bob Seger tune, but that was her boss' bag. The Bad Seeds, though, wove in and out of her life like the stitching in Batgirl's mask. Nick Cave sang "Loverman" like a rant; James Hetfield sang it like a seduction. She was asexual, but she could appreciate desire.

Talk of how Metallica respected their fans bled into talk of fan service. Raissa asked Rudella if she meant those panty shots in her darling anime. Rudella warned her not to blaspheme, then brought up how "Freddy vs. Jason" got fan service right. The slash of the titans could be enjoyed by someone completely new as well as those who knew what Freddy's middle name was or which Jason flick was "Frigay the 13th". Unlike some fan-centric movies that winked or nudged fans to the point of having a seizure.

Raissa wouldn't let the panty shots go, and asked why anime had so many. And why all the panties were white. And did she like them. Rudella let out a sigh of regretful resignation and tap-danced around answers she didn't have or want to share. Raissa saw the otaku's shimmering flop sweat, then decided to let it go since it'd be stupid to crash over animated panties. She asked Rudella to tell her about that geisha word again.

"That geisha word" was "karyukai", meaning "flower and willow world". Mineko Iwasaki, a geisha whose life was twisted into "Memoirs of a Geisha", said her sistren were uniquely beautiful like a flower, and benevolently enduring like a willow. Rudella went on to remind Raissa that Mineko corrected her story with "Geisha of Gion". Then, again, about how geisha weren't whores: they were exceptional party hosts and sex was ditched a long time ago. Raissa smiled and nodded, and was relieved by Rudella's steady driving.

Her nods took her to her phone, where she checked for messages and was amused by the clock being an hour ahead. Rudella didn't sing unless she was at a bar with a teleprompter, so Raissa was also amused that she sang along with Metallica's cover of Anti-Nowhere League's "So What". Quite enthusiastically not giving a fuck about going places, fucking the queen, fucking a goat, and many other trivialities, you boring little fuck.

This prompted Raissa to look up ways people 'round the world said they didn't give a fuck, then shared them with the beaming driver. Some examples:

- It can oxidize my ass.
- I don't give a frostbitten onion.
- It bothers me like a cardboard duck.
- It interests me as much as a kilogram of shit.
- Flowers on my dick and bees all around. (Raissa's fave)

Suddenly, an old cop car sped past then. Like, really old. The red siren on the roof was the size of a coffeemaker. When it was far enough to not be seen in its rearview, the geeks laughed at it like it was their favorite Three Stooges bit. That'd be in "Hokus Pokus", when Shemp hypnotized Moe and couldn't get him out of Sing Sing. A close second was the Niagara Falls gag with Curly in "Gents Without Cents". "I Love Lucy" had a great riff on that in "The Ballet".

Raissa rapped her knuckles on the glove compartment for a few seconds.

A few miles later, Rudella commented on how happily empty the roads were and complained about highway construction. Particularly how she never saw people working. Raissa said that if they heard her say that, they'd go on strike. Rudella scoffed and asked how could anyone tell.

Which brought Raissa to rant about how comic book companies mistreated their writers and artists. Rudella added that it wasn't the only art form overworking and underpaying the creative side, getting sidetracked by Hollywood accounting (always take gross profits, never net, lest you want to wonder why you didn't get royalties off a billion-dollar movie), and that it tended to happen because the creative side was either blinded by the razzle-dazzle or allergic to the business side. Raissa countered that the creative side shouldn't be taken advantage of, in the first place, and Rudella warned her to take it up with Burning Man instead of her.

Raissa wondered what that festival had to do with anything. Rudella explained how Burning Man was a desert sea of elitist pricks and those distracted by the razzle-dazzle. Raissa heard it was a haven for hippies. Rudella said whatever it was, it wasn't anymore, adding that responsibility to those types felt like a thousand handicapped orphans decimated by a hail of gunfire. Obviously, she was still amped from "So What" and didn't have the wherewithal to… expurgate herself.

Raissa thought for a few seconds, then brought up her annoyance with those who complain about getting older. Not people who're practically falling apart; the ones who "felt old" when a thing they liked ten years ago popped up, or that turning 30 was the worst thing that could happen to them. Rudella suggested their lives were so small, 30 probably *was* the worst thing.

The clock struck midnight EST as they passed Ann Arbor. They would've been there sooner, but Rudella drove at whatever speed limit was posted. Sometimes slightly slower. She did **not** want to give cops even a semblance of a reason to wield "local" justice on two out-of-state nymphs. That's the reason her paranoia whispered to her, anyway.

Raissa thanked Rudella for doing the drive with her since it'd be a pain in the tit to do alone. Rudella giggled, then mentioned the least interesting thing about "Night of the Demons": a gal put lipstick in her left tit. Raissa slapped Rudella's arm and asked why she hadn't offered that horror flick yet. Rudella said she didn't think Raissa would've enjoyed it, then apologized for being a misogynist. Apology accepted.

Thanks to her Rewind or Die education, Rudella introduced Raissa to many horror movies, the biggest section back home. Because all flavors of the macabre were at her fingertips, she wasn't burdened by distinction. She didn't give a fuck if the movie was directed by David Cronenberg or Charles Band, as long as it didn't bore her. Because of that, she assumed she was the only woman who appreciated wild swings in quality. Hence the misogyny.

Rudella also had a broad definition of horror, which made Raissa gun-shy of her suggestions. "Last Exit to Brooklyn" was a recent misfire; Raissa had to explain there's a difference twixt horrific and traumatic, and the misadventures of Harry Black and Tralala were definitely the latter.

Anywho, Rudella popped in the first disc of what could best be described as Metallica's orchestral best-of, "S&M". As in, "San Francisco Orchestra & Metallica", ya pervs. It has her favorite song of theirs, "No Leaf Clover", and she was particularly excited to belt it out when it came on. Raissa wondered why Hetfield sang differently, and Rudella explained that he growled in the studio and crooned onstage after blowing his voice out during the ...And Justice for All Tour.

Raissa checked her phone with a chuckle, tapped a few times, then chuckled again before telling Rudella there's a Lansing a few miles away. Rudella mourned the fact it wasn't her

Lansing. Raissa asked if her corset was bothering her, and Rudella said it wasn't, though she'd sound like Hetfield in the studio if she was bloated.

At last, they reached Detroit and only had around two towns north-ish to go. Two things amazed Rudella: the highway was significantly lower than the city, and the Detroit-Windsor Tunnel. If someone's whimsy was tickled, they could take the underground tunnel from Detroit, Michigan to Windsor, Ontario. Rudella had a numb bum, so she had no interest in being tickled.

Staying with assuaging anticipation, Raissa opened the glove compartment. She cracked her window and lit up a Virginia Slim. The smoke trail traded places with the cool air. Rudella noticed she was slightly sour, certainly dour, and asked if it was because of her uncle. Raissa took a deep breath and exhaled a confession.

They weren't going to see her uncle.

The MINI slowed on the empty highway as Rudella asked the obvious follow-up.

They were going to see Raissa's boyfriend.

The MINI stopped.

Rudella didn't know Raissa had a boyfriend and, after a long silence, explained as much. Then she asked how long they'd been dating.

A few months.

Why were they going to Grosse Pointe Woods?

That's where he lived.

Rudella was confused. How could they have dated for a few months with him in Michigan when Rudella never met him and Raissa never left Illinois.

They met on Reddit and have had phone calls and video chats since.

Rudella was pissed and, after a long silence, explained as much. Why the royal fuck wasn't *he* driving to *her*?

A coin toss.

How the fuck did she know he wasn't lying about that?

She tossed it.

What if he was a jagoff? Or a womanizer? Or a rapist? Or a murderer? Or--

Living in what-if would drive her mad; she'd rather burn than rust. Besides, those worries would be there if he lived down the street.

Why the ever-loving fuck did she make her tag along?

Raissa teared up as she told Rudella that she was her best friend and wanted the two most important people in her life to meet.

Rudella joined her, holding her hand. She let out a sigh heavy with frustration, acceptance, love, regret, and exhaustion, then asked Raissa why she couldn't be into women.

Raissa laughed, which was more of a pressure release, and wiped her friend's cheek as she asked her why she couldn't be Lee Ving. Then she held up two fingers and a thumb, and shouted "Vatos Locos forever!" with joy. Rudella smiled and did the same.

They rode through the curtain, onto the next stage of their lives.

CHAPTER TWELVE

Floundering Recovery

A shit aspect of recovery was when you weren't honest about yourself to yourself, then were surprised when the dominoes fell.

It was a few months before the malcontents were disappointed by the Mayan end. What they hoped would be an apocalypse was a clerical error, stuck with the fact they were the only ones who could save them from their manufactured miseries. Some would spend the rest of their lives waiting for catastrophe instead of spend a few years building bliss. Two hands working did far more than 1,000,000 hands hoping.

And if there was a quick fix to all of humanity's ails, what would humanity have learned? Not to appreciate that deus ex machina feat. Humanity would abuse the gift, sailing itself into another regret-filled morass, hoping for another miracle; not working towards an everlasting bliss.

Piri, still the Crustpunk, adjusted to Tender Revolution life well in her two years there, though she remained guarded. She had the same room on the first floor, and became Gaspara's unofficial right-hand dame. Between freak-outs. She never spoke for Gaspara, but she did wield a certain authority in the triplex (though less than the assistants). Like the best of those in power, it was power she didn't want, so she never abused it.

If life at Tender Revolution was a movie set and Gaspara was the director, Piri was the assistant director (with the assistants). To simplify, on a set, the director was in charge of the cast and the ADs and producers were in charge of everything else. All the major decisions were up to the director; the assistant directors facilitated said decisions on-set, and the producers off-set. The most important person on-set wasn't any of them, though. That'd be the caterer, and anyone who thought otherwise could work through their lunch break. Second-most? Payroll, unless everyone wanted to work for free.

Sometimes, the assistant director job was far more mundane. Many of the victims had violent reactions to men and blanket distrust of visitors. They also weren't good for much except recovering from trauma. But lawns needed mowing, leaves needed raking, and snow needed shoveling. Gaspara wasn't the kind of bitch who'd let Piri and the assistants do everything... but those chores weren't an even split.

All of it was responsibility Piri wanted, so she never felt taken advantage of. Tender Revolution was a kindness, but she couldn't merely exist while she recovered as best she could from her vagabondage. To a life without her perils. But her perils would not go gentle into that good night. Not until years later. For the most part.

Women weren't a monolith; as such, the victims of Tender Revolution needed different approaches to recovery. The shelter's third floor had an employer/employee situation. The victims responded best by doing a service and being rewarded or rebuked. Teacher/student was the lingua franca of the second floor. Those victims needed to be taught and tested. Gaspara's floor had a drill sergeant/recruit vibe. Tough love and routine made her victims, like Piri, feel at home.

A false sense of conscription wasn't nearly enough to pay Piri's agony debts; however, she did get better at hiding from everyone when her subconscious came to collect interest. She thought if they saw she still had freak-outs, she'd be locked in a padded room for the rest of her life.

She didn't know what triggered her, but she knew what happened when she was and was grateful it was slow in the coming. It began with a chill, which was why she always wore long sleeves when it was cold (so she knew the difference twixt nature and nurture). When she felt like she was wrapped in pins and needles, she knew she didn't have much time left. Then she felt like she was choking. Then it got bad.

Psychologists called it "depersonalization-derealization disorder"; Piri called it "a fucking nightmare". At this point of her clandestine panic attacks, she felt like she was on the outside of her body looking in, saw it do things she had no control over. She also felt like her thoughts weren't hers, and nothing was real.

These psychological calamities assaulted Piri for minutes at a time. Then, like the low tide, they went away without any sign they were there. Then she rejoined the (hopefully) clueless.

There were different rules for different floors, but they all stemmed from a base rule: "no disrespect". The women who Gaspara kicked out only kissed the pavement after breaking one of their floor's rules. Two or more became a habit, and habits such as that were viral. The woman currently being taken away broke a rule of the second floor. She lasted a month and a half.

The exile, as the car door was about to be shut on her, in a feeble and desperate act of defiance, berated Gaspara and called her a fucking buttonhead. Gaspara smirked and told her if she was going to be racist, at least get it right: Shawnee were Indians with feathers, not dots. Then the exile was someone else's problem.

Piri witnessed everything from the front doorway. Gaspara noticed her noticing her, then asked if she needed anything. Piri answered her question with a question, wondering if it sucked getting confused with India Indians. Gaspara chuckled, then told her not as much as banging her knee on her desk. Piri asked if she was angry about pilgrims. Gaspara shook her head and said it was hard to hold a grudge for more than 500 years, especially when she was around for only 43 of them.

She added with a sinister grin that she'd waste no time finding the best pro bono lawyer in the city if statutes of limitations were abolished. Someone was going to pay for the Indian Removal Act.

Piri was about to go back inside, then asked if Gaspara considered herself an American. Of course, she did. Piri asked what did being an American mean to her. Gaspara had been asked many questions throughout her life (half of them by Piri), but that one was new. She gave it the time it needed before replying since it was the sort of thing you get to answer just once.

Keeping the land healthy was part of Gaspara's Americana; she also explained how stupid it was for people to want to explore space when they couldn't take care of what was around them. Another aspect of being an American was respecting people enough to be fine with them not sharing your thoughts or beliefs. Her third was keeping the government working for the right people; as in, citizens instead of businesses. The one that got a cheer from the bibliophile was protecting and supporting the arts. Gaspara's last aspect of being an American was having the freedom to say and do whatever you wanted, while remembering causality was a thing.

Gaspara balked when Piri said she applauded her liberal tendencies since she voted for Bush twice. You could've knocked Piri over with a feather. When she regained her senses, she told Gaspara if conservatives heard about her, they'd call her a RINO (Republican in Name Only). Gaspara literally clutched her pearls, then let out a laugh that came from surviving over four decades of bullshit. When she was done, she told Piri that rhinos were one of the most dangerous animals in the world, way more dangerous than elephants, so getting called one immediately deflated their argument.

Gaspara didn't forget about Piri's reaction, and told her that the point of the two-party system wasn't one conquering the other. It was keeping things balanced, but not in a good-versus-evil sort of way. She had a hard time elaborating, then Piri said it was like the Lords of Law and Chaos in the Elric of Melniboné novels. The Lords were in eternal conflict, and the conflict was the point. If Law or Chaos won, the universe would fall into entropy. Gaspara said America wasn't that dramatic, but Piri got the gist of it.

Taking the win, Piri went inside.

Piri would soon be devastatingly exposed in a way only soldiers and children would know.

It was weeks since she brought Silencio to Terentia, without a word as to what happened. A word about anything, really. Piri hadn't seen her sex worker friends, either; the better to hide from Silencio's captors, my dear. Paychecks still arrived in her P.O. Box, so she was still officially on the Chicago PD payroll. An informant without anything to inform or anyone to inform to. She fell back into her old routines, proud of helping take down a sex trafficking ring.

One day, on the Red Line to Monroe St., Piri got a text. Terentia reaching out was a bittersweet feeling. It was a long time since they last spoke… but she was about to pop her Art Institute cherry. She didn't know there were free days, to it and Chicago's other museums, and was ready to overflow with culture. Even bought an old sundress and knock-off Doc Martens, AND a new hairdo (which was the result of the stylist freaking the fuck out at her viper's nest of split ends). But she'd have none of that without Terentia, so she met her where she was asked to.

At their secret place, Piri was stunned at the state of Terentia. What was once immaculate and starched was now slovenly and frayed. The detective's bourbon'd breath flicked Piri's nose as an apology fell out. Terentia didn't mean to go AWOL, but she needed time to think about what happened. Piri asked what she was talking about. Terentia stared at her disbelievingly, then said that the sex workers should've told her. Piri told her she hadn't talked to them since that night. Sighing, Terentia regretted she was the one to tell her: Silencio was deported.

When Terentia brought Silencio's taped confession to her captain, they were ecstatic. Until they went through the confession, and got to the part about the other victims. How some of them were Hurricane Katrina refugees. Terentia's captain told her trust in the government was low after how much of a FUBAR handling Katrina was, and America needed a win. That wasn't going to happen if people found out New Orleans women traded one victimhood for another. Better to keep them missing than reveal they were turned into whores. As for Silencio, Terentia's captain said her parents had to have been worried about her, so she'd be getting a first-class trip to wherever she came from. America could at least get a win from that.

Having told her story, Terentia wiped away her tears. Piri was horrified, recoiling when Terentia tried comforting her with a hug. The enfeebled detective told Piri not to worry, that her time away was spent figuring out how to make things right. She did, warning she would soon punish the one who failed Silencio and those who got in her way.

The AR-15 was military-grade ballistic might for civilians, and law enforcement got a discount. It could shred a human into giblets, with an aural terror whose echo slapped walls and trembled glass. As it did in a police station as Terentia stalked and slaughtered her way to her captain. After emptying a full clip into them, liquefying them into a platter of bone and sinew, Terentia turned the gun on herself. When Piri found out what happened the next day on the news, and convinced herself it was her fault, her mind tumbled down a path of derangement that eventually led her to Gaspara's doorstep.

Thus Piri's tale of revenge was complete; the two graves filled with her rapist's freedom and her sanity.

Fata Morgana

After her "chills" subsided, Piri was unnerved and ashamed to see Gaspara standing over her.

Gaspara entered Piri's room to remind her it was her turn to mop, but instead found her seized by a habit thought kicked months ago. Piri explained she couldn't figure out what caused her attacks, that she hid them because she didn't want to be sent away. Gaspara told her it was clear she needed help. Piri wrapped her arms around herself as if she was trying to squeeze the cause out of her, then tearily said she didn't want to get locked in a mental hospital.

Starting off by saying she wasn't proselytizing, Gaspara asked Piri if she thought about giving religion a try. Piri glared at her, and Gaspara repeated that she wasn't trying to convert anyone. She went on to say some people needed religion, some didn't, and one wasn't better than the other because of it. The point was to find the best shoes for you (or go barefoot), and to not make anyone wear your shoes.

As Piri considered, Gaspara suggested she visit all the major religious institutions in Chicago to see if any called out to her. Whichever one she chose, there wouldn't be any judgment.

The next few days, Piri took a bus or cab to all the important places. One that captured her imagination the most was the BAPS Shri Swaminarayan Sanstha Mandir. She spent hours at the Hindu house of worship, of limestone and marble. However, what took her breath away was its gorgeousity, not its purpose. Like the other houses of worship she visited, she didn't feel a connection despite being surrounded by those who did.

She told Gaspara as much when her touring was over, the only glimmer of hope was she felt she was on the right track. She just didn't relate to where the forks led. Gaspara suggested she make her own shoes. Piri said she didn't want to start a cult, to which Gaspara chuckled. Cults were about imposing power on people, by any means necessary; Gaspara only wanted Piri to get through each day.

Piri made a pages-long list of what she wanted from her new religion. From books she read over the years, she realized the more complicated the power structure, the easier it was to be corrupted. Her pages whittled down to a page and a half. The more rules there were, the harder they were to remember. Her page and a half whittled down to half a page. If she really wanted something, she wouldn't let it go. Her half a page whittled down to two sentences. Satisfied, Piri began her new life as a Pagan. She didn't feel like coming up with a fancy name, and she liked Pagans. She also liked the name "Gaia", so she gave it to her new deity and thanked Gaspara for her help.

Soon after, Piri had a moment of clarity. Gaspara should've given her the tap on the shoulder to leave a while ago. Piri saw although she was friendly to the women of Tender Revolution, she was Gaspara's friend. Friends weren't willing to let each other go, but Piri had burdened Gaspara enough and decided she should leave.

She was done with vagabondage and being the street-mad girl, and wanted to try out normalcy. Money to do that with gusto wasn't around; after Terentia's massacre and suicide, Piri had cut all her informant ties. She donated her Third World riches to the Sex Workers Outreach Project-USA, hoping SWOP-USA could fix her mistake. Gaspara gave her money for helping out the last two years, but that wasn't enough to restart a life.

Then she remembered reading about squatter's rights in one of her torn covers.

But where was she to go? She knew she wanted to stay in Chicagoland. The north side was out since she hated hipsters. Plus, it was probably easier for a squatter to be found out. She wasn't west much unless freighthoppin' took her there, so she didn't know what that area was like. South side it was, then. In a year, Palmisano Park would exist; Steelworkers Park, a year later. One was converted from a quarry, the other from a steel manufacturing site, and both would be signs to Piri beautiful change was possible from defiled places.

Piri initially thought an unincorporated town would be a perfect fit, but changed her mind. Unincorporated towns didn't have local governments, the only places where "we do things our own way here" was a point of pride as well as legally binding. She wasn't hot on police after what happened with Silencio, but local justice scared her even more.

She looked into suburbs where the housing crisis raped its way through. Harvey's motto was "At least we're not Riverdale." Riverdale's was "Fuck you, Harvey." After a while, her attention was drawn to Hegewisch.

Chicago's south side wasn't abysmally crowded like its north side. Comparative sparseness came at a price, which was the fact many of the things worth doing around Chicago were north. That's not to say the south side was boring, just that the north side was more fun. Those things meant the south side was more neglected, and fewer towns in the area were more neglected than Hegewisch. You'd think a steelworking town with a strike riot dubbed the Memorial Day Massacre would've at least earned a spot on the map, but it's missing more often than not. A hint of the well-earned chip on its shoulder.

To Piri, the feeling of disregard, one she shared due to how people reacted to her, was like a siren song. She decided to leave in two nights, when everyone was sleeping so she wouldn't be tempted to stay. When she left, she also left her beat-up copy of "The Man Who Laughs", with a note for Gaspara atop it:

Thanks for bringing her closer to becoming a safer person.

CHAPTER THIRTEEN

Salted Earth

Disease sunk deeper into Rudella's dreamscape, took note of precious pains, until she found the wounds she sought.

It was months since the Night of the Long Drive. Raissa's friendship dimmed in the presence of love's growing light. The grand distance with her Michiganian beau a mere crack due to technology's mercy. Mutual visits were frequent, yet they could oscillate so much before one of them had to make a destiny-drenched decision.

The sun glared mockingly through the window as Raissa taped her last box in her living room. Rudella watched from the kitchen table, her composure hung by a strand of shoddy spider silk. As she surveyed her corrugated spoils, Raissa looked at Rudella as if she just noticed she was there. She stifled what Rudella hoped were tears as she pronounced platitudes about everlasting friendship. Laughter soon flooded through pursed lips, whose attitude matched the sun.

The wicked snickering stained the walls, shades of gray streaked from floor and ceiling. The open door gave way to movers, disturbing parodies of comic characters the friends were fond of, who heaved Raissa's boxes away. As they did, the walls encroached upon Rudella with pained resonance. What could be confused as scratching and groaning was the sound of their memories obliterated in the scraping.

Raissa answered her phone with a warmth that had been a stranger to Rudella, then told the lucky man she was almost ready to see him. Annoyed by the transitional ruckus, and by the languishing eyes upon her, she went outside. After telling the obedient Rudella to wait for her.

The seeping gray resembled gnarled stripes, the walls continued their intrusion, and the obedient one was soon left with the stool she sat on. She could reach in any direction and effortlessly touch the pied stucco, such was their oppression. Years, perhaps decades, passed in wasted anticipation for Raissa's return.

When the silk finally snapped, it took the walls with it and left Rudella in a cage of disillusionment.

Behind her, a dream deterred. Rudella convinced Raissa her Michiganian wasn't worth the effort, then found her a local beau. When Raissa was in labor, Rudella was the only one allowed in the room, with advice that got the soon-to-be mother through delivery: better out than in. Rudella became the family's neighbor and a crazy cat lady; all the names rhymed with "Mur-

Mur", and none was the obvious "Purr-Purr". On their shared deathbeds, Rudella and Raissa were nothing more than inside jokes under matching duvets.

Before her, the arrant reality. Raissa and her beau built a joyous, sexless life together in Grosse Pointe Woods. Rudella's birthdays happened as they always have, but they were less of a concern for her old friend. Raissa became a Shutterstock mom with all its conventions. When she upgraded her phone, she didn't bother adding Rudella.

The reality further revealed itself. Raissa's children grew up ignorant of their mother's grand affair with sequential art. They also grew up specialists of living in two houses with neither feeling like home. When Raissa remarried, it was a second chance for all, and none wasted the opportunity. On her deathbed, surrounded by her nearest and dearest, Raissa admitted her lone regret was knowing Rudella.

The reality ended. Raissa would never know regret, or any of life's terrors and wonders, again. Her nearest and dearest mourned lovingly... and raged viciously. Then they noticed Raissa's caged regret and found a focus for their mismanaged emotions. They pulled and screamed and kicked and cried at the bars until, at last, the metal bent to their will.

It was instinct that sailed Rudella through the fresh gap and past frustrated hands. The maddened mob chased Rudella across chasms where her good times with Raissa once were. They forced her down a narrowing corridor that neither she could escape nor they could follow. At the end, an apologetic Honbria.

She begged Rudella to repair their friendship and Rudella, in her bout of immeasurable weakness, did.

Stockholm's Jest

Desperation for social creatures to live up to their name led to choices obnoxious and regrettable and desirous.

In place of usual things that made up streets and buildings, those of Rudella's surroundings were countless sheets of asymmetrical paper. Each sheet had printed its section of the whole it constructed; all of them made an incredibly soothing sound as they fluttered in the light breeze.

The whole was a collision of Downtown Chicago and Tokyo. Seemingly daytime, but the mash-up disappeared past a certain distance. No flora, as if the pulp metropolis used every tree possible to create itself, and animals of origami. No vehicles, though people, resembling banshees and lamias, were too badly drawn to use them.

Rudella returned to her short skirt, long jacket phase (with long hair to match). In front of her was a sign from Honbria: "Seek Me". Under the sky streaked with warnings about Honbria too obscure to read, Rudella obeyed. As she searched, the sketchy homunculi avoided her.

There was nothing behind the sheets, so she at least knew Honbria wasn't in a building or under the street. The "people" were too avoidant to help. It was a lack of feeling that led Rudella to her old friend. The closer she was, the less dignity she felt. When she was utterly insecure, Honbria was around the corner.

She was greeted with a smile and a wave, then a scepter appeared in her waving hand that she gave to Rudella. Pink ivory with a gold crescent moon atop it. As Rudella held it, she was filled with euphoric nostalgia. So much so she glowed bright enough for even the sun, wherever it was, to be ashamed.

When her radiance receded, Rudella noticed two chain links of jade at the end of her scepter. They were the same two links dangled from a pink ivory bracelet Honbria wore.

Rudella tucked her drapes behind her ears with her free hand, still brimmed with halcyon delight, then asked Honbria what they should do first. Sternly, Honbria replied that she wasn't satisfied with Rudella's acceptance of her apology. That it didn't matter much with the threat of the angry mob. That clear-headed words mattered more. That actions spoke louder than words. That Rudella should lick the soles of her shoes.

Rudella did what she was told, taking her time with each slab of dingy rubber. Anything for a friend.

Honbria grabbed the swooning Rudella's shoulders, stood her up, and gave her an approving hug. In a smooth motion, Honbria broke the hug and stepped behind her, then slowly spun with her. Gesturing to their environs, Honbria bragged about them having unending things to do there, though everything had a price.

Rudella did what was suggested, giving Honbria all the money she ever had. Anything for a friend.

The folded animals interested the enchanted Rudella, and she began approaching one. Unlike the "people", the fauna didn't acknowledge her bubble, and a unicorn cantered toward her. Until Honbria became a wall between them, then the paper mimic galloped away. She told Rudella it was years since she was distracted by her so-called life, and demanded her undivided attention.

Rudella did what was requested, giving Honbria all the time in her world. Anything for a friend.

Entranced by nostalgia, remnants of anguish clung to Rudella. She shared her dilemma with Honbria, who had a simple solution. Insecurity came from not knowing one's worth. By that reasoning, if someone had no worth, they also wouldn't have any insecurities. Honbria didn't want the burden, but she asked Rudella for her self-worth anyway.

Rudella did what she was told, and absolved herself from even a dime of pride. Anything for a friend.

If a word is repeated often enough, it loses meaning. The instance is called "semantic satiation". As time passed in the fool's paradise, that was what happened with Rudella and "nostalgia". Her affection towards collegiate memories waned as one's tongue numbed from sugared overindulgence. Eventually, youth lost its thrill.

Honbria had Rudella's pride, her acceptance, her attention, and her wealth. What she didn't possess was her awareness. Like Neo at the beginning of his sixth Matrix escape, Rudella was aware her trappings were such, yet didn't have the knowledge of escaping them. She only knew she desired to leave, and desire was another treasure that eluded Honbria's hoarding.

Rudella's captor wasn't an idiot, and could see her enraptured becoming less so. Anyone could be broken if beaten enough, but Honbria put the caress before the whip. She stroked Rudella with the threat of loneliness, the pain of inconsequence, the fear of irrelevance, and the chill of loss. Honbria cradled her with the belief those horrors and more waited to rape her if the safety of their friendship was annulled.

Knowing this, Rudella took the red pill, dropping Honbria's ivory tether to her and shattering it like so many dreams.

As Rudella's self returned to her, the shards spread throughout the paper metropolis like a thousand speeding bullets. Like a thousand speeding bullets, each was hot to touch. They ignited the paper, and the conflagration was beyond reason. Rudella looked up as the flames encroached upon her and, too late, saw the warnings in the sky.

Also the object of their admonition as she summoned towers of ash to bury her betrayer.

Limits of Engagement

The bitches in wedding gear stood satisfied over their smothered friend in the charred ground alive with anarchy.

Raissa crouched in her frayed bridal gown, then smacked the dirt. Again. And again. And again, as if it were a disobedient lover. Until Rudella could blink and breathe. Until Rudella noticed her with a flush of enmity and bliss. Until Rudella saw she wasn't alone, and gazed upon Honbria, in her jogging pants and open uchikake, with similar insistence.

Honbria tells you, if you're curious, "uchikake" goes "YOU-chai-cake".

The bitches looked at each other, then Honbria took the lead in the conversation. She explained to the buried one they would ask her two questions; if she answered wisely, she could escape. If idiocy danced on her tongue... Honbria gestured towards her rusty shovel.

Rudella asked a most obvious question, and Raissa told her it was to see if she would fall into her old traps with Piri.

Before Rudella could protest, Honbria slammed the edge of her shovel into the chaotic earth, and the thick air was filled with pained screams. They were in the Killing Fields, after all.

Raissa lifted Rudella's chin so they held eye contact, for a sense of truth and lies, then asked her why didn't she stay buried. The gesture worked, and Rudella was threatened with potential judgment as she deliberated. To stay buried meant hiding parts of herself. The things about her that would hurt the most to share.

By not sharing them, Piri couldn't wholly accept her. In that sense, partial love was ultimately the same as no love at all.

Rudella waited for acknowledgment or discipline, but received neither.

Was Rudella changing for Piri or herself, Raissa inquired with transfixed eyes. This consecution of dreams began because a crush turned into a like. Her reconstruction of self to be a better person for a woman. But what if the woman didn't want her? Or worse, didn't want Rudella Amended? Would Rudella be satisfied with herself after being discarded?

She thought for a heartbeat, for an age. She would be filled with the agony of love lost… but she would still love herself.

Honbria grabbed Rudella's long hair, then ripped her from the turf like a mandrake.

Raissa gave two angry stomps, which splintered into existence a dilapidated stage of wood and commerce.

Honbria stripped Rudella as if peeling a potato, then forced her into a burlap sack and onto the stage.

Humiliation and woe conquered Rudella's nerves as she wavered under the spotlight, planks groaning underfoot as she shifted in place. Raissa stood at the podium to her left and addressed the Killing Fields, introducing the latest item up for auction. Honbria clapped to raise the putrefied versions of Raissa and Rudella from their eternal slumber, then pointed their attention to Rudella.

The average person made around $2,000,000 in their lifetime, so Raissa asked that much for Rudella. No takers. She cut the price in half and reminded the undead Rudella was a mortician. To the cares of no one. The bid eventually dropped to an overpriced cup of coffee, with the same indifference. Desperate, Raissa offered a fuck, then a shit. The decedents went aground.

Honbria cackled and pointed out that not even dead people gave a fuck or a shit about Rudella. Raissa couldn't help but join in.

Rudella had enough. She launched herself at Raissa, choking her and slamming her head into the wood. Until both broke. However, Rudella didn't lessen her grip until her fingers dug into her friend's flesh, then tore what was left of her neck open. Blood and giblets dripped onto the frayed wedding dress.

Honbria didn't wait for Rudella's attention she once coveted. She ran through the Killing Fields. For days, she ran. Through the Forest of Denial, the Cave of Forgotten Dreams. Through the Fire and the Flames, the Birthday Massacre. Without pause. Without regret. When she finally tired, near the No Leaf

Clover, she collapsed to her knees. Rudella bludgeoned her into chunks with a sign that said "Seek Me".

Satisfied with newfound liberation, she took in the sights until Disease tapped her shoulder.

Self-Infection

The twins beheld each other, matched also by their disgust of the façade stood in the glassless mirror.

Rudella's disgust of Disease due to her seemingly endless suffering. Her vast self-mutilation and self-repair present in her body bound in vinyl tape, black and glossed, and twine, dull and shredded. All for love. Disease's disgust of Rudella due to her lacking signs of anguish, and her profound feeling of victory.

They found themselves in an orchard, mangled branches ripe with peaches, video cassettes, and skulls. Ruptured concrete beneath their bare feet; chain link fence across the sapphire sky.

Disease made the first move, slowly circled Rudella and scanned her as if looking for traps on her flesh. Rudella's pursued gaze was the only thing that betrayed her stillness. A stillness born from her unwillingness to slice her feet on shards of concrete Disease was impartial to, with a bloody trail to show for it.

On the subject of Honbria, Disease inquired as to how Rudella conquered her. The debased twin's voice quivered with frustration and sorrow. Honbria's death was an instinctual act, so Rudella chose to appreciate it instead of question it. But she knew Disease would consider that a non-answer, and thought of a proper reply.

Nostalgia became a dull burden, and she wanted to create new memories, not fade with old ones.

Disease broke from her path to pluck a cassette and purposefully unspool it, magnetic tape crinkling to the jagged ground. Rudella's focus, and her position, remained. On the subject of Raissa, Disease inquired as to how Rudella conquered her. For irony's sake, Rudella couldn't help but feel that she didn't, but she wasn't going to let Disease see that. She found a way to satisfactorily twist the truth.

If abandonment was overcome, it was because she beat it beyond submission and reason.

Disease felt begrudgingly satisfied, then bound her feet with the cassette's innards. As she did, Rudella noticed the sky began to rust. Disease wiped her sanguined hands on a tree trunk, then leaned her back against it. On the subject of Piri, Disease inquired as to if Rudella's intentions still lingered. Her answer was swift as breath after choking.

All chances not taken were missed like the desert missed the rain; better to had failed at trying than had succeeded at regret.

It sounded like the breaking of thousands of iron bones. Corrosive flakes fell as titian snow. Rudella tried her best to muffle their clamor, keep their stinging from her eyes. When she was able to steal an upward glance, she saw the cause of the sudden miseries.

The sky was falling.

Chain link pieces plummeted, their aim at her immediate surroundings. She had nowhere to run, nowhere to hide. Disease watched puckishly as the iron crashed around their target, decimated the concrete and sent the debris below with Rudella.

The metal and masonry streaked as they dropped, then turned into drapes of the softest silk. Rudella slid down them into a dimly lit cave, onto a floor of potpourri. Her burlap sack was replaced by a velvet nightgown that trailed farther back than she could see. Her hair that teased her waist now danced above her shoulders. Her eyes found Disease with her, unchanged.

Curtains of silk made a labyrinth of the dusky cave. Disease would be Rudella's guide. Or, perhaps, her Minotaur.

The twins wandered through the silken sad uncertain until a fluttering caught their chestnut eyes. They approached the rhythmic stillness, soundless save for dried petals and Mylar crunching underfoot. As they ventured deeper, fluttering turned billowing, yet they could see past the silk once they parted it. Disease stopped at what had to be the center of the maze, and gestured wickedly at the billowing circle.

As Rudella entered the veil, the sudden sound violated her. The sight was worse. The silk's rhythmic stillness was caused by Piri's rhythmic breathing. On her hands and knees upon a satin pedestal, while someone fucked her from behind. The sound was her ecstatic droning interrupted by thrusts so heavy, they rocked her throat. The one gripping her sweaty hips was violently blurred; Rudella couldn't tell if they were a man or a woman.

Disease stalked her way to Rudella, and spoke loudly to weather the moans with a warning this could be an eventuality. Piri might be too much for her, and her roaming eye could find someone better suited. Maybe even while still with her in arm's reach. Piri managed to keep her balance with one hand while the other, rocked by her partner in carnality, reaching out for Rudella.

With the detachment of heartbreak and acceptance, Rudella told Disease she was right. But she also might be too much for Piri. Or they might find another reason to cheat on each other. Or they might never cheat. Part and parcel of the dating game.

Piri's fucktoy disappeared as she got up and walked to Rudella until they felt each other's breath. Rudella wanted to touch her, but she couldn't. She thought Disease gripped her wrist, but she was behind Piri. It was the silk. More sheets bound themselves to her arms and legs, made her unable to move forward or back.

Then the ground fell from under her again.

Crack became rift, rift became canyon, canyon became the world. The world was beneath Rudella as she dangled from her bindings. Below her, as far as her eyes could see to her left and right, the unending overhang of a raging waterfall. Its foaming plunge pool glowed as if smothering a galaxy of fireflies.

When she looked up, she saw her trappings suspended from Piri's fingers. Chains slunk down to greet her with their hooks into her splintered skin. As Disease slid down them to meet her, hands gripped taut silk and feet supported on dangled thighs. All soaked in blood. She warned Rudella this could be her eventuality. Piri might be manipulative. She might take advantage of her under threat of dropping her over the edge.

With the determination of worry and lessons learned, Rudella told Disease she was right. Also that life taught her to be mindful of red flags when they sprouted. If she ignored them, she deserved whatever maladies Piri made her heir to.

Then Rudella was gone. Disease wept for there were no more worlds left to conquer, which meant she no longer needed to exist. Then she was gone. The consecution of dreams couldn't go on purposelessly. Then it was gone.

However, an unknowing parting gift remained to be handled in the waking: Rudella's abandonment issues.

CHAPTER FOURTEEN

Greasy Spoons

Shed a tear for those whose livelihood meant dealing every working day with assholes, dickheads, raging cunts, and smuggerfuckers.

Teachers and med heads were obvious, but bakers and servers were also deserving. What're the four most important days of the year? That's right: Valentine's Day, birthdays, weddings, and Christmas. Pastries were the centerpiece of each; often literally. They're not only expected, they're **demanded**. If a loaf-keeper fucked that up for you or yours, it'd be a very bad time for all involved. Perhaps apopleptic.

As for servers… let Piri's Lake Stop life take you on a journey through the service industry. She did her job well, but not all her coworkers deserved praise. One waitress was arrested on the job. Surprisingly, not the one whose chemical romance gave her a habit of nodding off. Another was fired for bringing politics to work, which was a nice way of saying she hassled customers who didn't fall on her side of the two-party line. Betcha wanna know which. There was also the one fired for guilt-tripping customers who didn't tip big enough for her next casino visit. And so on.

But don't think those workplace fallacies never involved management. The owner did their time behind the apron and avoided going to any diner. Because of that, the manager was Lake Stop's feudal lord. In any profession, incompetent people floated to the top due to their confidence. Sooner or later, everyone figured out the gimmick and the charismatic bumblefuck was fired. But not before food was micromanaged for breaks, staff offered no less than a limb to leave for family emergencies, a waitress miscarried, plus many other ineptitudes.

Sure as the dawn, the worst part of any job was the customers. Waitresses got a particularly bad view of humanity since many people on the other side of the menu felt entitled. Besides being wrong, it's also ironic since they're literally beneath the wait staff while they sat. Along with constantly getting the wrong kind of attention, the ass pinching and slapping kind, Piri had binders full of shitsquibs. Two stood out, to the point where Rudella could finish her stories about them (she eventually learned to put a moratorium on "split pay" and "comp meal").

Shit occasionally happened and people found they had less on their debit card than they thought. Piri tried to be nice about it whenever it happened since she's the last person to give someone grief for not having money. Most were appreciative. Some were defensive. One was obnoxious. One was with a group who neglected to tell her they were splitting the bill, then spent another eight minutes figuring out who had and owed what. One kept trying to push parts of their order on others. One was pissed at Piri when she broke the news about their card, then said she drained their bank account. One had a friend who took care of their bill and wasn't their friend the next day.

Shit occasionally happened and the odd typo snuck into the menu. In Lake Stop's defense, a possibly vindictive manager turned off Spell Check and no one knew how to switch it back. Whenever a customer pointed any of them out, they got a No-Prize. Piri also hummed the chorus of Louis Prima's riff on Irving Caesar's yankee riff on "Just a Gigolo". Of course, there's always someone, or a pair of someones, who wanted to wreck fun for profit. Like the couple who seemed to flit from diner to diner as if they were sport-fucking to their next comp meal. Meals were free if the order was screwed up, not for a No-Prize. But these were goddamn Americans, goddamnit, and they didn't ask for a goddamn chesseburgee. Giving Piri the worst kind of attention, a customer called the police on *them*.

When Rudella eventually introduced Piri to comics, she did so with the first part of Mimi Pond's two-volume magnum opus to waitressing in late-'70s Oakland, "Over Easy".

She had to buy a new copy thanks to the plentiful, bleeding papercuts from excitedly reading.

Squatting was meant to be as temporary for Piri as waitressing's permanence, but she now desired a swift exit from both.

She thought she'd be fine with the hazards of slinging plates; she survived a life of vagabondage, after all. What she realized during a bike ride to work was that, terrible as homelessness was, the bad parts were spread out in terms of frequency and location. She could count on something bad happening to her each time at the diner, and had nowhere else to go 'til the end of her shift. Plus, she was a time bomb of agony debts. She managed to manipulate her life around her panic attacks, but an unavoidable and apocalyptic one was inevitable.

As was losing her squat in Hegewisch, though the housing crisis swinging its big dick through the working class meant there was a good chance Piri would be committed before she was evicted. Neighbors were clueless thanks to her mastery of stealth, but an anxious Realtor could still ruin everything. A semi-charmed life could only get her so far.

The problem, rote as it was, was money. Many benchwarmers and panhandlers ended up that way trying to woo Lady Luck, so lotteries and casinos were out. Getting another job would threaten her routine too much, leading a nosy neighbor to call the police. Stealing led to jail; fine 'til her sentence was over, then she was back on the street with a record. Assuming her informant past didn't become a conversation topic between her and a shiv.

Then Piri remembered a brave way to make a few bucks, and called a few of her old friends still in the biz.

It had been a long time since the Silencio incident, so she wasn't sure who was still working. Or alive. Her burner phone was smashed ages ago, but she was from an era when people bothered to memorize phone numbers. After knocking the cobwebs off a few and getting varying shades of good and bad news, Cassandra Luxx had everything she needed, and was willing to share. Ms. Luxx had been a sex worker for around a decade, and sampled as many ways to hustle her pussy as she could in that time. Knowledge that Piri was keen on discovering.

Chicagoland was a damn fine place, but there were patches of annoyance. Take Pilsen, for example. There's nothing wrong with it except its name was easy to confuse with Posen. Didn't help they were far enough apart to hate yourself for mixing them up. Ditto Forest Park and Park Forest. Of course, Ms. Luxx wanted to meet in Pilsen; then, to be closer to Piri and the south side, Park Forest. Piri thought she meant Posen; then, to be closer to Ms. Luxx and the north side, Forest Park. Then they said fuck it and met at Buckingham Fountain.

The first thing Piri asked was if Ms. Luxx, in one of her many pairs of Pleaser heels, still had her license plate. She's originally from Hawaii, which blew Piri's mind the first time she saw her Scion xB, apart from the fact it looked like a giant cube, because she still had her plate. Piri must've stared at that rainbow on aluminum for five minutes, like the closet rube she was. It came across the fucking ocean, for cryin' out loud. Then she admired Ms. Luxx's French tips.

With that bit of innocence out of the way, their talk turned caffeinated and naughty. Piri had buckets of questions about sex work; Ms. Luxx had one: was she sure? Ms. Luxx would be the last person to say sex work was wrong, but she'd be the first to say it wasn't for everyone. Apart from the obvious… overexposure, oodles of workers neglected the dangers and the business side, leading them to chemical dependencies or a sudden zealot life. Not everyone, but people from both sides of the camera, and watching the show, had no problem taking advantage of those who weren't careful. Cruelty was genderqueer.

Piri listened, then asked how that was different from any job.

Fear was the coffee of emotions, and Ms. Luxx was pleasantly surprised Piri was fine with her venti white chocolate mocha. Usually, sex work talk with normies had the intensity of

Frederick Douglass and Oscar Wilde debating apples and oranges. There was no middle ground with her, so Piri's acceptance made Ms. Luxx let down her hair like a studded bra on a marble floor. Metaphorically. Her strapless wonder, to the disappointment of the distracted, stayed snug under her blouse and over her dirty pillows. And she spent too much time with her updo to let anything short of one night with Heath Ledger's ghost or Rachel Weisz mess it up.

The first topic of conversation, to the dismay of passersby, was what kind of sex work Piri wanted to do. Ms. Luxx brought up streetwalking because of Piri's old life, and knew a few ok places with reliable johns. Piri wanted nothing to do with streets anymore unless it was about getting from Point A to Point B. Escorting was next; at least, until Piri said she didn't wanna fuck anyone but herself. She didn't say it was because she'd probably puke on the other person... but don't ask, don't tell. Ms. Luxx congratulated her on having a zero chance of rape, and a poor mother had to stop her giggling toddler from chanting "rape".

Solo work had a lot of variety for Piri despite being by her onesies. She could use her fingers or oh, so many toys. Toys that buzzed, poked, or prodded. Toys that could be ridden, tied, or blown. She could dress up, too. There were also other, less damp options for sex work. The unicorn was being a financial domme, which was basically making someone spend money on you without anything in return. Ms. Luxx knew a financial domme, 'til she tried stealing her client. The more typical gig was being a foot model; very high maintenance since the feet have to stay pretty, but the pay was worth the grief. The only catch was getting asked sometimes to step in some weird shit. May or may not be literally.

The best thing about being a camgirl was that it was legal; as far as the IRS was concerned, anyway. But if taking money made Piri nervous, she could make a wishlist on her ecommerce site of choice and let her customers buy her things. Half the things in Ms. Luxx's apartment were wishlist grants. Including the Juicy sweatpants currently enjoying her curves. Another best thing was making her own hours. If she wanted to make a video after breakfast or at two in the morning, the only thing stopping her would be Aunt Flo.

Piri's head was swimming with possibilities as if it was dunked in the Fountain. Ms. Luxx's last bit of advice, before sliding on her feather-collared coat, was to pick a professional name, lest she wanted to deal with fairy-dusted idiots with too much time and misguided dedication on their hands. Which shocked Piri because she thought Cassandra Luxx was her real name. Poor thing.

Ms. Luxx's *other* last bit of advice was to make Firefox her default browser. It's the best at keeping privacy private. With eventual addons like uBlock and Ghostery, Piri would never have to worry about sites invading her with ads and trackers. Which meant perverts couldn't take advantage of data they couldn't find.

The beach was across the street from the fountain, and the day was nice enough to enjoy it, so Piri copped a squat on some sand and thought about what she wanted to do. Still nursing her mocha, wrapped in a bright orange raincoat despite the clear blue above, and Lake Shore Drive's traffic whooshing behind her.

She wondered what her sex name should be. Whatever it was, she didn't want it to be obvious. Tits McGee had a certain charm, but it's a novelty act, at best. She thought about sexing up a name, but Shakira was already at its erotic saturation point. She then thought about the kind of attitude she wanted to have as a camgirl. Like a wave on the shore before her, a cackle flowed from her lips. Kilhanna. Camming would be temporary, and she'd want to get as much from it as possible. For some reason, that made her think of the burn-out glory of Kill Hannah's "Kennedy". A perfect fit, if ever there was.

How Kilhanna looked meant the most to Piri; mainly because she wanted to hold onto anonymity. Customers would often see intimate parts of her, which was part of the gig, but she didn't want to be found in the wild. Bastions of morality might tar and feather her, and idiots might expect... handouts. Theatres tossed out old costumes, so she could dumpster dive for bits and bobs while she was downtown. She thought to go one step further and make what would pass for a set in the basement with cardboard and fabric; that way, bastions and idiots couldn't know where she was.

Like any product or service in an abundant market, Piri knew her first few videos would have to be free. Only an idiot would expect strangers to pay for something new when there were plenty of free alternatives. But if she reeled them in with freebies 'til she had an audience to get the right kind of attention from, money and ejacu-- adulation, that was genius.

However, none of this mattered if she couldn't get off without feeling catastrophic. Agony debts and all. A quirk of her narrative, though, was that she never attempted self-love. She figured the rollercoaster of troubles that popped up whenever she had sex applied to all kinds of sex. She also figured she could fake orgasms as Kilhanna. If she was wild enough, who'd care, right? If she *could* scratch her record without any fuss, though, it'd be fantastic for all parties involved. Cameras, by nature, liked rewards. Few things were as rewarding as a well-earned orgasm. She didn't want to test her theory in what passed for a bathroom at the beach, so she took a bus to a place she knew had a nice, single-occupancy one and executed her hypothesis.

Dear reader, it was, to put it mildly, a success.

Regeneration

Days became months, and the lust of hundreds brought Kilhanna thousands on a platter of toys and kinks.

Parts of sex work were fun, but it was still work and work could be mundane. Upkeep was the most important thing, and also the most mind-numbing. Waxing was never an option for Piri; she'd rather shave often than deal with ripping once in a while. So she shaved her legs and 'pits and, delicately, landing strip. Her customers hated bush, and the strip was a compromise. She went bald once, terrified of female genital mutilation with each razor stroke. The grind of a pumice stone in the shower kept her feet soft and smooth.

As Kilhanna, she wore various half-masks and wigs, but she still used a facial scrub and kept her pixie cut well-groomed. The only makeup she wore was neon lipstick; the better to not be noticed in the wild, my dear. Riding a bike kept her fit, but vanity took over after and she started yoga. Her customers appreciated her flexibility and muscle tone. Especially around the glutes. Her nails were constantly trimmed; nothing ruined a session like a hangnail scraping her girly bits (fellas, one of the most thoughtful things you can do for your gal is clip your nails). Then she got lazy, and fetish-y, and started wearing black latex gloves.

Each video began with Chris Charisma's remix of DJ Yoeri's "Fuck on Cocaine" and ended with Slim Shore's "Syren". She used to play music during, but customers thought it was distracting. She liked getting off to songs, so she had tunes pumping through her wireless earbuds.

Sexy times were fun times, yet there needed to be variety to keep all parties interested. At first, they were fine with fingers and the occasional pillow-hump, then there were desires for more. Piri didn't have a gender preference, but she *did* hate <u>anything</u> going inside her. No one saw her first dildo video since most of it was her freaking the fuck out before she kicked the camera away. Vibrators were more than welcome, though. When she could afford a Sybian (basically, a buzzing saddle) a whole new world opened to her. She had to cut back on it and vibrators since her fun button started going numb. Bad for business and morale. All the while treating each video like a kinky, quasi-costume party.

More than half of her paycheck came (heh) from pictures of her feet. Thanks to Ms. Luxx, she found a decent site, then was warned its patrons were notoriously picky. That pumice stone and lotion did the trick because they accepted her piggies with open arms. And wallets. Some wanted them bare, others wanted them in heels, and the big spenders wanted them playing with food. As long as they didn't want them amputated and their payments cleared, Piri didn't care how they wanted her tootsies.

To keep things personable, she posted things on her blog, Four on the Floor, once a week. She mostly rambled adorably and suggested songs, but there were also acts of revenge. Attempts at shaming her popped up in the comments and, once in a while, she gathered the best ones and wrote elaborate takedowns of their shallow arguments. As a rule, pro-lifers who weren't also anti-war or anti-death penalty got it the worst. For some reason, guys felt the need to send her dick pics. Even after pinning a post to the top of her blog about why she didn't want them. So she started posting them, writing the most vile things about them, and outing their senders. The pics screeched to a halt after a week. The clit pics didn't get the hint, however, 'til she blogged about how one looked like a pug eating mayonnaise.

A misconception of mobile home communities is they're just pits of decay. Sure, trailer trash exists, but many are nice. When Piri had enough money, she moved a few minutes away to Chicago's only one: Harbor Point Estates. Close to highways and loaded with nature, it had everything she needed. Plus whatever her customers donated to her P.O. Box. A permanent, legal residence also gave her a library card; a privilege she abused with glee. She had one of the dazzling houses, with thick walls. She's a screamer when sex brought her to a natural conclusion, and she was crabby about holding back at the squat. Hard to avoid neighbors' attention if they could hear her ecstasy from the basement.

Though the camgirl life was quite good to Piri's bank account, she knew it could quickly turn bad. Which was why she got into the reselling market. Sleeping rough 'round Midway and O'Hare airports, she found out people routinely scammed foreigners who just arrived. She also found out airlines sent unclaimed baggage to, waitforit, UnclaimedBaggage.com, where people could buy those left behind things for a spectacular markdown. From there, any enterprising, formerly homeless woman could resell them online or at Swap-O-Rama for however much she wanted. She also had no problem sharing the wealth and donated to charities that helped her. Like the gals back at Tender Revolution.

She *also* wanted to pay back all those musicians whose music she stole for her mix CDs, so she started buying their albums (CDs, unless they were only available digitally).

Women were smaller than men; that's a fact of life. Women were usually overpowered by men; another fact. Piri was a scrapper, but she told herself that she'd learn to do better the first chance she had. That line of thought brought her to Aikido. A completely defensive martial art style that used the opponent's energy against them. She locked onto a school that taught Kokikai Aikido, which was a minimalist version. There were brutal versions, but she just wanted to effortlessly embarrass her attacker and get away.

Since she didn't have to worry about her hiding hole being found out, or about Roman hands and Russian fingers, she started wandering around Hegewisch like a normal person would. And showed off her eye patches she began designing. And avoided those of the… NIMBY persuasion (she giggled when she thought about what she got away with for so long in their back yard). She didn't realize so many streets were just letters. Her greatest thrill was riding Hardstyle to Supermercado El Tapatio #3 for groceries because she was able to go whenever and buy whatever she wanted.

Her thrills didn't stop next to the Manzanita or with Kilhanna shenanigans, either. Cassandra Luxx took her to burlesque shows near and far. For awesome lessons on the Burly-Q, read Liz Goldwyn's "Pretty Things", Jo Weldon's "Burlesque Handbook", and Dita von Teese interviews. All hail Bettie Page and Lili St. Cyr. For something burlesque-adjacent, read "Ziegfeld and His Follies" by Cynthia and Sara Brideson. For something more awkward, look up "Baby Burlesks", at your peril.

Despite her… openness online, and the fact her Kilhanna wear would fit in swimmingly, Piri was too shy to go onstage and dance the hoochie coochie. She had no qualms about appreciating other dancers, though. And she appreciated them weekly. Just the shows; she was nowhere near ready to see if camming made companion sex a thing yet. Still, she wielded an enthusiasm during the shows like it was the '60s, The Pill just came out, and nothing could kill her. She also began her tradition of having the current Olivia De Berardinis calendar. Can't love beautiful women and art without having anything painted by her.

Although she still rode her bike, money meant she didn't have to suffer Chicagoland weather when she had to work at Lake Stop. Yes, she still worked there. Not as often, but she had to get out of the house out of fear of turning into a chronic masturbator. Just kidding, she liked routines. Anywho, she took taxis to and fro, always four blocks away from Harbor Point, lest any drivers had stalker ideas.

Then, once upon a September, a cute mortician entered her life.

CHAPTER FIFTEEN

Bell Tolls For Desolation

Now we know their pasts apart, the time has come to entwine Rudella and Piri's present, and future.

September changed its mood, fortunately
Allowing the ardor twixt them to spread
October and its wicked wonders next
Then into the arms of February
No sweets shared, though, from lady to lady
The damaged cases still swayed and baited
By trauma freaks lurking in their closet
Those, in dreams, Rudella conquers keenly

As May flowers bloom, one finds bravery
The Mortician, as fixed as she could get,
Asks Piri out as she drops off her check
The Maiden, willing despite her worry
The Staff, exhausted from months of flirting,
Tears the roof off with claps and cheers and sweat

Rudella's geek flag flies around Piri
Encouraged to flutter caffeinated
She takes the fresh-won chance to fill her head,

Draw her eye to a four-color party
Comic book conventions come vast and wee
The Mortician, with no moment wasted,
Finds a modest one in a foyer-shed
To not overwhelm the Maiden with glee

Books are laden with continuity
So introductions are complicated
What catches Piri's eye and fills her head
Are the devoted dressed fancifully
Rudella describes the lot eagerly
While Kilhanna gets ideas for a… "skit"

Convention life ends most successfully
The Maiden's a fan with tastes eclectic
Shows her X-Men love with a pinback X
Her Catwoman love in ways more kinky
(The Mortician doesn't yet know, sadly)
Her Rudella like with a great request
Another date; a place she intended
Fair's fair, and love's built on equality

The arcade still tickles Piri's fancy
Though Rudella's game skills aren't lauded
She has fun on her date's dime and token
Next, to Little Palestine for some tea
And meals the Maiden's desperate to eat

While the Mortician expands her palate

Endometriosis wrecks their next meet
Rudella, flushed with redundant regret,
Promises Piri to push past distress
And to go clubbing downtown (by taxi)
Tucked in an alley, Neo is firstly
A club where Black Clads go to lose their shit
Lively tunes with melancholy lyrics
Swaying under morbid lights carelessly

The night's young and so are they, so they flee
First to eat, then to turn into clubheads
Berlin's close and Piri wants to work it
To Rudella's enjoyment, boy, does she
Because this club's a big rainbow party
Pumping aural cocaine heard past Halsted

Despite their obvious fun and mutual attraction, not one of these dates are sealed with a kiss.

Fourth Time's the Charm, Rudella

The progress she's yearning for is finally at her proverbial door; with threats of the monkey's paw that'll come scratching later.

With all she's been through
She thinks the worst is over
Yet she doesn't have a clue

If only she knew
There's much more Piri to uncover
With all she's been through

Delight in baby steps has left her askew
She assumes what it means to be together
Yet she doesn't have a clue

It's not her fault, she's made due
With scraps from her almost-lover
With all she's been through

Good and bad times will flow down her avenue
In torrents of nature and nurture
Yet she doesn't have a clue

What she knows is she's overdue
For something spectacular
With all she's been through
Yet she doesn't have a clue

Problems she let brew

As they go to the theatre
Forcing them beyond her purview

"Mad Max: Fury Road" is onscreen, wide and true
While she sacrifices cuddling to wonder
Problems she let brew

Mixed signals constantly join the queue
She's taking them, loud as thunder,
Forcing them beyond her purview

To her, Piri is harlot and ingenue
An evidenceless bother
Problems she let brew

She feels her paranoias renew
The vehicular carnage distracts her
Forcing them beyond her purview

Credits roll and someone wants their shoe
Still, wrong thoughts wander
Problems she let brew
Forcing them beyond her purview

In a place worthy of Siouxsie Sioux
Among tombstones and dreary weather
She'll soon know what she got herself into

The idea to picnic here is… guess who
Her date enjoys it, even with a bit of laughter
In a place worthy of Siouxsie Sioux

Mourners don't approve the ballyhoo
The Mortician, however, is rife with pleasure
She'll soon know what she got herself into

In her head, Dave Clark Five's "Glad All Over"
Thanks to the oldies station her parents prefer
In a place worthy of Siouxsie Sioux

Rudella puckishly asks to hear something taboo
Piri rants about Rose Mackenberg
She'll soon know what she got herself into

A good time is had near a solemn statue
Her worries fade into the ether
In a place worthy of Siouxsie Sioux
She'll soon know what she got herself into

However long love takes to debut
That's how long she chooses to linger
This is fine, this is fine, too

Even if hope begins to mildew

Following desire's will to fester
However long love takes to debut

Even if her dreams make a hullabaloo
About the perils of St. Anger
This is fine, this is fine, too

Even if anticipation beats her black and blue
And regret makes her feel like a sucker
However long love takes to debut

Even if madness and despair ensue
Entertaining thoughts of murder
This is fine, this is fine, too

The alternative is letting loneliness hew
At what she worked hard to deter
However long love takes to debut
This is fine, this is fine, too

Along the steps to Piri's front door, Rudella gets what she
wants and all the wicked wonders it's heir to.

Fourth Time's the Charm, Piri

Since Rudella did the asking, Piri feels she should take the lead, yet forgets the rules modernity has broken.

The lack of progress makes her ache
Where she stands, she still can't tell
She wonders if she was a mistake

Rudella won the chance she couldn't take
She should, by now, be her belle
The lack of progress makes her ache

So many urges are now awake
Yet Rudella hasn't forced her out of her shell
She wonders if she was a mistake

Doesn't the Mortician know it'd be a piece of cake
To take what she wants, like the lion and the gazelle?
The lack of progress makes her ache

She knows her feelings aren't fake
She thirsts to be the Mortician's mademoiselle
She wonders if she was a mistake

Her melancholy could fill a lake
As disenchantment spins her carousel
The lack of progress makes her ache
She wonders if she was a mistake

Perhaps the lead she must take
While riding on the Fury Road, Rudella does dwell
Unless ambition leads to heartbreak

The thoughts wind in her mind like a snake
Not knowing which to quell
Perhaps the lead she must take

Placing a hand on Rudella's thigh, for sanity's sake
Might place the Mortician under her spell
Unless ambition leads to heartbreak

If only the Mortician wasn't so fucking opaque
She wouldn't be slave to anxiety's bell
Perhaps the lead she must take

Maybe she should let her inhibitions flake
That'd be really swell
Unless ambition leads to heartbreak

Mutual indecision makes her quake
The movie ends, her desire back in its cell
Perhaps the lead she must take
Unless ambition leads to heartbreak

She wonders if she was a mistake

If their disconnect does fortell
While her date grips distraction like a keepsake

That their dates were just her dreaming awake
That their picnic is a farewell
She wonders if she was a mistake

Rudella could scorch her worries like a drake
A little attention would be a bombshell
While her date grips distraction like a keepsake

A touch, a caress would undertake
Her devotion to the deathly damsel
She wonders if she was a mistake

Talk of Rose Mackenberg makes her break
From confusion and most harmful thoughts that befell
While her date grips distraction like a keepsake

Conversation becomes like velvet cake
And though most doubts have wailed their knell
She wonders if she was a mistake
While her date grips distraction like a keepsake

What would surrendering her heart forsake?
An answer's taking ages to jell
The lack of progress makes her ache

The strong Piri everyone knows is fake
And exhausting; she wants to rebel
What would surrendering her heart forsake?

Being Rudella's means she can break
In private; for feminism, an infidel
The lack of progress makes her ache

Dash Berlin's "Till the Sky Falls Down" bites like a snake
Though she wishes it would dispel
What would surrendering her heart forsake?

They stop for a milkshake
Anticipation clamors like a bell
The lack of progress makes her ache

Fed up and knowing what's at stake
We come to the end of her villanelle
What would surrendering her heart forsake?
The lack of progress makes her ache

The pain is sated when they go inside her home, debts she
thought were gone for good lurking under the floor.

CHAPTER SIXTEEN

Young Americans

In which our couple discovers what it means to love and be loved in return.

How does a new relationship change a person? Unlike everyone at Lake Stop, none at Sunset Shores knows about Rudella's off-work life. So when the queen of snark and brooding starts showing up with pep in her step and a crooked grin, they didn't know how to take it. Her partner in granite grime draws the short straw and asks, half-expecting a strange tale of revenge. The other half was hoping for one. When he hears the whole romantic story, he's surprised she found someone and they're a woman. Rudella asks if any of that's a problem, and he tells her only if she visits.

As for the Lake Stop crew, they see the Piri they've always known. Until it's close to her quitting time. Then it's a roulette wheel of which Piri they'll get. She doesn't stop being a waitress, but everything else is up for grabs. Antsy is the funniest. Longing takes her the closest to trouble. Cocky leads to bigger tips, for some reason, and she's too oblivious to take advantage. Happy is typical, and some of her coworkers like trying to burst her bubble. Once, they said she had yellow fever; she said it was incurable. A customer quipped about waiting 'til their first fight, with a round of knowing laughter.

We check in two months after the start of their relationship, one night on Rudella's couch. It's neither Piri's first nor second time here, but she's still amazed by all the books and movies Rudella managed to fit in her apartment without feeling cluttered. All the bookcases handmade and stained since Rudella saw how much cheaper it was, and knew someone with a circular saw. Each shelf has doilies since no one stopped her.

They're couchbound because Rudella introduced Piri to "Hannibal", and they've been watching it from the beginning in anticipation of the encroaching series finale. Piri read all of Thomas Harris' novels and, like any gal on the wild side, loved his cannibal psychiatrist, Hannibal Lecter. "Hannibal", the show, filters "Red Dragon" and "Hannibal", the novel, and "Hannibal Rising" through a gorgeous, High Gothic lens while presenting an intense relationship twixt Hannibal and Will Graham, an FBI profiler damned by getting Dr. Lecter's attention.

Rudella and Piri agree the first season spent way too much time saying "Garrett Jacob Hobbs". Don't make a drinking game out of it: you'll be dead before the commercial break.

The Viewsome Twosome finish the tragically sanguine final episode of the second season, wrapped in an afghan and sharing a carton of butter pecan. Rudella enjoys the rewatch like a warm cup of Cinnamon Apple Spice, but Piri is a million miles away.

Rudella notices twixt spoonfuls and asks Piri what's wrong. She replies with roundabout worries that don't say anything, yet express her anxiousness. The Mortician comforts her, after a fashion, by telling her that she can't react worse than what they just saw, so she shouldn't take the winding road to her point. The Maiden forces a smirk, admits everything about her Kilhanna life, then takes a long time before looking at her couchmate for a reaction.

Does she fuck anyone else? No, just herself.

A welcome indifference greets the camgirl, with a warning to keep it that way since her girlfriend's too selfish to share.

Rudella picks up Piri after work, whenever she can. Piri counts her tips during the ride, and Rudella occasionally pretends to roll down her window.

This time, Rudella places her hand on Piri's thigh. She **SLAPS** the hand, sending singles and fives all over the dashboard and front seats.

Rudella swerves her car, surprised by Piri's reaction and the fluttering distractions. Luckily, it's late so there's no one to swerve into. She pulls over, then understandably wonders what the fuck aloud.

Piri panics, gathers her money, and apologizes. She doesn't know why she reacted that way. But you do. She kisses the hand she slapped, unsure whether to stroke Rudella's hair or rub her shoulder. She tries both, but is shrugged away.

The short drive to the mobile home goes in slow-motion, time stretched by awkwardness. Only when parked does Piri ask about her girlfriend's day. Fine, 'til it felt like driving in a snow globe for no fucking reason. Piri's mea culpa: a cup of coffee and a foot rub. Rudella reminds her waitressing means one of them needs both more than the other. Piri reminds her she gets free refills all night, she has awesome insoles, and Rudella spends work in sculpted heels.

Nursing her java in her blood-stained mug, Rudella enjoys the massage tips Piri learned from a torn cover. People tend to rush through a rubdown when it only gets better the more time you take. Piri is on molasses time.

As Delerium's soothing "Chimera" album spins in her stereo, Piri wants to test her limits. She can make-out with Rudella and get herself off without a dire reaction; can she get Rudella off? She tests the waters by focusing on a foot, inching her way up to a calf, then up to a thigh and under a fringe skirt. No nausea. No shakes.

Piri works her way to Rudella's hips and red cheeksters, ready to run away if she feels a situation coming. Nothing happens, not even as she slides the pinstripes down and kisses her way back up. She pauses, but that's because she notices Rudella's pubes are straight. She's only seen them curly, or gone. She strokes them, and Rudella didn't know a tickle could be a turn-on.

Being Kilhanna taught Piri so many wonders about her panty hamster. Since she's her own torn cover, she should share her knowledge. It didn't take long for an orgasm to electroduce itself. Piri hides a tear as she nuzzles a thigh; she can be at least this intimate without anything going wrong. She expresses her enthusiasm to Rudella, doing things to her that make her useless in the morning.

When Rudella eventually gets up, she has barely enough time and willpower to go to work. But she does, and her coworkers are even more distracted. In her leather-jacket-and-flapper-dress phase, like a ghoulish Louise Brooks, she's virtually a musical number the whole day. Fosse, not Sondheim.

She finally settles down when she gets to Papercuts, picking up Trina Robbins' history of lady comic creators, "Pretty in

Ink". The clerk tells her someone sold their "House of Secrets" omnibus, and they want to know if she wants it. The complete series of a woman forced by a haunted house to help judge people's secrets? Fuck yeah, she wants it (discounted). And spends her afternoon rearranging her shelves to hold it. Happily, due to her latent OCD.

Piri has the day to herself before work, so she finds a trail to walk. She avoids Erie Lackawanna since it's tied to Lake Stop, but the area isn't lacking choices. She finds another trail, then chains Hardstyle to a bike post and goes on her way.

The first thing catching her attention is the bridge over a creek. And the gnats swarming it. Down a little ways, a clearing with towering power lines to her right. A little farther, a doe. Harmless, but a terribly territorial buck is probably nearby.

She'd rather not die, so she goes back to the entrance, cops a squat on a bench, and pulls out Alan Moore's "Voice of the Fire". She made a deal with Rudella, who had twinkles in her eyes, that if she liked the novel, she'd read one of his comics. As she reads the 6,000-year tale of an English locale and the motley crew of weirdos peppering its timeline, Piri can't help but feel Rudella played dirty.

In a healthy relationship, there's a baseline of self-satisfaction you should meet. Once you do and it can be left alone, you should keep the other person happy since it works both ways.

Unless you're asexual, it's wrong to think sex isn't an important part of a relationship. Along with the obvious pleasure perks, sex is the ultimate trust exercise.

Sex has been happening a lot lately with Rudella and Piri, though always one-sidedly. The former, after her latest thrill, tells the latter she feels guilty she's the only one going through Georgia Summers. Piri never heard about her humidity woes, and Rudella knows explaining would get them off-topic. Instead, she explains how she wants to make Piri feel as good as she makes her feel, hinting at toys she bought at Spencer's.

Piri tried a few times to finger herself like she did to Rudella, with the same panic attack to make her regret it. She wants what they have now to be enough. Who wouldn't want someone to make them feel good without any effort? She presents the question to Rudella, blowing up into a rare argument about mutual gratification. Usually, the complaint is about a person not wanting to do a helpful thing, not the opposite. But Piri's not ready to tell the whole truth, nor does she know how to, so both go to sleep angry.

In the middle of the night, Piri wakes up to a faint glow from the other side of the bed. And a familiar sound: her moaning. Grogginess flies away from her as she realizes Rudella's watching a Kilhanna video, and using it for its intended purpose. She tries to ask what's going on, but she can only stammer part of her question. Rudella asks if she can fuck her, but both know what the answer is. Or isn't. Piri asks if Rudella has to do that in bed, hoping she'll stop. Rudella takes her phone to the bathroom and closes the door. Kind hearts don't grab any glory.

Days pass, bridges are mended as best they can, and neither sleeps at the other's place. Or rather, Rudella keeps that door shut. Phone calls are pleasant enough. Ditto dates. However, Piri can't escape the feeling her girlfriend's hanging something over her head she can neither escape from nor overcome.

Mur-Mur and Rudella had a lot in common. One thing was both didn't lash out much. If they felt bothered, they'd run away from the object of miseration to a safe place. Occasionally figuratively. If they were followed, they'd get small and quiet. Not to hide; to warn. After that, it was the object's fault whatever happened to them.

The Mortician isn't in a safe place, with regard to the Maiden, but she plays with the key to the door. She doesn't desire loneliness, and it would be foolish to choose it. Still, being unable to do for Piri what Piri does for her tempts idiocy. Because what would that dangling thread in their relationship unravel?

Piri knows what Rudella wants, and knows she can't give it to her. She asks Gaia for guidance as she looks for answers. There are other things she wants that Rudella could give her. Her patrons do it all the time. She imagines their smiles when she opens a package from her wish list. She wouldn't have to imagine with Rudella. That would make up for the other thing. Right?

Then Rudella's apartment building catches fire.

Faulty wiring and a lazy landlord. The flames are so fast and intense, the flanking buildings are caught in the conflagration. They manage to survive with scorched bricks and shattered glass. Rudella's building, less than cinders and more than heartache.

Rudella knows something's wrong by the sound of helicopters. It's not strange to hear them around, with the Lansing Municipal Airport nearby. It *is* strange to hear them staying in one spot. On her way home, she hears them. As she gets closer, they get louder. The park district burns trees to keep forests healthy, so she stopped noticing smoke years ago. She couldn't ignore it this time. Or the sirens. Or the blackened wreck that is her life.

Piri hears about the fire in the middle of her shift. She thinks the worst when Rudella doesn't answer her phone. She can't get out of work early because it's homecoming night, and Lake Stop is packed with teenagers. A panic attack hits her so fiercely, she almost passes out by the dumpster; her usual refuge taken over tonight by gossip. She forgets to clock out when her shift's over, then speeds on her bike to what's left of Rudella's apartment.

The area around the remains are yellow-bound. Piri sees a few familiar faces; Rudella's neighbors. She rushes to them, begging them to tell her Rudella's alive. The shorter one calms her down by telling her they saw her after the helicopters came. That she was safe. That she left soon after.

Piri drops to her knees in relief, then cries with a jumbled union of joy and frustration. She calls her beloved again, and is thanked by a voicemail for her trouble. Rudella could be anywhere. Or dead. Or worse.

After making a mental list of all the places Rudella might be, Piri gets a taxi and makes sure her bike can go in the trunk. Those homecoming teens tipped well, so she doesn't have to worry about fare.

Three hours of searching leaves Piri with no results and almost no money. She's dropped off a few blocks away from Harbor Point, mumbles a semblance of gratitude, and walks home with her bike after the taxi leaves. She doesn't have to work 'til the next evening, so she decides to search again when she wakes up. If she sleeps. She doesn't know where else to look; maybe the same pl--

Rudella's sitting on her doorstep.

Piri runs to Rudella, who tells her, in a daze, she forgot she worked tonight. Before she can finish, she gets a swift, loud slap across the face. Before she can react, Piri melts in her arms. Rudella holds her tight and strokes her hair.

In the morning, Piri calls Sunset Shores and tells them Rudella's situation is why she won't be in today. Rudella's too asleep to agree or argue. Piri doesn't usually wear her eye patch at home, but she has an unconscious need for protection. She's glad Rudella's alive and in her bed; at the same time, she didn't plan on that and her routine's off because of it. The chaos of last night is also catching up to her, so she needs whatever buffers she can muster.

As she makes breakfast or lunch, depending on your view of time, she thinks about how she can make the catastrophe better for Rudella. Then for herself. It'll be a while before insurance does its thing; she can share her house with Rudella for however long she needs to. Which, so she believes, will *have* to make up for her being unable to give herself the way Rudella wants. She leaves triumph in the wake of her smile as she brings the Mortician her meal and tells her about her Sunset Shores call.

Finishing what she can of her lunch, Rudella meekly thanks Piri for everything, and returns to losing her attention to the window. She hasn't taken off any of what she wore yesterday, so she frantically searches her inner jacket pocket when something grabs her attention. Thumbs and fingers tap and flick 'til they find what she's looking for: pictures, stretching back to when she moved in, of her apartment. The things inside it, in particular. The most recent set of pics is two months old; at least she won't miss much on the insurance claim form.

However, this is only a respite from her dazed state. It's not what was lost in the fire that bothers her, it's what she attached to them. She put in a lot of time and effort into earning that mortuary science degree. The rollerblades were the last thing her appa bought her before she left for Illinois. The squeaky bathroom door and her silencing it kicked off her DIY stint that she'll always be grateful for. The "V for Vendetta" graphic novel was what kicked off an amazing night with Raissa. And on and on.

An hour or so later, she checks her bank balance. She only has the clothes on her back and she wants to take a shower; kinda pointless to get clean only to slide into the dirt again. Piri offers to buy clothes for her, but she turns her down and says the drive's for more than just that. Her sweeter half understands and says she'll be here when she gets back.

Before Rudella allows herself to continue feeling guilty, she goes to the Lansing police station and asks if anyone died in the fire. No, fortunately. While there, she handles all the insurance things, then finds a bar to do a Four Horsemen shot. Enjoying the numbness brought by Jack Daniel, Jim Bean, John Jameson, and

Johnnie Walker as she nurses a glass of water, neat, she steps back into self-pity. Then she grabs an armful of whatever fits at Goodwill, a pack of cheap panties at Walmart (she doesn't feel like wearing bras for a while), and drifts to Piri's shower.

She doesn't bathe so much as she lets the water run over her at its hottest 'til it runs out. The renter left for work while she was scalding, but not before leaving a get-well note next to two slices of pizza. Rudella's been over plenty of times, yet she's never really looked at Piri's house. She's amazed by how strange it is. She doesn't know about her vagabondage nor her resell business, so she doesn't understand why things are so random. There's no reason or rhyme to anything, which extends to her movie collection made of discards from various places. She's up for any distraction with her slices, so she picks "Inside Daisy Clover".

A cynical rags-to-Hollywood film from 1965, "Inside Daisy Clover" has one of the more unique endings of the subgenre (**<u>nothing</u>** comes close to 1975's "Day of the Locust"). Said ending is too close to Rudella, and what little enjoyment managing to squeeze through her malaise is tainted. She zones-out on the DVD menu for hours, until Piri gets back from work with cream of potato soup and french fries.

Piri's been through enough of others' bad times to know not to pry. Instead, she looks at her darker half's tangled, henna-red hair, gets a wide-toothed comb, and gently gets all the knots out. She leaves the TV alone, wondering why that film was picked, and flashes back to Gaspara standing in her room while she stood at the window. When she's done, she kisses Rudella's neck. The only movement she's done in hours is shrugging her away. The next is holding her hand.

The following morning, Rudella has to remind herself that she's in Piri's bed. And why. She goes to the kitchen and makes a joke about being up for breakfast instead of lunch this time. Piri giggles, then asks if Rudella wants coffee. Because she's been waitressing for so long, she picks up on ways people say certain words. A coworker obliterated how normal people say "coffee" with how she says it FOH.

If you're curious, Piri's brainwashed "coffee" goes "koe-WAH-fee".

Realizing she hasn't said it yet, Rudella thanks Piri for letting her stay 'til she figures everything out. Piri tells her that's what girlfriends do. A thought distracts her, then she asks if Rudella could leave for a little while. She has a weekly schedule to keep with camgirling, and she dances around being obvious since it's still a sore topic. Or rather, part of it is, in an atypical way. Rudella gets the hint; she isn't happy, but she doesn't want to fuck up Piri's livelihood. She's lost too much to be a bitch.

Harbor Point's a big enough place to wander around in, so that's what Rudella does while Piri does her Kilhanna routine. It also lends itself to easily taking the wrong turn at Albuquerque, so she doesn't wander far. Autumn being what it is, she gets by with an oversized black sweater, and her old shitkickers she wore the day of the fire.

She's still in the shock phase as she wanders closely, which means her view of what happened is clinical. She thinks about what to do about her mail. Will it be dropped off on the ashes? Does the post office hold it, or return it? She pulls out her phone from the hem of her cheap panties, but it's dead. The charger's a melted mess with the rest of her life.

She comes across a neighbor who thinks any time's a good time for a barbecue. He points out he's seen her around Piri's occasionally and asks if she likes cochinita pibil. She has no idea what that is, but knows it smells good. He offers her a Modelo; she turns it down since she can't drink beer. One wild night at the bar and she's fine, but give her one beer and she's having a paint party in the bathroom. If she makes it there. He calls her a bad lesbian for turning it down.

She asks what kind of music's playing. Ranchera (Miguel Aceves Mejía's "Malagueña Salerosa"), and she'll hear some Son Jarocho if she sticks around for the next song (Son de Madera's "Siquisirí"). She does, making a mental note to look into both genres, then is handed a paper plate of pibil wrapped in foil. Her malaise is easy to see so, before she leaves, he tells her it can't rain all the time. Her smirk is tiny, yet genuine like her gratitude.

Back at Piri's, she almost goes inside, but hears someone isn't done with her routine. Rudella waits for a few seconds, listening to how great Piri won't let her make her feel. When she's fed up, she sits in the backseat of her Civic and eats her warm gift. As she does, Piri's denial coupled with the fire destroying everything embellishes her abandonment issues. Her tears come quietly, but they flow long enough for her gift to turn cold.

Sticky business now taken care of, Piri calls Rudella after taking a shower. It going straight to voicemail concerns her. The fourth time worries her. She rushes to find her like two nights ago and, like two nights ago, she finds Rudella on her front steps. She's relieved until she sees her paramour nursing a bottle of apple cider, and flashes back to a decade of homeless drunks ruining their lives and those around them.

Piri snatches the bottle and pours what's left on the ground. Rudella, rightfully, wonders aloud what the fuck. Piri orders her to not drink in her house, and Rudella points out she's not in her house.

Piri, almost bullying, tells Rudella she's not going to date a drunk. Rudella tells her that she bought only one bottle, which doesn't even come close to being a drunk. Plus, she's had a shitty few days, if Piri didn't notice, and needs the relief.

Placing her hand close to her breast, Piri tells Rudella she could relieve her better than alcohol. Rudella backs away from the hand and tells her she wants it the other way around, but she only cums for paying strangers.

Not wanting to have that conversation, Piri says she called a few times. Rudella tells her that her phone's dead, but she bought a charger. Piri tries being a snob as she tells Rudella that she should've charged her phone instead of drinking. Rudella, ever the emotion sniper, tells her she would've, but it plugs into a wall and she was too busy using a vibrator to notice.

Piri stalks her way to Rudella, then whispers in her ear that she was raped. She lists in monotone each violation and violator; they come easy to her because they often command her nightmares. Rudella tries to get away from the intensity, but Piri locks her arms around her and continues. Stoic whispers still. Her arms drop to her sides when she's done, and stands as if a feather could knock her down. Or a word.

Rudella has two: I'm sorry.

Morning eventually arrives, with Piri alone in bed. Rudella left to deal with mail problems, and restock her pain pills for when endometriosis hits since she was **NOT** going to let the fire make *that* worse (not by a damn sight). Her frustrations involving compassionate sexuality humbled by pity, she could only muster trivial questions to her lover. At least she knows Piri doesn't work tonight.

The Maiden looks at her hand as it hangs off the bed; the way you do when you use any reason to not get up. Then her fingers slowly play an imaginary piano. Then she thinks about what she admitted to her lover last night. Theda opened the door to moving past rape with a grin, one of the scant things Piri looks back fondly of in what passed for their friendship. Opening the door and moving in are different things, though, and take different strengths. She survived… but she suffered.

She gets up to do her laundry. As she loads her cart, a panic attack hits her. She almost knocks over the TV when she drops to the floor. She knows her triggers and plans her life around them, but this one is unexpected. And hard. She's lucid enough to muffle her screams so no one thinks she's being murdered. Her grip around her mouth is strong enough for her teeth to accidentally cut the flesh inside. When the attack finally passes, she sees it's only a tiny scratch. And that she pissed herself.

Even after one so intense, she moves on as quickly as possible and buries the attack deep in the closet of her mind. A little mouthwash goes a long way, and she is going to the laundromat, anyway. Plus, all the pee was in her pants, so she doesn't have to mop.

Since Rudella isn't back when Piri's done with clothes, she takes care of some Kilhanna business. Actual business, not the sticky kind. The subscription service she uses pays her biweekly; a direct deposit's coming soon, and she's checking to make sure the numbers add up. They do.

She checks her "requests" folder, and spies a few for feet pics. They're reasonable and reasonably quick, so she pulls out her foot nook and fulfills those lucky few. Then she puts her clothes away after doing another round of mouthwash.

With a bunch of money coming soon and a depressed girlfriend to cheer up, Piri decides to take her out tonight. A quirk of sapphic relationships is usual rules don't apply. Like, who pays for dinner? The decrepit law of the land is the guy does. Relationships should be equal across the board, but that's talk for another part of this novel. Anywho, the decrepit law always makes Rudella and Piri squirm when the check comes, so they settle on it going to who did the asking.

A way Piri keeps her trauma underground is smothering it with her love of cats. She doesn't think she's together enough to own one, but she finds them incredibly soothing. Since her vagabond era, she cut pictures of her fine, felidae friends and glued them in an ever-growing collage book. Whenever she has time to daydream, she takes out her kitty grimoire and smiles her troubles away. As she does 'til her thanatophile gets back.

Rudella's made dating blunders before, but she feels pushing sex on a rape victim's the biggest, so far. She wants to show she's sorry, but she'd hate to get flowers. She doesn't know if Piri feels the same, and doesn't want to dig a deeper hole. Thinking about it, she's not sure what to offer. Everything in Piri's house being as random as it is, Rudella kinda feels anything goes. Unless there's a code she hasn't cracked yet. Does not cracking the code so soon, if there's one, mean she doesn't care? Or does cracking it mean there's not much mystery left in their relationship? Caring's tough.

When Rudella raps at her chamber door, Piri's surprised (and slightly bummed) to see her with a large pizza box from Aurelio's. When she sees "I'm Sorry" written in pepperoni and spinach, she can't help but be charmed. And slightly confused. She asks Rudella why she's sorry, to which Rudella stumbles out that she was pushing sex and she shouldn't have because… y'know. Piri kisses her cheek, then tells her she can't apologize for something she didn't know.

The two eat the apology pizza, with ginger ale nearby, and watch a double-feature from Piri's random collection. "Bitch

Slap" is a clever riff on exploitation and sexploitation flicks. "Return of the Living Dead III" is a sadomasochistic, "Romeo and Juliet" riff on zombies and sequel (of a sequel [of a sequel]) to "Night of the Living Dead". When they're done, Rudella asks her paramour what's with her movie tastes. Piri tells her that, until a few years ago, movies weren't her thing. Then she lived at a place where a rental store dumped off its stock, and she reveled in the bizarre choices. That sort of feeling bled over to how she buys movies.

Rudella chuckles, then tells Piri about her parents' store, Rewind or Die. She doesn't tell her about "Mannequin"; instead, she rants about the fight movies she's seen and Cynthia Rothrock. Piri asks what's a Cynthia Rothrock. A martial artist who went undefeated in tournaments for five years before retiring, then appeared in 80's Hong Kong action movies and is the only American woman to headline them. That's who Cynthia Rothrock is. Rudella suggests Piri start with "Millionaires Express"; she doesn't star in it and it's not her first flick, but it's a great intro to her. Plus, it has Yuen Biao, and you can't go wrong with him.

Piri can't let all this martial arts talk go on without humblebragging about studying Kokikai Aikido, each Japanese syllable ramping up Rudella's attention. Rudella asks if that's the kind where you punch out someone's heart, and Piri disappoints her with talk of using energy that doesn't involve fireballs. Rudella's teasingly dismissive, saying martial arts don't count unless they have at least… twelve ways of punching and/or kicking a motherfucker before they eat dirt.

Piri doesn't want to hear any more slander of her style or her sensei, gives Rudella a couch cushion, and tells her to run at her and hit her with it. She can even go for her blind spot. Rudella checks out the cushion, making sure a) it's super-plush, and b) the zipper side's towards her.

Satisfied, the Mortician walks to the other side of the living room and sizes up the Maiden, who slowly takes her fighting stance. Rudella looks at the cushion, then at Piri, then the cushion, then Piri.

Piri beckons Rudella to her with a kissy face, also thinking her sensei would be proud of her form.

Rudella charges.

Rudella eats rug.

Piri puts the cushion on her lap, Rudella's head on the cushion, and asks if she's ok. More than anything, Rudella's grateful she didn't bite her tongue. Piri wonders aloud if she has anything to say about Kokikai Aikido, and Rudella tells her that it makes her ass hurt. Her better half breaks the sad news to her that her sensei doesn't teach bum massages.

Regaining her composure, Rudella says she has two questions for Piri. One: can she move in? She'll pay half the rent and bills, and she doesn't have much to move in with. Dealing with mail stuff and other problems today, she realizes it'd be better for her to have a new place to live as soon as possible. It'd be kinda like "Nana", except they're dating. "Nana", one of her favorite anime, is about two very different women, an art student and a punk musician, named Nana who share an apartment and live fucked-up lives. Piri says she can and, with a smile, she knows what'll happen if she doesn't wash the dishes. Abandonment issues: sated (for now).

Two: can she kiss her? Piri leans over and answers her question, though she doesn't break away. The kisses become longer, passionate. She could kiss her for hours. Rudella sits up and cradles her lover's face. She pulls her in for another loving exercise in longevity then, instinctually, her hand trails to a breast.

Rudella stops both, remembering Piri's reaction, then she realizes Piri didn't stop her. Piri, with trembling hands and voice, grips Rudella's hand and tells her to not put anything inside her. Rudella nods, then returns to Piri's breast, over the fabric. Piri will always be amazed Rudella can find her nipples over her bra. Now, arousal and astonishment are pronounced in her mind.

Rudella enjoys Piri enjoying her, but she's also making sure to stop as soon as Piri stops enjoying her. She tests the limits of her new playground by sliding her other hand down Piri's sweatpants and over her panties. She doesn't go far before finding out how drenched she's making her better half. She also doesn't want to ruin a good thing, so she keeps her fingers over cotton as she rubs her the right way.

Piri responds wonderfully, then unexpectedly as she tells Rudella to pull her hair. Rudella does, while licking her neck, and Piri melts. Rudella doesn't have to rub anymore: Piri rocks her hips in the palm of her girlfriend's hand.

When Piri cums, she feels like she's floating on clouds and waves of fizzy water.

And she knows this time, she got lucky.

Rudella stares at the morning ceiling, trying to make it the new normal. She feels great having finally made her beloved feel as awesome as she does to her. She wonders where she is and finds her by following the tunes. However, as the Xxl Mix of Noemi's "In My Dreams" guides her, she's surprised by what she finds.

Piri usually finds time around Rudella to pray to Gaia, but since they're living together… Prayer, for her, is mainly a recollection of the previous day and an affirmation of the current one. She offers both to Gaia and hopes the balance continues; if yesterday was rough, let today be better. If yesterday was fantastic, prepare her for the pain of today. Keeping in theme with balance, she sits cross-legged on the floor as if she were scales.

All religion baffles Rudella, but she's not enough of a bitch to tell her girlfriend who just let her move in she thinks she's wrong. Instead, she jokes about hoping she doesn't try to convert her. Piri senses snark, but simply replies her beliefs don't require her to. Though she'll accept tithes. Rudella asks why Piri isn't Wiccan since they've been around forever, to which Piri points out that Wiccans only existed since the early-20th century and *Witches* haven around since the dawn of time and were humanity's healers before--

Speaking of donations, after breakfast, Rudella goes to, you guessed it, Goodwill (Lansing AND Hazel Crest) to properly buy new clothes. "New" clothes. Not before visiting the remains of where she used to live, flicking through photos in her phone taken for insurance purposes but now acting as memorials. Being a mortician, she's intimately aware of the purgative power of mourning. No one died, but she still lost her life.

She'll miss the surprise of fauns on Autumn days. Waking up alone, though that's due to habit. She'll miss her favorite stories being in arm's reach. She'll miss knowing where everything she wants is, by heart. She'll miss her pillow, the perfect softness and malleability after sleeping on it for years.

She says farewell to the shelves she made. To the bed where dreams and things were lain. To her curated collections of escapism and reality. To her stash of vanilla Charleston Chews. To the sink she learned how to fix. To that one step that only squeaked when it was hot. To her years spent growing into a different person. To whoever she was going to become if she stayed there.

She realizes she hasn't told her bumonim yet. For some reason, she wants to keep it that way. For a while.

After buying practically every black article of clothing at Goodwill that fit, and more cheap panties, Rudella goes back to Piri's. It doesn't feel right to her to call it "home" yet. Nor should it; she "moved in" last night. She doesn't know how it made its way so far north, but she was more than pleased to have found a Waffle House t-shirt. A little bit of Georgia across her chest.

Piri left Rudella a "gone fishin'" sign on the kitchen counter. She has no idea what it means and hope it's not literal, so she calls her sweeter half to see what's what. She'll be gone 'til the afternoon. It's not that Rudella doesn't trust the folks at Goodwill to do their job, she just feels comfortable after washing the clothes she buys. Since Piri's hamper is half-full, she takes it with her to the laundromat.

Done with being the doting kind of lover, Rudella sees she has time to kill. The weather's decent, so she gets more familiar with Harbor Point. When she tried a few days ago, she was overwhelmed by all the new. Now, she sees it's an easy area to get around. Nowhere near the winding disaster that was her old Bourbonnais haunt.

What strikes her the most is how much water there is. On one end, there's a pond with a fountain, but Wolf Lake dominates the north. Chicago's industrial mountain range can be seen beyond it. The estate is peppered with and surrounded by trees, keeping the arbor leitmotif going for places she lives.

It's quiet, but the odd person does their thing outside listening to music. Like the one watering their garden to "Protons, Neutrons, Electrons" by Cat Empire, a... Latin ska/jazz/alt rock/reggae/funk band from Australia. Or another one sketching to "Holocausto" by Mónica Naranjo, Mexico's favorite Spanish import (a pop princess who disappeared for years, then came back as Batman). She makes sure to stop by and thank the guy who gave her the pibil. After remembering where he lived.

Piri almost writes "fission" instead of "fishin'" on her note to Rudella. She knows the difference: she just hasn't been able to shake a pun she heard years ago. She hopes nuclear scientists don't make the same mistake. Ditto rocket scientists and programming feet instead of meters (which would be Robin Williams' fault).

It's an errand day for her, starting with a bike trip to the post office to see what Kilhanna has a-waitin' in her P.O. Box. A bundle of coincidences, apparently. Though she stays in contact with Gaspara and Miss Luxx, she's too paranoid about police who don't care to tell anyone from her vagabondage where she lives. The P.O. Box is a compromise that Gaspara and Miss Luxx don't seem to mind since they send Piri letters, like the one a-waitin'.

Piri keeps the letters to herself, so you can't know what they say apart from, in Gaspara's case, the bits of thanks for the bits she donates. The bundle steps in here: with the letter, a few packages from her wish list. She opens them enough in the lobby to know what's inside. Some are for herself, but most are for Gaspara. She slaps new shipping labels on those with farther to go, puts the ones for her in her bike's wire mesh basket, and goes about the rest of her day.

The roads of South Chicago Suburbia are at the mercy of rivers, trees, trains, and corn. You can't drive down a street too long without at least one of them cutting you off. It's as frustrating as you think when you have someplace to go in a hurry. Though it's an errand day, Piri's in no rush to finish up before work (a perk of starting early), so frustration breezes past her like Autumn leaves.

One of her favorite words is "antepenultimate", surprised something was before "penultimate". She never cared to see how far that daisy chain went, however. Her antepenultimate errand is getting groceries. Not a lot; her bike basket's not a car trunk. Just enough to dinner-surprise Rudella with.

Pete's Market has the best selection, part and parcel of being a massive store, but it's a little farther than she wants to go. Baltimore Food and Liquor is closest, but it doesn't have what she wants. Goldilocks settles for Supermercado Tarimoro.

A lot of attention is focused on Aunt Flo showing up late, but people forget she can also come early. Until Piri found stability in her mobile home, her periods were all over the place, for all the stress-induced reasons you can imagine. Since then, she can set a watch to when she needs a pad (**<u>nothing</u>** goes inside her). Which is why she's shocked when she feels like she's peeing next to the canned potatoes, and sees Aunt Flo rolling out the red carpet.

As Rudella rocks out to Manfred Mann's "Doo Wah Diddy Diddy" (their cover of the Exciters' "Do-Wah-Diddy"), the sole consolation of losing her CD collection in the fire being it's also on her phone (including Piri's random mix CDs), she folds laundry on the couch and puts them into "mine" and "hers" piles. She doesn't want to take over any closets or dressers, so she bought a large plastic storage box. She lost all passion for fashion, so the randomness of whatever's black up top doesn't bother her.

She's about to watch "Shoot 'Em Up", one of the best action movies of the century that people forgot, because she didn't expect Piri to have it. But Piri calls her, freaking out and asking to bring her a pad.

Embarrassment keeps Piri in the shower longer than it takes to clean up. When the feeling finally leaves her, she dries off, puts on fresh everything, and puts the day's clothes in the hamper. She notices it's empty, then asks Rudella what happened. Rudella tells her about her day, and Piri is pissed.

For reasons she won't understand until she's in therapy a few years from now, Piri feels violated by Rudella washing her clothes. Coupled with her frustration with what happened earlier, Piri unleashes irrational anger at her confused darker half. The conflict teachings of Rudella's eomma keep her from taking it for long; she grabs the "hers" pile, tosses it at Piri, and tells her she won't touch her fucking clothes again if she's going to be a goddamn bitch about it. Then she storms out and broods on the trunk of her car.

Piri at least understands Rudella didn't like her reaction. She doesn't get why she did her laundry, though. She'd never do that to anyone. That's so cruel. She tries calming down, then remembers, tucked in the back of a cabinet, a jar of comfort food she forgot was there. She eats the peanut butter with a spoon on the couch, watching the door among the scattered fabric.

It was around an hour later, under the twilight sky, that Rudella was able to shrug off her cozy shroud of brooding. In that time, she thought about the Persian phrase that everyone else tries taking credit for: "This too shall pass." Whenever something good happens? This too shall pass. Whenever something bad happens? This too shall pass. Pain and pleasure are transient so, as long as either aren't overwhelming, it's worth it to wait out (or wait for a return). She knows that Piri has issues, but she feels they're livable issues. Or rather, that's the conclusion she came to after brooding for almost an hour.

When Rudella goes back inside, she's met with an uneasy glare from her girlfriend. She apologizes to the couchbound one, a half-eaten jar of peanut butter at her feet, telling her there'll be a clear laundry boundary line between Rudellatown and Piriburg. The glare doesn't flicker. Southern sass creeps in when Rudella tells her lover it wasn't that serious.

Then Piri bolts to the bathroom like a caffeinated racehorse.

Being homeless for as long as Piri was, she came across peanut butter jars that were either full, or full enough to scrape maybe four fingers-worth of the good stuff. When they were full, they didn't last. Because of this, when she took out the one in her cabinet, she didn't think anything of the fact it was cracked since it was so old. But she should've thought instead of eating half of it.

The only thing Rudella can hear from the bathroom is confused vomiting. She wants to know what's wrong… but she also doesn't want to get puked on. She cautiously approaches, gurgled whining becoming more pronounced, then slowly opens the door. Very slowly.

The toilet seat looks like a slimy, brown disaster. The toilet bowl's worse. Nothing's as bad as the smell.

Rudella almost runs outside, but Piri grabs an ankle and begs her to not leave her like a child begging their mother. Far too sick to be ashamed. Rudella almost kicks her in the face, but she remembers that the spewing creature on the floor is her troubled better half.

Then Piri sits on the toilet, almost sliding off twice, before she sprays the wall behind her, filling it with another slimy, brown disaster.

Nothing's as bad as the smell.

She begs, again, her beloved to not leave her; Rudella's practically dry-heaving while seriously considering breaking up so she can jump into the pond and breathe through her nose so the burning can make the stinking stop. But she stays. Even as Piri gets a worried look in her eye and her cheeks puff up with yet another disaster.

Rudella grabs the tiny trash can by the sink like a cobra striking its prey, then shoves it in front of Piri's face and smacks her in the back of the head. The force makes her lean forward and unload into the can, *almost* sliding off the toilet.

Desperate for air, Rudella leaps into the bathtub, knocks over a shampoo bottle, yanks open the window, and sticks her head out with deep breaths. A neighbor sees her and asks if there's a problem. She begs them to go to the store, buy a jug of Gatorade and the best fucking air freshener they can find, and that she'll pay for both with a tip when they get back. They ask what for; Rudella gags as she tells them that it's a matter of survival.

A loooong time from now, Rudella will make jokes about how Piri could've pinwheel'd out the window and over Cook County.

Many people think love means dying or sacrificing for your lover. They're wrong, of course. Love means staying in the bathroom while your lover violently pukes with explosive diarrhea to make sure they don't pass out, and keeping them hydrated while they're a snotty, shitty, shivering mess. Love is the suspension of disgust, after all.

Months and a new toilet seat later, Rudella and Piri are settled into their life together. They shared their first New Year's kiss, which is the level of intimacy they've had since... that night. Rudella has a hard time seeing Piri as sexy, which suits her since she doesn't want to tempt her rape agony debts. Sex is an important and healthy part of any romance, but only if all parties involved want it.

They're not dating to fuck, they're dating because they enjoy each other. And they have plenty to enjoy, and they have plenty to temper their bonds. One of Piri's favorite things to do is drop random facts she learned from her torn covers on Rudella's lap. Like how your eyes ignore your nose (close either eye and you see it, open both and you don't). And how your nose is as long as your thumb. And how your thumb is as long as your pinky. And how your index finger is as long as your palm is wide. Rudella was massaging her hands, at the time.

Although Rudella is long done with mourning what she lost in the fire, and has a buoyant bank account thanks to the insurance check, she has no interest in rebuilding her geeky life. Piri told her that she didn't mind a bookcase or two, but space isn't the issue. Losing her books and movies, with the memories of obtaining and enjoying them, was like losing her best friend. She lost one or two, so she knows what she's talking about. To her, buying replacements is like trying to replace friends. She'd rather them be gone.

Why didn't she feel this way about the thievery? She did, but it was with a case of at-least-a-thing-like-this'll-never-happen-again.

Doesn't stop her from being a geek, though. And a funny relationship thing happened. The comic convention she took Piri to last year did nothing for her library, but did lots for Kilhanna's wardrobe. Piri's library would get much more sequential art after Rudella gave her Mimi Pond's "Over Easy" for Christmas. The Mortician doesn't do Christmas, but Piri bitched SUCH a fit (Valentine's Day was even worse) that she bought her that book. A geeky fire was properly lit in the Maiden and she took the slack, with a little focused guidance from her paramour.

During a slow night at Lake Stop, Piri refills all the sugar shakers. As she does, she thinks about how she spent most of her life surrounded by people. About how she's done with it now. About how Kilhanna and reselling pays better than waitressing does. About how she mastered poverty. About how it wouldn't be terrible to make being a hausfrau of sorts her new routine.

About how it'd be nice to only worry about Rudella grabbing her ass (whenever that happens again).

When she finishes, she puts in her two-week notice.

Two weeks and a farewell party later, Piri figures out what to do with herself. Being a notoriously light sleeper, she wakes up, as always, seconds after Rudella does to go to work. She usually has things to do throughout the day, so that's not the problem. It's her nights, now free of waitressing, that make her stare at the ceiling. She thinks for far longer than she should, mostly being distracted by other thoughts. It's when she starts bitching to herself about how redundant "I personally" and "me myself" are that she decides she's spending too much time in bed.

After her daily Gaia praise, she does yoga while watching "Meet the Applegates". It's a heartwarming tale of mutant praying mantises who disguise themselves as a nuclear family to shut down a nuclear reactor that's poisoning their homeland, but get sidetracked by various vices. She goes about the rest of her day with her usual routines, agitation descending upon her like the sun to the horizon.

When Rudella gets home, she sees her sweeter half in an anxious state that kinda reminds her of huskies when they don't get what they want. Telling Piri that wouldn't go over well, so she keeps it in her pocket. Instead, she asks what's wrong and her girlfriend tells her she needs something to do. Inspired by what she has in her pocket, she half-jokingly suggests going for a walk around the estate. She bites her tongue when her husk-- her other half bounds off the couch and sprints to the door.

The nightly walks are a thing, for a while, and something always happens afterward that keeps Piri focused. Goth as she is, Rudella can't be a night owl as often as she likes (though her job's an awesomely morbid excuse), so Piri's focus doesn't involve her past a certain hour. Never sex because the memory remains. When Rudella's available, they watch movies and shows, but mostly, they lie around and play Uno. I'll let you wonder who's more intense than she should be. When Rudella's not available, Piri's either putting puzzles together or reading 'til she passes out.

One night, Piri wants to go for a ride. Rudella's too tired, which leads to an exhaustion-fueled spat that ends with her telling Piri to get her license before storming off to bed. The Maiden grumbles on the couch for a while, then realizes that's not a bad idea. A day later, to her one-eyed surprise, she gets her permit and bribes Rudella, with foot rubs, into helping her get her required road time in her Civic.

The morning Piri gets her license, she also gets a call from Miss Luxx. She checks in, from time to time, and asks how sex work life is treating her. She used to give Piri tips on how to make her videos better; Piri felt awkward, at first, but she couldn't argue with results and eventually stopped needing advice.

They talk shop while Piri waits outside the Secretary of State office 20 minutes away, in Midlothian (Rudella always thought the town sounds like an Elven suburb in Middle-earth) for Rudella to get back from the gas station near the street. The couple took the Civic, Piri used it for the test, and Rudella filled it while Piri settled things. Those nearby hear quite the one-sided convo about orgasm denial stories from the porno pirate hag. Piri chuckles puckishly at their reactions, then tells Miss Luxx about her new license. Then about how she needs a car since Rudella's not gonna share hers for much longer.

Then Miss Luxx chuckles. She tells Piri that another comrade in lust is selling his car for a dollar. Piri asks what kind (a Toyota Paseo) and what's wrong with it (not a damn thing). In fact, it's as good as it was the first day off the lot back in the Clinton days; he and his local mechanic kept it in superb condition. Why is he selling it? He bought it for his girlfriend a few months ago, she turned into a cunt a few weeks ago, and he took it back along with her share of his life a few days ago. Spite sales are the best sales.

Before Piri gets even more excited about her good fortune, Miss Luxx tells her there's a catch. If she wants the car, she'll have to go to Indianapolis, Indiana and drive it back. She wonders how she'll do that, then smiles warmly as if remembering an old friend. In a way, she is. She can take a train.

Buying a car across state lines can be tricky, but Piri gets lucky with the Paseo. After PayPal'ing the guy a dollar (plus a few more cents for the transfer fee [she's not a monster]), he mails her the title and a bill of sale with his John Hancock. It's weird getting insurance before the car, but she takes care of that when the title comes in. From there, she gets the title transferred at the Secretary of State office. She also brings two forms for out-of-state shenanigans: VSD 190 and RUT-25. Uncle Sam loves his taxes. She's more than a few dollars poorer, but she's the proud owner of a car half a state away.

The night before Piri picks up her new-old Paseo, she asks Rudella if she wants to come with. She'd go if she could since she's mildly suspicious of the whole thing, but she has work. Piri assuages her by pointing out a) she's picking it up at the train station, and b) she knows Kokikai Aikido. If he tries anything, she'll flip him into traffic. Warily satisfied, Rudella kisses her g'night and tells her she wants constant updates. If she wasn't afraid of being struck blind by a panic attack, Piri would tell her how wet her concern makes her.

Piri could take the Metra to Union Station, but she doesn't want to sully the long train ride with a short one, so she takes a bunch of buses at the crack of dawn. She wants to keep a semblance of her routine so, while she waits to board the train, she writes a post on Kilhanna's blog. Those are always random, which is appreciated by her fans, so she riffs for a few paragraphs on her phone about how weird it is people don't forget how to ride a bike. The song she chooses to put a button on her subconscious thoughts behind the post is Hex Hector's remix of Mikaila's "So in Love With Two".

All the while, she keeps Rudella updated with texts, who occasionally replies with a subtitled pic of a crowbar that says, "Don't gimme no reason." As in, that's what she'll drive to Indianapolis with if that guy tries anything.

Of course, Piri buys a private room ticket. She may be excited to ride a train again, and to be the kind you're supposed to ride, but she isn't settling for anything except the best seat. Especially when a pillow was her cushion of choice/necessity. Plus, she didn't want to risk a beautiful experience being ruined by mouthbreathers, anklebiters, or rude-as-fuck passengers. Otherwise, she'd use her paramour's crowbar before she gets a chance to.

The train lurches forward to start its five-hour trek to the heart of Indiana. Piri splays on the couch like a giddy napalm bomb, letting her head and dangling limbs gently rock with the rest of the train. She thinks about what her life was like when she used to take trains, and how much better it is now. She thinks about how she can buy a car instead of walk past them and ask for change. She thinks about how her mother hated her, and how Rudella loves her. She cries happily, and holds herself as congratulations.

Then the shivers begin, and she realizes she can't even enjoy this.

Five hours later, Piri's the proud owner of a Paseo, though she has to fill the tank, and Rudella doesn't have to unleash her iron brand of justice. The incredibly straightforward drive takes about the same time as the ride. She passes Monticello but, more importantly, she passes Indiana Beach. All her life, she's seen commercials and billboards for the amusement park that reminds people there's more than corn in Indiana. Seeing how easy it is to get to, she has a new Summer destination.

Another five hours later, Rudella approves of the purchase, then understands she'll be going to Downtown Chicago more since she can't use her Pilsen/Bronzeville excuse anymore. Damnit.

When she was growing up in Conyers, Rudella discovered "Doctor Who" thanks to one of the coroners who let her visit the morgue. They were part of the tape trading scene, back when fans worldwide had to rely on each other instead of the BBC to watch the show. People recorded episodes, found others who did the same through fan clubs, and expanded their libraries. No one could have all of the, at the time, nigh-700 episodes since the BBC erased some early on for new episodes of something else, but Rudella's coroner Whovian did their damndest to hoard what they could. Even if some tapes were a copy of a copy of a copy of a copy, making the quality somewhere twixt sludge and cotton.

For those who need a refresher, before streaming and DVD, after wax cylinders and teletype, there was VHS (Video Home System). Pop a video cassette into a VCR (Video Cassette Recorder) and you could watch movies and shows whenever you wanted instead of waiting for theatres or TV. You could also record things off TV, two to eight hours worth (more hours = less quality), and the tapes were reusable. The tapes were also big and clunky, so you can imagine how much space the coroner's massive collection took up in their basement.

Rudella was introduced to "Doctor Who" because the coroner kept making jokes about turning the corpses into Cybermen, and she finally asked what the fuck a Cyberman was. Kids say the darndest things. Instead of telling her, the coroner gave her the first three stories of the First Doctor on tape ("An Unearthly Child", "The Daleks", and "Edge of Destruction"). They told her if she still cared after watching those, they'd tell her.

She did care, and she wanted more. It took her a year, but she caught up with all the "Doctor Who" that's available since 1963. Having all of time and space open to an alien who solves problems as a thinker, not a stinker, was immensely cool. However, what made Rudella linger for hundreds of episodes was she saw the show as a metaphor for imagination and creativity. To her, the Doctor represented an artist, and each story was a piece of art he created. All of time and space served as imagination's potential. The monsters that recurred throughout the show embodied themes artists (un)consciously return to.

It didn't hurt the pubescent girl that the Doctor tended to travel through time and space with attractive women. She felt her first… stirrings with the Second Romana, a Time Lord like the Doctor who (heh) was very much his equal. The only reason Rewind or Die didn't have any episodes is because Rudella left for Lansing when she found out the DVDs existed.

The fire burned Rudella's interest in the show and its revival, as it did with everything else she enjoyed. However, it did reintroduce itself through Piri in an interesting way. A reason the Doctor travels with someone instead of by himself is see the wonders of the universe through their eyes. Otherwise, he'd be bored or angry or both. Instead of being bored or angry or both about going downtown with Piri, Rudella decides to see it through her eye and love it all over again. And does she.

If you want to find out (a lot) more about "Doctor Who" and the US of A, check out the second printing of "Red White and Who: The Story of Doctor Who in America", edited by Steven Warren Hill.

One April Fools' morning, with neither ceremony nor jest, Rudella gets an email telling her she's fired. The owner of Sunset Shores sold it to a private equity firm that would rather have a fresh staff start instead of inheriting employees. In other words, cheaper labor. She and her coworkers are getting a month's wages and are welcome to apply for their previous job once the business reopens, but their time is done and whatever things they don't pick up today will be discarded.

Piri is startled awake by her lover's bawling. It's the first time she sees this, and she doesn't know what to do. Rudella's not much for tears, and they're feeble under the light of the blue moon. But next to her in bed, under the cold light of day, Rudella is a heartwrecked child gripping her phone and repeating desperate denials. Piri tries keeping it together, knowing this isn't how she wants Rudella to find out about her panic attacks, until she finally asks the obvious question. The Thanatophile tells her she just lost the most important part of herself for no other reason than dollars and cents.

The following days, Rudella fulfills the lust of those expecting the Goth-charmed to be a tormented mess by becoming such. Until now, she has been Piri's anchor. Though being together for almost a year, Piri still keeps her vagabondage secret and safe for reasons that will be known only when they break free. Despite her clandestine distrust, she depends on Rudella for all beyond her private past. No matter what happens, she can lean on her morbid knight in velvet armor.

Until now. Her days are flanked by Rudella weeping into her pillow, crumpled so tight that her spine and ribs threaten to burst through her skin. When Rudella does get out of bed, malaise turning her early mornings into high noons, her time is spent doing mounds of nothing to a nihilistic beat.

Piri feels herself cracking and makes a big attempt to cheer Rudella up before she doesn't know what she'll do. She doesn't like spending as much for shipping as she did, but "Night Shift" arrives the next day instead of the next week. A comedy about coroners who turn a morgue into a bordello; she thinks is tailor-made for them. When she offers it to Rudella for date night, Rudella doesn't even let her finish the sentence before she goes to bed.

The next day, Rudella lumbers from her slumber to find a note on Piri's pillow: she's going out of town for a few days. It's hard for Rudella to make friends, due to being a loner and atypical tastes. She cut herself off from her geek friends after the fire. The Sunset Shores orphans aren't speaking to each other. Her college friends… She doesn't do social media because it doesn't allow you to move on or to let friendships run their course. Piri is all she has, and she left her alone with only a note to keep her company. She has no one.

Actually, she has two.

She visits them every Hallowe'en, and spells it that way since she found out it's short for "All Hallows Even". Their only time seeing each other, but that's fine since they call so often. Despite their lifelong intimacy, she still hasn't confessed that her apartment building burned down. She needs to see them in a hurry, and is needy enough to make them come to her, so she calls and breaks the news to them. She'll have to spend the night alone, but her bumonim will take the red eye to be there in the morning.

They're surprised to see her living in a mobile home, but they're glad she's ok. She greets them in tears; sadness and relief, but also to get the affection and attention she hasn't gotten from her companion. They give her what she wants, holding her in the doorway until her tears run dry.

When she pulls herself away to take them in, she smirks at how they still dress the same. Her appa, shades of cowboy; her eomma, shades of hippie. One loves Peter Gabriel, the other loves Phil Collins, or maybe the other way around, but they meet in the middle with Creedence Clearwater Revival, for some reason. Both with a tan her flesh has long been a stranger to. Her henna-red hair's a long-suffering mess. They point out her flesh looks a bit… squishy; she tells them her rollerblades were lost in the fire. Her appa shakes his head with grief.

Her bumonim look at their ttal's place, then at each other, then at her, and tell her she's going to their hotel. She doesn't have much reason to stay, and there's nowhere for them to sleep, and it's a free hotel trip, so she agrees.

When she was wee, it took a long time for her bumonim to understand the difference twixt a motel and a hotel. A motel ("motor hotel"), your car goes in front of your room and is meant for quick stops; a hotel, your car goes in a lot and is meant for as long as you need them. There are other differences, but you can extrapolate what from that info. Anywho, Rudella still feels the need to make sure they know the difference (they call her when they think the TV's broken when they just need to press the "Input" button), and is pleased when they park their rental in the La Banque Hotel lot in Homewood.

Downtown Homewood is one of her favorite places to be because of how olde tyme-y it feels. Sometimes when she's bored, she goes there just to sit and wander. She makes it a point to at least pass La Banque Hotel, if not stare at it from the bench across the street like the closet rube she is. It's not big but, from what she can see of the lobby through the window, it's classy. She never considers staying for a night; partially because she didn't want to do it on a whim, and partially because she built it up too much in her head. But now she has a reason. As long as she reminds herself hotels don't have dungeons, she won't be disappointed. Weird that her bumonim chose it out of so many other hotels near and far... but why ask why?

For two days and nights, she was cared for at a level Piri never tried to. Nor asked if to. Her appa talked movies with her and they tried beating each other with intense games of Six Degrees of Separation. They even have house rules with the latter: no Robert Altman films, Samuel L. Jackson, or Udo Kier. Otherwise, games end quicker than a mosquito's fart. Her crowning achievement: connecting Christopher Lloyd to Humphrey Bogart.

With her eomma... The first thing Rudella does is convince her to not beat with bricks the stupid fucktards who fired her ttal. It isn't easy, but Stoli helps. They end up learning a new toast (¡Arriba, abajo, al centro, y pa' dentro!), and slurring heinous torments to inflict before passing out. The rest of their time is spent sightseeing and showing off. At one point, her eomma shows Rudella her baby pic on her phone. Seeing herself happy in her car seat and onesie, thinking about her life now, she weeps without ego and constantly apologizes. Her eomma holds her until she stops, making the mistake of thinking those regrets are for herself.

Knowing they can't convince her to go with them, her bumonim take her back to her empty home. Before they leave, her appa gives her one large, and one larger, box. The large is a new pair of rollerblades, and the larger... He tells her he closed Rewind or Die a few months ago since the kids love Netflix, so he put all the DVDs in binders to give to her. Buffed all the scratches out, too. He didn't sell any of the movies since he knew she'd hate him if he did. Especially that damn mannequin movie. She's hit with the double-whammy of yet another part of who she is being taken away, and of having that part placed in her arms to live forever.

That damn mannequin movie's the first thing she pops in, of course. Whenever she bought a movie, she "suggested" her appa should buy it for his store. He listened, mostly, and she has most of her collection back. She could've bought it all again with her insurance money but, remember, it's the memories she attached to them that kept her from doing so. Knowing her appa listened to her and didn't forget about her are pretty good successor memories, wouldn't you say?

She notices the date on her phone after picking it up, how inactive it's been since waking up to that note, and realizes Piri has forgotten their first anniversary. She puts her phone down.

A day later, Piri sits at the lip of the pond in Harbor Estates as if she's a whisper away from falling in. She's been sitting there for a while, listening to Allure and 112's cover of Lisa Lisa & the Cult Jam (with Full Force)'s "All Cried Out". Whoever wrote "Apology not accepted; Add me to the broken hearts you've collected" should feel proud, and better. She knows she fucked up and is preparing herself for the inevitable break up. She's also been watching her home, and Rudella's car, taking mental snapshots of areas with various memories. Happy memories. Infertile memories.

Piri's intensity and stress coupled with unusually cool Summer air put her under the sandman's sway, heavy lids and lapping water. Then earth and grass become her mattress; despair and longing, her blanket.

Come one, come all! Underneath this aurora of tumult emotions, Piri invites YOU, lowly dog, to behold her traveling, wonderful, BEAUTIFUL, **EXCITING** Atrocity Exhibitions! This raver-ribboned sky beckons you to these gates bound in loneliness and hesitation! Make haste! These Exhibitions are roaming, thus can linger in this Manic State for only so long! Admission? Shame, of course!

Feast your eyes on Piri's first Atrocity: the Phonograph of Matronly Rancor. Don't be fooled by its craftsmanship; it is a dastardly thing that spews bile and other malice at young daughters expecting love and tenderness. Be amazed by its burnished crank; its sole source of power glimmers from chronic use. But whose? Mother, or daughter?

Beyond these heavy tent flaps lurks another Atrocity. Do you dare ride the Carousel of Violation? Piri had no choice. Upon these undulating fingers, pricks, and tongues, she was forced to let them have their way. Notice how they change with each revolution, never belonging to the same person. Remember: cruelty is genderqueer.

You might have had your fill of this land, but fret not! As the Atrocity Exhibitions journey to their next habitable terrain, the boring old is replaced by the vibrant new! Piri ABOUNDS with horrors, so worry not of dreary repetition, meager fool! Not as her roadshow ventures from the Manic State to the State of Denial!

Who is this morbid mistress of death and ink awaiting at the gates? Be this Rudella? The folly of this one; she believes she's ready for the Exhibitions. She doesn't understand that those places on display for her are to keep her from exploring too deeply.

Such as the Pool of Comeliness. It shimmers the splendor of prism sky sublimely. Its scent entices any proud or scandalous appetite. Warmth as cozy as tender, loving care waits to embrace. But it's shallow.

Of course, there's the Exhibition that drew her in, in the first place. The Servitude Homunculus offers a humble meal, one that anyone can provide for themself. What happens when money's put in its slot is the unique service? Countless ways of feigning interest and making one feel important, so they can furnish a little more money next time.

These delusions aren't her, Rudella. They exist for you to feel better and to not pry. Think on that as we leave you for greener pastures.

Ho-leeee shit! The stubborn broad follows the Atrocity Exhibitions across the River of Doubt! Not only that: she wants to be the caretaker of Piri's gloom patrol! To see those which are too abhorrent, too neglected, too truthful for the masses! Be she brave, or be she naïve? On with the show, sullied cow!

This... specimen is one of the Taboo Atrocities. The Aversion hides in shadows to protect you from its horrors, Rudella. But look: a spotlight. Aim the revelatory beam into the dark and regard the grotesque majesty. Regard the freak with mounds of putrid flesh folded over one eye. Regard the freak who wants your love.

Still with us, Rudella? Perhaps the Tarnished can send you fleeing. Slathered in stringy pearly-white, with dollars and cents and presents caught in the wake of the freak's snail trail. Sounds positively orgasmic, doesn't it? Cameras record every spasm for those you'll never see and always know.

And yet, you linger. I suppose that has nothing to do with this being the State of Grace. Or everything. Fine. You've earned the *privilege* to be Piri's caretaker.

But! You have not seen all these Atrocity Exhibitions have to offer! To love one at their best means to love one at their worst! You, Rudella, awed at the Exhibitions and tamed the Atrocities... but can you embrace Delirium and the Damned? Let us see, greedy hussy!

You won't even make the attempt. Run, then, Rudella. Run away and betray Piri. Throw her away and turn all this into the State of Decay. You don't des--

The glinting sunlight off the rippling pond welcomes Piri's waking eye. Not much time has passed despite all that happened in her reverie. The familiar Civic hasn't left its spot, which means she can't do the easy thing and change the locks of her house. But her dream convinced her Rudella can't handle her deepest disdain, so there's no reason to delay her perceived inevitable.

Rudella's making corned beef and pickles on rye when she hears keys at the door. Knowing it can be only one person, she grabs a butter knife with the sadism of slashers she's seen in so many horror movies, then rushes to the door. She slams into it to stop, the impact shocking herself and her girlfriend, hearing a bundle of metal and a body drop onto the lawn.

A person can't help but be some sort of product of their environment. Rudella was a loner in Conyers, yet certain Southernisms crept into her being. Good manners, for instance; an -ism that was at home in the Midwest. She's not much for smiling at strangers, or anyone, but she managed to throw a nod or a wave to those in passing. Thanks to her "cousin", Calantha, Redneck Rudella made her presence known when she was fucking pissed. That's who opens the door, two steps away from being the ENTIRE Firefly clan.

Their arguing is fierce, and long-brewing. Not in just the time Piri's been away, but in the whole of their relationship. If a person thrives on conflict, leave them, but conflicts that need to happen in a relationship need to happen so bridges can be built instead of walls. They avoided addressing whatever problems they had with each other, unknowingly building walls between them. At this point, labyrinths existed in their mobile home. They live in their own worlds because they don't think the other wants to join.

Everything spills out onto their lawn until patterns emerge. Rudella wants Piri to admit she doesn't love her. Piri wants Rudella to abandon her. Piri confuses Rudella's aloofness with the notion of her not caring enough. So she feels unwanted. So she doesn't feel she can be vulnerable with her. So her panic attacks find new reasons to flare up, and stay hidden. Rudella feels abandoned although she's done nothing but be there for Piri whenever she needs her. If Piri had a problem with her stoicism, she should've said something so Rudella could try being more open. Not blame her for not being a mind-reader.

Desperation makes Piri blurt out her history of vagabondage and panic attacks. She doesn't know if she tells her tale to lure or repel Rudella. She only knows she's emotionally spent when she's done. And lighter. Ages pass in the seconds it takes to look up at her thanatophile, not sure if she'll get what she wants. Or even *what* she wants.

Rudella looks down on her street-mad girl with pure bewilderment. Mostly because Piri felt the need to keep that away from her. She tells her as much… but she wants to say more. She wants to yell at her for not trusting her enough to tell her sooner, and variations of that theme. But she knows, at this point, it would become a fight for fight's sake, so she jokes about how their home's a nice upgrade from a park bench. It gets a laugh from the Maiden, of acknowledgment and relief. Piri's also glad Rudella says "homeless" and not "unhoused", another link in the circle jerk of nomenclature (as if calling it another name will end it).

They admire each other as if seeing their gorgeousness and gorgeosity for the first time, then Rudella glances across the street. Three guys have been watching them. Her neck gets redder as she aims her butter knife and asks why the happy, high-flyin' fuck they're rubbernecking. After some grumbling among them, the one in the middle admits their wives always say the woman's right in an argument. They wanted to know what would happen if both parties were women, so they partook in a secondhand phenomenon.

The problem with some women is if you get them to think they matter to you, they'll pave the cliff you make them leap from. Piri's one of said women. Rudella, however, is fine with paving steps. In the days since the blow-up, their labyrinths are changing into museums and their worlds are becoming a Venn diagram. Piri has been preparing for other things, too.

When Rudella made her cum, she thought it was because of the rubbing but, after many self-experiments, she found it was because of the hair-pulling. She wasn't sure what that meant, and the burden of learning is on the curious, not the knowing. Research led her to someone in the Threshold Society. After mistakenly calling the Sufi one instead of the kink non-profit. They were helpful in educating her about what she learned was her pain kink, and understanding that binding did nothing for her. Whips, not chains.

Rudella's fine with not fucking Piri; she just doesn't want to have a one-sided pleasure experience with her. Thanks to the peanut butter incident, her libido was nonexistent. Since the lawn incident, though, she's gotten rather horny. And Kilhanna clips can do only so much for her. Imagine her surprise at the serendipity of Piri saying she wants to try a sideways thing that night.

Piri explores her new kink with enthusiasm and success. Rudella enjoys making her better half feel as much pleasure as she does, even though it involves pain. It also awakens something in her. As Piri breathes lustfully anticipating another drop of hot wax on her breasts, Rudella's comfort with being in control leads her to thoughts of being her own boss. Not now, though. Now, she's getting wet making her slave moan and twitch while the Afterlife Chillout Remix of Amber's "Sexual" wafts through the air.

Rudella and Piri settle into their new normal, their dull flames of desire burning strong. Because she was fired instead of quitting, Rudella gets unemployment checks. Her eomma didn't raise a fool, so she also gets state aid for food and insurance. Her cost of living is low, and she has plenty in her bank, so she lives comfortably while she builds an audience with her latest passion

(Piri's joke about working at the nearby Ford factory didn't go well). Her desire to be her own boss leads her to writing an educational blog. Jenkins' Death Babble teaches people about aspects of death through the titular serial killer character, borrowing the idea of song posts at the end from Kilhanna's Four on the Floor blog. It's early days, so money is barely trickling in. She loves doing it, and getting horrible pics you'd only find on Something Awful. She breaks them down on her paid Patreon posts and adores the comments.

Piri's recent night routine involves watching old shows. "Xena: Warrior Princess" was first since she wanted to see what the hubbub was. It didn't take long for her to adore it, because what's not to love about a campy romp with a woman who futilely tries redeeming herself after being a warlord who gleefully slaughtered countless people? She adored it so much that it bled into sexy pain times, with her making a costume and telling Rudella to tame the warrior princess.

Still in the mood for women punching bad guys in the face after "Xena" ended, Piri began "Alias". Spy games and relationship issues were a strange mix, at first, but Sydney Bristow eventually rocked her world. Then Piri jumped into the spy cheesecake that was Emma Peel's run in "The Avengers", with Rudella reaping the frisky benefits.

Piri ditched the violence, but stayed in the UK with "Downton Abbey" and "Upstairs, Downstairs". Both are about turn-of-the-20th century life and the decline of the British aristocracy. "Downton Abbey" is newer and has the (much) bigger budget, but "Upstairs, Downstairs" has the better writing and characters. Her crush on Sophie McShera can't keep her in Yorkshire for long, so her night routine is spent watching the Bellamy misadventures. Nervousness creeps in as she gets close to the end since she'll need a new routine, then remembers video games exist. Rudella worries Piri won't be as attentive, but Piri remains the consummate girlfriend. Unless she can't pause the game.

Piri also wants to wear out the tires of her license. She drove them to Kenosha, WI's Bristol Renaissance Faire (their first) a few days ago. Rudella, as the Twelfth Doctor (medieval reenactors love a time-traveler), made a misshapen bowl she uses for breakfast, or whenever. From afar, Piri, as a literal pirate hag, spent a chunk of her time watching a woman pretend she was a faerie, gently and wordlessly greeting people as she gave them daisies. She didn't get one because she didn't want to ruin that beautiful pocket of time, and Rudella heard about her regret all the way home. Now, she convinces Rudella to go on a road trip with her to Cahokia Mounds, "the largest pre-Columbian site north of Mexico". Her selling technique? Similar to Jesse celebrating science with Walter White: "Yeah, bitch, history!"

Going to Southwestern Illinois takes a little over four hours, and Rudella eventually appreciates not driving.

The ride's quiet, apart from pips of conversation. Around Decatur, Piri suddenly gets serious and says that a hundred years from now, no one will care about her. Rudella kisses her fingers, presses them on her lover's cheek, and tells her that if those century folk won't care about her, it's stupid to care about them. That she should think about those who care about her now. That we're all dust, anyway. This sort of nihilistic comfort is one of many things keeping their mobile home a happy one.

This too shall pass.

CHAPTER SEVENTEEN

Jill-in-the-box

In which Rudella uproots and discovers a new aspect of herself, and Piri's agony debts eventually come to collect.

The election for the 45th Presidency is a shock, and a symptom of trauma still lingering from the Towers falling. In the proceeding years, fear turns into distrust aimed at all but those who spread lies instead of build foundations. Then distrust becomes profitable, and fact-checkers cow in the presence of bluster. While the dominating force in pop culture makes spectacles of doing the right thing against all odds.

Rudella is overwhelmed with disappointment. What keeps her from doing something hazardous is rewatching every George Carlin stand-up special. He was as angry as she is about similar things, but he was far more eloquent, vulgar, smarter, and funnier than she can imagine being. She doesn't agree with everything he said, but she doesn't agree with everything Piri says (and she puts her tongue in her). He didn't punch down. He saw the line, dragged people over it with him, and made them glad he did. He also reminded them they're all the same instead of carving yet another social divide. The most important thing he did? Made you stay curious about humanity and the world you're in. When

"It's Bad for Ya" gives Carlin his final standing ovation, she's in a much better place.

Piri is devastated with resentment. What keeps her from doing something grotesque is playing "Dead Rising". Choosing video games as her night routine benefits her greatly since she had around five decades of history to sift through, and her being late to the party makes the sifting cheap. When the election is over, she wants to hurt people until she stops hurting. She has enough presence of mind to know doing that would be… trouble, so she picks a game about killing a mall full of zombies in quite imaginative ways to assuage her. There's a story, but she just slaughters her way around the Willamette Parkview, night after night, until she can look at another human again who isn't her Goth.

They kiss each other again at midnight of their second New Year's together, also ushering in their new tradition: watching "The World's End". A comedy about the apocalypse of nostalgia is the perfect way to say g'bye to last year, and they time it so the world ends at midnight (for NTSC readers, start at 10:25:06PM, New Year's Eve). The night's a damn fine break from the fallout, which is needed for what's next.

Women take the election the hardest. The President in the queue is an ardent misogynist; among many, many, many, many examples in an Access Hollywood recording, he says women let you grab 'em by the pussy when you're famous. Not every woman relies on Carlin or zombies to make them feel better. Many don't want to feel better. Many want to be heard and make a difference, leading them to a worldwide protest the day after his inauguration.

Piri pays close attention to news about the Women's March as it gets closer. Specifically, where it is and how she can get there. When she finds out it'll converge in Grant Park, she makes her battle plan. As she does, she's excited by the fact that she'll share one of the most important and positive American events of the 21st century with the love of her life.

The day before the March, ignoring the news cycle, Piri sets aside her signs and crowd kit (so she can stay hydrated and potentially be a nurse). She expects the morrow to be an all-day-and-night gig, so she figures out how to alter her routines and stay sane (including "Tetris" on her phone for night gaming abroad). It'll be unseasonably warm, but that's becoming the unfortunate norm (it doesn't have to be), and she lays out her Punk-as-fuck clothes (including a spiked eye patch). She asks Rudella what she's gonna wear; she replies she isn't going.

To say Piri is fucking baffled and repulsed would be an understatement, and expresses as much. Rudella knew this was coming and put it off for as long as she could, yet she still isn't able to clearly convey her thoughts. Doesn't help that Piri's apoplectic.

After pausing, Rudella says that Piri's an activist. That an activist screams loudly and pounds pavement, whereas she offers support from the sidelines (both are fueled to do good, not to feel good). She's never going to be someone who marches and protests, but she is someone who makes signs and points to where people need to focus. She adds that Piri, or any activist, shouldn't expect everyone to fight. Some folks are helpful, but some don't want to be involved at all. Forcing them to do otherwise would make her the fascist she rallies against.

Piri is incapable of agreeing. She feels if it's a cause worth fighting for, everyone breathing needs to join in and they need to be on the front lines. Evil wins when people don't care. Pushing women back at least a century is what those in charge want, and that's evil. She passionately brings up how global the March already is, which is glorious, but having every woman in the world along would make it a war they can't lose. She acquiesces that even if all women don't join in, things have to get better in the face of those who are there.

Rudella unfurls a heartbroken smile as she thinks hard about saying what she wants to. She sighs, letting come what may.

She says she wants more than anything to be wrong, but she doesn't think much will change. The Women's March will be magnificent... then what? Women aren't a monolith, and there are plenty who want those kitchen days to come back. Even worse: they're the loudest ones.

Then there's the benevolent sexism. Putting women on pedestals and telling them they're The Best means they can't make <u>one</u> mistake, or else they're knocked into shit and become The Worst. Women aren't perfect, they're human and humans have the right to fail recoverably. Likewise, treating women as if they're daffodils when they're closer to cedar. Woe to the ones who bend and snap back instead of wilt and crumple. Fewer women need protection than the world thinks. Every woman doesn't need to be nurturing, either. Some can't even be trusted with Sims, and that's fine.

Protests are meaningful, but recent ones taught the pricks in power to be patient. They'll lose the battle, but they'll win the war because movements rarely think beyond the next day. And a women-centric movement? Guys can be assholes without ruining men. One broad with a mic fucks up and womankind has to answer for it. An entire gender is unable to fail recoverably.

On the verge of tears, Rudella asks if the March can survive a bitch, and if there's a plan beyond tomorrow. Disgusted, Piri locks herself in their bedroom and is gone when Rudella wakes up.

The Punk wakes up angry. Angry at the reason why the Women's March exists. Angry also at her girlfriend not joining in, and for comparing protests to shitty start-ups. However, she wants healthy anger to get her through the day, so she reminds herself of what Rudella has done. She helped make signs, made sure she knew how and when to be where she needs to, and said she was proud of her Shield-Maiden. It's when Piri checks her phone that her unhealthy animosity goes away completely. A surprise playlist, titled "Crowbar", filled with the protests of Atari Teenage Riot and System of a Down, the dystopian threat of Nine Inch Nails' "Year Zero" album, and Metallica's "King Nothing" buried in the middle. Piri almost kisses Rudella in thanks, but she doesn't want to wake her up. Instead, she does her Gaia routine, writes a quick Kilhanna blog about how women rock, too, and sets out for some ideological ultraviolence.

Flicking through her phone over waffles and ALAGA, Rudella sees how the March is going and how far their rumbling is felt. Worldwide and fervent, just like she was told it'd be. She's pleasantly in awe of the nooks and crannies expressing their rage. Tiny towns she's never heard of and never will hear from again, united in a need to be treated better. One protester makes her laugh with admiration. She's been dabbling into being the geek she was before the fire, watching "Supergirl" flirt with politics (Piri loves the pseudo-science of "The Flash" [they adore the batshit "Legends of Tomorrow"]). Melissa Benoist, the Maid of Might, smiles as she holds a sign warning the pussy-grabber that hers is made of steel.

Rudella almost thinks this protest will ignite the change women have needed for centuries, but she still believes what she said last night. Years after the March, is she gratefully proven wrong?

After finishing breakfast, Rudella thinks about her day. She was too busy anticipating Piri's reaction that she never thought about what to do while she was gone. But she's gone, hopefully not yet hoarse, and the world still turns.

In the recliner, once she kicked off the blanket and pillow, Rudella flips through one of many giant movie binders. Kids have the strangest tastes. It's an unwritten rule that everyone who loves "RoboCop" was too young to have seen it their first time, but it's not the only premature viewing experience Lil 'Della had. Not by a damn sight. She thought about why she picked "Blood In Blood Out" that day, then figured she might've thought it was a horror movie. She's right, in a way: what happened to those Chicano cousins, especially Miklo, was horrific. Didn't stop her from sneaking it away from Rewind or Die more than she should've. Or stop her from popping it in now.

One of the cousins, Cruz, ditched gang life after it wrecked him and became a painter. Rudella's seen this squillions of times, but this time's the first she's inspired to look into painting. She doesn't want to make a career out of it, and she's fine being her only fan. She just wants to express herself in an oil-based or watercolor sort of way, and to not copy to Olivia De Berardinis (or compare and despair). She's checked out of the film now and focused on where she can paint. How isn't a problem, she knows where a few hobby shops are. But their home is too small, and she wants to keep it private so outside's a bother. She giggles at the absurdity of the idea that strikes her, then looks up something on her phone.

Success. As long as she makes her monthly payments, the owner of a storage unit she found doesn't care how she uses it. Thinking about Piri's resell gig, she also asks about bidding on abandoned units. People who don't make their payments get their things tossed, but the mysterious contents can be bid on sometimes. The owner says she's free to give him more money whenever she wants.

The March was everything Piri hoped it would be, and she's enjoying the come-down from her Crowbar high with her new friends in a studio apartment. Everyone knows her as Gwynplaine because she finally found a way to be her literary hero. Dead Weather's fucking awesome first album, "Horehound", makes for great come-down tunes. She texts Rudella her address and a group pic of everyone she's with. Her galpal tells her to have fun, and she's not jealous since she's dating a professional spank bank (hard to be green-eyed when piles of people get off on the object of her affection). Adding a lewd smiley, Piri thanks her for the help. She also jokes about not leaving her alone again since she's suddenly a painter.

Unsure of whose apartment she's in, Piri becomes a social butterfly until she finds someone interesting. Many of the groups have opinions on women that sound more like college theses than conversations, so she avoids them. Ditto the groups lousy with micro-aggressions.

By one of the floor-length windows of block glass, she finds Jenn. With a mimosa in her red cup and ribbons in her hair, Jenn toasts Piri's ginger ale. Piri asks her what her shirt of a crown stomping a knight's helmet means. When people are knighted, men are sirs and women are dames. In Medieval Times, sirs took orders from dames ("Yes, m'lady.") so, technically, Sir Sean Connery could've been bossed around by Dame Joan Collins. Piri giggles long and hard at the idea of James Bond getting punked by The Bitch.

Jenn asks Piri if she came with anyone; Piri sees this as an opportunity for petty revenge and replies that her girlfriend was supposed to, but she got a fierce case of the boot-scoots. Jenn sympathetically shakes her head and says period shits are the worst, adding it's ok to be a protesting feminist on the toilet. Piri truthfully tells her Rudella doesn't call herself a feminist because she doesn't want to join a club where no one agrees on the rules. Jenn chuckles, saying that she expects the anti-trans sect to start a ruckus whenever someone cracks open the Spirytus. Piri piles on with sex worker-hating raiding party, which makes Jenn ask what are they raiding. Panties, of course: sex workers buy the best.

Things escalate twixt the imaginary feminist factions 'til they get too absurd to go on. Piri looks around the apartment and points out that more guys than she thought were part of the March. Jenn agrees, then admits she feels kind of sorry for them, including her boyfriend. Women have a choice between being brave or scared; men don't, and you could find a paper trail from most of the world's woes to the fact that men aren't allowed to be scared. Piri says that letting men be afraid and letting women be emancipated would be quite the Indian gift. She quickly explains that an Indian gift is a present with an expected equivalent, but certain people bastardized the idea into "Indian giver".

Jenn gets another four fingers of mimosa. Piri gets antsy and plays "Tetris", telling her she's still listening but this is something she has to do. Jenn, with ribbons in her hair, is amused. What Rudella said nags at Piri, so she asks Jenn what her plans are in regards to the March. Jenn feels the consensus is it's obvious the world has to pay attention to women now, so it's only a matter of time until things get better for them. Her drink abruptly takes her to cakewalks: how slaves walked around and mocked their owners on Sundays, and owners misunderstandingly thought it was so cute that they gave cake to the best.

Oh, fuck, Rudella might be right.

Enter Troy and Helen. Because he's with her, everyone thinks him harmless. Plus, guys can also want equal gender rights, as the day has shown. However, some want to watch the world burn, learning the wrong lesson from "Dark Knight". Troy's about to get a refresher course as he approaches the wall of block glass with his horse. He'll learn something else: he just fucked with the wrong Mexican.

Piri and Jenn see their new company, with the former's danger sense fluttering on, forged by almost two decades of vagabondage and waitressing. The latter's too buzzed to care. Helen spends too much on her body trying to achieve an ideal she thinks men want, but she's trying to be in disguise as the girl next door, so she looks like a Walmart model by way of Egon Schiele. Troy tries the same subterfuge, but still looks like yet another smuggerfucker.

Theirs is a two-handed scheme: Helen leads them down a road, then Troy beats them with his contrarianism. Tonight, they want someone in this gaggle of feminazis to admit men are better. And why not? All the world's successes can be placed on the shoulders of great men, and women bend so easily over tables.

If you think people don't go to gatherings just to start shit, you haven't been to enough gatherings.

Troy sees Piri as the more stubborn and sober of the two, so he focuses on her, out of earshot of the rest of the party. Unfortunately, Piri is also forged by Bugs Bunny logic: roundabout attempts that go to absurd lengths to get her to (dis)agree or reveal secrets. Helen acts the heartbroken cheerleader. Jenn doesn't get what's going on, but she's enjoying the smuggerfucker's growing frustration.

Then Troy starts turning hostile, and Piri's physicality changes. She turns her body to her left so her right shoulder's facing him, sliding her foot gracefully 'til she looks like 9:00, on the dot, from above. Her hands are steady; her gaze is locked.

Jenn's seen enough action flicks to know when someone's about to get knocked the fuck out, and tries warning Troy.

Helen eggs him on, saying that getting beaten like a man'll teach that bitch.

Jenn sees Piri's perfect bladed stance and warns Troy again, then backs away with an excited grin and ribbons in her hair.

Troy's fuckin' fed-up and throws a punch backed by a few months at the gym and a night of aggravation.

In one serene motion, Piri grabs the punching arm with her right hand, kicks his ankle so he slams into the floor, and palm-slaps his arm out of the socket with a little help from gravity and her left hand. Kokikai Aikido isn't brutal, but he deserves… a variation.

Coldly, calmly, she drops to one knee, digging it into his spine as she holds his dislocated arm like a sinewy broomstick over a pile of ashes. She knows pain. *She knows pain.*

Partygoers rush to Troy's unending screams. Piri's death stare stops them in their tracks.

She leans over until she can almost taste his panicked sweat. She tells him in a whisper to shut up. He obeys. Whispering still, she tells him to admit women rock, too. She shakes his lifeless, throbbing arm until he does what he's told. Satisfied, she pops his limb back in its socket with a violent yank, then leaves with a purpose. Rudella's eomma would be proud.

Helen, world torn asunder, rushes to her beau, the same, with newly stinky jeans.

Jenn giggles into her cup and tells everyone Gwynplaine warned him.

A few days later, Rudella settles into her painterly life, over a year into her baggy, don't-look-at-me phase. The day after the Women's March, she went to every secondhand store in a ten-mile radius. Canvases are expensive, but if a clever Georgian bought a bunch of cheap paintings, big and small, and some primer, she'd save a few bucks.

The day after that, she went to her climate-controlled unit to wipe slates clean and arrange her workspace. The unit's a good size for what she needs. Her now-blank canvases lined one end like fallen dominoes. She made an easel after doing the math and seeing how easy they were to construct. Next to that, a stack of milk crates acting as a stand for her palette (made that, too), as well as "drawers" for her oils and watercolors. Behind the easel, more crates that'll be her laptop stand.

The day after *that*, she bought oils and watercolors. Don't be fooled by her frugality: she spends money when it counts, and she wasn't going to buy cheap paint. At least, not until she found out which cheap paints worked as good as the primo stuff. Her chatelaine came in the mail, making her giddy. A chatelaine is basically a fancy, metal keychain that can be customized to hang all sorts of things. Like paintbrushes. She also bought an old robe because she's just going to wipe paint on it.

Now you're caught up, and we're spying in on her first day as a hobbyist painter. Rudella loves the films of Rainer Werner Fassbinder, Gaspar Noe, Darren Aronofsky, Claire Denis, Kenji Mizoguchi, Michael Haneke, Abel Ferrara, Catherine Breillat, Lars von Trier, and Sion Sono. They make fucked-up, dreary films; comedies for deep people. As in, she finds comfort in them like other people do in comedies. Not that she thinks they're funny.

Even she's not brooding enough to laugh at "Requiem for a Dream" or "The Piano Teacher". In a few months, when #MeToo exposes cruel truths of crueler people, her separation of art from artist will be tested by some of those directors.

Piri can't stand comedies for deep people, so Rudella has to wait 'til she's not home to watch them. Or rather, had to, thanks to her new sad-cave. However, the women in those films are… prone to hysterics (Piri says Rudella's favorite genre is House of Psychotic Women), and the last thing she wants is someone thinking her unit's a murder shack, so she wears headphones while she watches a few minutes, paints for a few minutes, and on and on.

For (much) more on Rudella's favorite genre, read Kier-La Janisse's book about that building of mortar, derangement, and femininity.

What does Rudella paint? Whatever she feels like. For her, it's not about making sense of anything. She gets inspired, then purges onto the canvas. She has no intention of showing anyone, not even Piri, so she has utter freedom. No matter how abstract or disturbing or beautiful the end result is.

Although Piri is permanently denied from seeing what Rudella's up to, she's loves seeing her Goth buzzing with excitement after her first day. She doesn't even mind watching "Head of the Family" (a B-movie about a vengeful, greedy, mutant Southern family, with a surprisingly good performance from Jacqueline Lovell) during dinner. A nice trade-off.

Early the next morning, Rudella rubs one out in the shower before breakfast. It'd be weird to wake Piri up just to sit on her face; orgasms are great for the heart, and she starts her day clearheaded. She wonders what it'll be like to paint with an energy drink, so she goes to Walgreens. She's unable to pick a drink (if she was at Jewel, she'd dart to a bottle of Bawls) 'til she sees a column of NOS. Many a Bourbonnais Banshee night was fueled by those blue-and-orange cans. She buys a regular one... and a Chick-O-Stick. Willpower? Ha.

She told the clerk she didn't need a bag, so she figures out which pocket's safe for her candy as she walks to her car. She doesn't want to eat it yet, and she doesn't want it to break when she sits down.

An SUV hops the curb and **SLAMS** her car through the brick wall, into the empty photo department. Dust and debris smother the Civic's crushed remains. Skidmarks and motor fluids streak the linoleum. The door chime that she's known for almost twenty years crackles dead.

Redneck Rudella comes back with a vengeance. She beats the fuck out of the concussed driver with NOS, bouncing his head off the deployed air bag like a bloody ping pong ball. Beats him for ruining her day, for wrecking her car. For maybe killing someone, for almost killing her. For taking the last thing she had since she moved to Illinois.

She screams at him about how much of a raggedy-ass pile of shit he is, almost feral.

The can bursts open and sprays everywhere. She doesn't care: she beats him with whatever's left in her hand. Even when she can't tell whose blood she sees.

All of this happens in seconds.

When the adrenaline wears off, and she's dragged to the other side of the parking lot, she comes to her senses. A clerk does their best to her bloody hand with a bandage they got off the shelf until an ambulance shows up for her victim. She's trance-like in her despair.

As the medics carefully remove him from the driver seat, he yells something about not being worth it. The medics try to console him, but they misunderstand him. He doesn't mean he's not worth it: he means the pain. "It" being an insurance scam. He admits as much through his yelling, well within earshot of Redneck Rudella.

They sedate her before she manages to pull a tire iron out of what's left of her trunk.

The irony of the poor, unfortunate insurance scam is Rudella has full coverage. All the sweeter since she obviously isn't the one at fault. The other guy's lawyer drags things out because of… her enthusiastic reaction, and launches a byzantine scheme to get her to pay for his medical bills. Her lawyer counters with whatever the legalese for "hillbilly rage" is to put an end to that. When she eventually wins her case and gets her money, she drags her feet on what kind of car to buy until she makes the choice you'd think she make when you read about her hanging out in a morgue. She buys a used hearse (pride of the Midwest), and loves it like, well, like a Goth loves hearses.

But that's in the future. Right now, a worried Piri sits next to a doped-up Rudella in a hospital while her hand's properly mended. The scratches from the shredded can are long and numerous, but also shallow. Skin glue in lieu of stitches, and they're out the door.

They only have to adjust to one car in the time it takes to pick up Rudella's insurance-provided rental: an orange Hyundai Veloster. Piri affectionately calls it Rudella's safety cone. Rudella, like everyone else, can't fight a nickname.

Apart from the occasional judicial interruptions, nothing changes for Rudella. She still paints, with her other hand. She's annoyed, at first, but convinces herself that her art while she heals is her sinistral era. When she's better, it'll be back to her dextral era. Jenkins' Death Babble is a pain since she types with both hands, so she makes especially sure the thanato-facts are worth blogging.

The Women's March didn't have the intended consequences in Hegewisch. In fact, it's like it didn't happen. The residents are big supporters of the new guy. Our peculiar heroines are the kind of folks who make his followers feel threatened, for some existential reason. They are THEM, and THEM are the problem. THEM are taking away jobs, not greedy bosses looking to spend less money on workers to have more money for themselves. THEM are taking away rights, even though equal rights for all don't mean less rights for some (equality isn't a pie). And on and on.

Dread hangs over everything Rudella and Piri do in town. Not so much because of what the local red hats do, but because of what they're capable of. The news reminds everyone daily of shitty things red hats do across the nation. Piri is particularly panicked about their potential, to the point where Rudella steps in and says they're moving. Piri's regretful, and thankful.

Lansing sings its siren song to Rudella, and she finds a condo off Ridge Rd. that she's wanted to live in since she moved there. But the hunt goes on, keeping options open and all that jazz. They consider a rental house in South Holland 'til they see the separation of church and state is literally four lanes on South Park Ave. An apartment that shoots to the top of Piri's list is in Glenwood, about ten minutes west of Lansing. It's near train tracks, but it's also near all the important places (including a forest) and a place that's still close to her heart.

She doesn't regret not being a waitress anymore, but she does miss the atmosphere. The back of the apartment overlooks Gabe's Place, a cozy diner she can smell from an open window. She loves the idea of being a regular there, quietly judging the wait staff like she does at any diner. It'll pass her tests with flying colors, and she'll become addicted to their turkey croissants.

The Glenwood apartment costing much less than the Lansing condo seals the deal, and Rudella looks for ways to live near trains without blowing her brains out.

A week later, they manage to move all their stuff in one trip. A mobile home can't hold a lot, so their lives fit in the Paseo, the safety cone, and a U-Haul truck. Miss Luxx, in stylish coveralls only she could find, has the honor of driving the third one. It's the first time Piri allows home life and sex work life to intersect so openly.

Miss Luxx is the quintessential femme, but she has no problem being butch when she needs to, which is how the three get their furniture up the stairs without much fuss. After a stumble when one calls the others "partners". The Georgian says they didn't join the force or form a business or somesuch shit: they're girlfriends.

Since she's a mystery, Miss Luxx makes sure to always be near Rudella while they move things. The feeling's mutual, which is why Rudella asks as many questions as she answers. About herself, about Piri. By the end of the day, they're delighted to know the other's alright, and to have a list of Piri like Alice when she was ten feet tall.

The whole time, Piri feels like her ex-wives are comparing notes. Doesn't help that they delight in tormented her during a break with "Rubber Johnny" (watch at your peril). Ditto that Miss Luxx is in awe of Rudella's humble-bragging about seeing David Bowie Is, an immersive exhibit of the Spaceboy, at the MCA (first group on opening day). That's right: Rudella suffered downtown traffic for Bowie.

It's too late for Gabe's Place, with hours from six to three, but Dos Caminos, a seafood-and-more restaurant, is open and two minutes away. Everyone's starving, no one's been here before, and it's the Twosome's treat. In other words, it's a night of expensive experimentation for Miss Luxx. Rudella and Piri decide to share a rib dinner, and Miss Luxx takes a chance with Oysters Rockefeller. Both dishes take a while to cook, so they're left with a lot of dead air.

Or would be, if Rudella didn't ask Miss Luxx how she came up with her name. She admits to being a big fan of Carla Gugino, who was in two ensemble comedies as a porn star ("Women in Trouble" and, waitforit, "Electra Luxx"). Rudella thinks about what

she's seen Gugino in, Piri says Frodo ate her hand in "Sin City",
and things click. Miss Luxx urges Rudella to watch Gugino's
movies with Sebastian Gutierrez before dreamily saying she
reminds her of Marilyn Monroe, if Monroe was taken seriously.
Rudella thinks about Monroe in "Niagara" and Gugino in the first
season of "Wayward Pines", the wiggle they share, then nods
approvingly.

Piri chuckles, then gestures at someone across the
restaurant who keeps looking at Miss Luxx. The object of desire
smiles and suggests they're probably a fan. She waves at them,
making them blush and knock over their drink before rushing to
the bathroom.

While admiring Golden Age of Hollywood's wiggles,
Rudella brings up Barbara Stanwyck's. Miss Luxx agrees, then
brings up how Stanwyck had the career Pam Grier should've.
They had a similar "tough broad with a soft side" charisma, so
Hollywood not passing the torch between them is the world's
tremendous loss. Rudella thinks about Stanwyck in "Night Nurse"
and Grier in "Friday Foster", then nods approvingly.

Rudella asks Miss Luxx if she's seen "Womb", about a
woman who clones and gives birth to her dead boyfriend, then
raises him as her son while the film asks uncomfortable questions
about humanity. Piri sighs disapprovingly… but Miss Luxx leans in
and says she hasn't. Rudella tells her she should, as well as the rest
of Eva Green's filmography, adding she's proudly carrying the

"complicated woman played with no ego" torch Bette Davis wielded. Rudella tells Miss Luxx to watch Davis in "Jezebel" and Green in "Cracks", who nods acceptingly.

Besides that "Womb" hiccup, Piri enjoys the conversation. Or rather, enjoys Rudella showing off her smarts. She's grateful it's about cinema instead of death. She's also annoyed her food's not ready, but that's what happens when you order a chunk of cow.

Intrigued, Miss Luxx asks Rudella what she's watched lately, who tells her about "Autopsy of Jane Doe". Piri was grateful too soon. The whole movie's an authentic autopsy of a woman, with spooky dealings happening throughout. She excitedly brings up "Kissed", about a mortician who really loves corpses, "Curdled", about a serial killer geek who becomes a crime scene cleaner (with an awesome Cumbia soundtrack), and "Neon Demon", which has a mortician but is about people's infatuation with youth and beauty (with an awesome synth score). Miss Luxx warns Piri she better hold onto Rudella (with an intellect and a savoir-faire).

Rudella returns Miss Luxx's question, who tells her she watched "Opening Night" for the nth time. The one film by John Cassavetes she hasn't seen yet; the Goth hears its themes are akin to "Neon Demon", with NYC grit instead of LA gloss, and gets even more excited about it.

A hangry Piri stops their fun. Miss Luxx jokes about giving her surströmming (fermented herring [yes, it exists]), then Rudella steps in as the responsible girlfriend who knows her lover's limits. She comforts the Punk by telling her dinner should be out pretty soon, then asks her to keep things New York and tell Miss Luxx about Richard Kern's films. Piri lights up and rambles about his sexy, abstract short films in New York's underground, then how he fits into the Cinema of Transgression of the '80s.

As their food, at last, comes, Miss Luxx says she gets a kick out of them sharing the same birthday with the weird ways they act like twins (Goth being an offshoot of Punk, for one), then asks how presents work. Piri's gone BBQ feral, so Rudella explains that they each put twenty bucks in a jar every week, then split the pot on their birthday as gifts to each other. Their first birthday as a couple was a complicated mess, and the jar's a tidy remedy.

Before she dives into her oysters, Miss Luxx asks the still-rational of the two if they want to go with her and her friends to this year's Pride parade. She knows where there'll be a Floralia afterwards; a sex worker gathering named after the festival for Flora, the Roman fertility goddess of flowers and Spring. Rudella says she's never been to a parade, and doesn't want to. Miss Luxx arches an eyebrow. Rudella explains that she doesn't feel who she prefers needs to be celebrated. Or hated. She just wants to live her life. She also doesn't watch most sapphic flicks since they tend to have one woman in a hetero relationship; as if her love only counts if she's with a man first. Piri grumbles something like an affirmative.

After the quite filling dinner, the Twosome tell Miss Luxx she can spend the night instead of driving back so late, but she'd rather keep the feminine mystique of no one knowing what her toots smell like and goes home. Plus, she doesn't want to be the one keeping them from… dancing the Lambada.

Although moving was her idea and she's pleased with the new apartment, Piri's filled with melancholy as they go up the stairs. Rudella's spousal sense tingles, so she switches from enjoying the view in the skinny jeans to asking what's wrong. As she unlocks the door, Piri says that she wishes things were different.

They survey the disarray of their lives and aren't interested in wading through it to the bedroom. Rudella suggest making a blanket fort; Piri asks what it is, and Rudella remembers her girlfriend won't know a lot of things she took for granted growing up. The Ex-Mortician tells the Shield-Maiden to get ready for bed while she builds one. The latter does what she's told, deciding while brushing her teeth that she doesn't want to search for pajamas, and strips down to her chic lingerie before seeing in the living room what the fuck a blanket fort is.

It looks like what she's seen many a hobo make, but she hides her bafflement in the face of Rudella's pride. Rudella, however, can see her lingering melancholy, and invites her in the dimly-lit fort. Piri goes in, and is pleasantly surprised to find it looks like a harem (the decorative pillows they're going to sell soon helps). What little light there is comes from a smartphone with a movie paused and ready. The flick that put trashy Troma Entertainment on the map, and one of her faves, "Toxic Avenger". Rudella has no idea why a mutant nerd in a tutu and a mop brutalizing thugs in New Jersey ranks so high, but this isn't about her. Her girlfriend's depressed, and she's right in thinking it'll cheer her up.

Piri doesn't make it through Toxie's first adventure, but Rudella makes sure she's knocked out. Watching her while she sleeps, in a precious moment of vulnerability, Rudella sings The Bangles' "Eternal Flame" like a lullaby. She surprises herself with a tear that she wipes away before joining her in slumberland.

Weeks pass. The Twosome bike and 'blade together almost daily. Rudella's still in her painterly groove, filling the walls of her storage unit with canvassed stream of consciousness. She even convinced Piri to let her bid on a unit that's soon to be tossed. They fought about it because the Shield-Maiden wanted to be the instigator of their resell gig. The Artisan won by telling her they can also use the unit for the stuff they already have, nice and organized, instead of them living like proto-hoarders. Piri didn't like losing that fight, so Rudella cheered her up by singing "Elephant Love Medley" from "Moulin Rouge!" and getting her to join in (as Satine, of course).

Days pass. One of many, many, many, many perks of libraries most people don't know is as long as a library has a book in the network, it can be borrowed from any library. That's how Piri recently read Mel Gordon's erotic histories of Paris (1920-1946) and Weimar Germany, "Horizontal Collaboration" and "Voluptuous Panic". In her vagabondage, she loved spending time at the gorgeous and ginormous Harold Washington Library. Though she inherited Rudella's hatred of traveling downtown. She can't even take a train anymore since she'd have to leave her car at the station, and thieves have come to love catalytic converters.

Because of these things, Piri picks up a book from the lovely Glenwood-Lynwood Library, from a faraway place (the West Side). Tanith Lee is a fantasy and sci-fi author who's been on her to-read list for time immemorial, but she never thought about reading her when the opportunity presented itself. Until she found out she's dead. Piri starts at her beginning with "Birthgrave", about an amnesiac woman who wakes up in a volcano and hangs out with a barbarian tribe. What a debut, right? And it's part of a trilogy. She spends most of her day reading it at Gabe's, figuring out the new normal of drinking something with a lip ring.

Piri goes the few steps home since her hangout spot closes midday. Lucky for her, Rudella's in court so she can admit aloud having all the resell stuff in a unit was a fantastic idea. Their apartment's bigger than their mobile home, but not by much. It's like a rectangle with the lower half taken up by the living room, and the upper half sharing the bedroom and bathroom with a hall leading to the kitchen.

As she checks her usual news sites (she swears by Teen Vogue and The Onion), she sees a familiar face. Jenn, and a few others from the March's afterparty, were arrested earlier for doing something anarchic, shouting something about looking up what they recorded on WITNESS (a site that "helps people use video and technology to protect and defend human rights" [and remember: one call to a politician is worth much more than a thousand viral posts]).

A repugnant seed in her mind is nursed with brackish water that will erupt into something grotesque.

Hours pass. The novelty of dyeing her hair by herself wore out when she let it grow out (wrapping it in a bun when driving, of course), so Rudella asks Piri to henna her up when her roots show. Piri didn't like doing it until, over a series of reddenings, she built a character who does enjoy it. Which is why, as accepted as the dawn, Rudella gossips with a hard-livin' hairdresser named Mavis. They had the wonderfully cheesecake "Charlie's Angels: Full Throttle" on in the background, but Piri didn't want to fetch the drool bucket. So Rudella put on a playlist of geeky, peppy songs she loved in college, like Witches' "There She Is!!". Piri sneaks in the B4 ZA BEAT Mix of Jennifer's "If You Were Here With Me". She's glad the soundtrack's far happier than last time. Rudella made a bleak, D.A.R.E. playlist that started with A Perfect Circle's "The Package" (the addict) and Nine Inch Nails' "Closer" (the drug), and descended from there.

Mavis asks Rudella what college life was like. After staring at the wall for a while, she says it's like "Genshiken". An anime about a club that involves watching anime, reading manga, and playing video games for college credits. Mavis admits she didn't go to college because her deadbeat second husband left her with three kids, and none of them came out of her. Rudella asks what their names are: Pookie, Dookie, and Trafalgar Square (because the baby mama's from London, Ohio). Rudella, stifling laughter, asks where they are now: Dookie left with Pookie to start an electric Jew's harp band, and Traffy S. didn't come up for air after getting sixth place in a rock-eating contest. Rudella loses it somewhere around "band" and "and". Piri pinches her thigh so she doesn't break character.

Mavis is done after Rudella reminds her (as always) to clip her ends, and Piri reminds her freshly-coiffed babe to not renege on their deal. Mavis works, Rudella cooks. Pasta's on the menu, so Rudella trails olive oil around the pot's rim (to keep water from boiling over) before using it.

While she simmers the orecchiette and sizzles the sausage, she plays the adorably campy video for Sugizo and the Spank Your Juice's "Super Love" three times, as a stopwatch. Meanwhile, her mind goes to those important people in her life during her college days. At the time, she considered them bottle-breaking friends. Y'know, friends you'd break a bottle to use like a knife and defend. Then she found they were ships in the night, and the only bottle she broke was to send them on their way.

She debates putting sewer cheese on the orecchiette with sausage and spinach, but settles on Romano. Piri's knee-deep in her nightly routine, so she eats between battles in "Xenogears", the most philosophical game with giant robots and mental disorders you'll play.

One morning, Piri goes to the post office to see if anything's waiting in her P.O. Box. Almost goes. She had a nightmare about cops breaking Jenn and making her tell them about all involved with the Women's March. They found out Gwynplaine was really that homeless bitch who corrupted Terentia into slaughtering her fellow compatriots of the thin blue line. They were going to find her and make her pay.

She mistakes her subconscious rumblings as prophecy instead of as memos. Which is why she waits two blocks away from the post office, with her phone's camera zoomed in on it. Looking for someone, anyone, who might be suspicious. Cars that are parked too long. Birds that might be drones.

For four hours she waits for nothing. But maybe that's because they're too good at hiding. She walks home, taking the most convoluted way to make sure she's not followed. She'll get Rudella to close her P.O. Box tomorrow.

She tells the Artisan, then asks her to do that thing she does for headaches. "That thing" is mixing drops of peppermint essential oil with coconut oil, then massaging her temples for one minute. As Rudella plays her part as the helpful girlfriend, Piri thinks about what else those cops might do to track her down.

Using Kilhanna springs to attention so, just like that, she decides to end her sex work career. She loves it, but nothing's worth getting done what those cops will do to her for causing a massacre and marching with an anarchist.

Rudella asks if the headache's that bad. Piri says she doesn't hurt anymore, and Rudella asks why she's crying. Piri makes up something about the ending of "Edward Scissorhands", thanks her for her magic fingertips, then goes to her laptop.

She shuts down her video hosting account, and spends a half-hour tormenting herself about how to end things on her blog. She never gets further than a paragraph before deleting everything. How to say goodbye without saying why? To people who have seen more of her than anyone besides Rudella, and have given her so much? Money, gifts, strength, confidence. Unexpectedly, the things she was asked and paid to do as Kilhanna taught her to live shamelessly. Fortunately, not also as an attention whore: being a whore-whore was enough. At least she gets to leave that world on her terms and a "good" note.

She settles on a title: "Release the Flesh No Longer". In place of a blog, she posts a song. In her choice, her subconscious shows a reflection she won't notice: The Verve's "Bitter Sweet Symphony". Then she logs out, deletes her saved password she was never able to remember, shuts down Kilhanna's email account. Tosses all her masks and her foot nook in the garbage, her Pavlovian keys to Kilhanna. Cuts all remaining ties to her camgirl life, then listens to the song, not understanding the message to herself that's blatantly clear, until Rudella helps her into bed.

The repugnant seed germinates, piercing its taproot ready to putrefy into fertile innocence.

Post-pimp liberation, some women can't shake the mindset. Their relationship is one of the fiercest cases of gaslighting. It must be, or else why put up with living it? Under their pimps, if a woman acts out, she's punished. That warped expression of attention becomes such an important part of her life, she seeks it out. She'll act like a brat just so she can get yelled at or worse because, to her broken self, that's love.

None of that is a problem for Rudella in her post-Kilhanna life. There are one or two relics, though. Kilhanna may be gone, but Piri's libido didn't disappear. It's a surprise to Rudella; pleasant, then she realizes she's part of a routine. She's a night owl when it comes to sex, but Kilhanna always worked midday. Rudella happily adapts, of course, but she has to adapt. And Piri fucking Rudella at night is much different that Rudella fucking Piri dayside.

For Rudella, sex is about the destination, not the journey. Though there can be many destinations. Piri, however, enjoys the journey of sex, and doesn't mind not reaching her destination. Her paying fans loved her longer videos; years of playing the long game with her panty hamster conditioned her to love the feeling at least as much as the release. Something that doesn't click with Rudella (mostly because Piri assumes she knows), so she occasionally wonders why Piri doesn't cum after diddling her for half an hour.

Another Kilhanna relic is Piri's love of cosplaying and role-playing during sex. It must shock you knowing Rudella's also a fan. You can be knocked over by a feather after reading that. Up is down and cats bark after rea--

One secret Piri didn't share as Kilhanna is her penchant for masochism; a gift only for Rudella because it goes beyond the trust of typical sex. Sovereign trust she doth bestow; timidity she doth protest. It wasn't easy for Piri to signal sexy pain time until Rudella's kinky double-feature: "Story of O" and "Hellraiser". Piri enjoyed the masochistic devotion in former, though she read the book by Pauline Réage years ago. The latter, however, lit a fire in her as well gave her the signal she needed.

A few days later, while Rudella went about her day carefree as a jellyfish, Piri gave her a box. Not just any box: a Lament Configuration replica. In "Hellraiser", it's a puzzle box and the device that beckons the Cenobites (demons to some, angels to others). Anyone can solve the puzzle but... it isn't hands that call them, it is desire. When the Cenobites arrive, they give their patron an experience beyond limits. Pain and pleasure, indivisible. Just what Piri wanted from her sexy pain time. Whenever she offers the Lament Configuration, it's her way of beckoning her Cenobite.

The paranoia of her "crimes" almost overwhelms her, and she yearns for the only relief pain can give her. She waits for Rudella to come home from painting. In the afternoon, when the Artisan arrives, she sees Piri on the couch with her hands clasped around a box of lacquered wood and polished brass.

But anticipation makes the thighs grow warmer. Rudella pretends to not see her as she takes her time putting things away and washing her hands. Nervously, Piri looks at her, almost handing her the replica as she asks if she understands w--

Her Mistress coldly tells Piri to shut up, and a quivering smile spreads on her face as she obeys.

By now, Her Mistress has perfected the symphony of pain on her orchestra of flesh. Conducted with whips, not chains. Moans, not words. Not even those for safety; Piri gives herself utterly to Her Mistress, so absolute her trust, so extreme her threshold. But nothing goes inside her.

On their bed and with her back to the door, Piri sits on her knees. Nude, save for a silk scarf of violet draped over a shoulder. The setting sun bathes her in its pumpkin glow as she awaits sensuous release from her anxieties. Then she hears Brian Reitzell's brooding, avant-garde score for "Hannibal"; season two, volume two. Then she knows it's time.

Her Mistress is a master of silently stalking, so Piri only knows she's close when she feels the silk pulled off her shoulder. She keeps her gaze downward, until her head is yanked back as the scarf is tied as a blindfold.

A kiss is forcefully stolen from her.

Minutes pass, then she feels a finger curl twixt the silk and her cheek, allowing her to peek at what waits for her on the bed. Her breath quickens as she glimpses Her Mistress' voyeurs of utter destruction. Then the finger teases her back into darkness and anticipation.

Something tiny and hard is placed on either side of her lips. As they trail down her neck, she tries to guess what they are. When they open passing her collarbone, she has an idea. When she gasps as they close on her nipples, she knows. And she wants more.

Another kiss is brutishly stolen.

She's shoved forward, still on her knees, and lies with arms stretched in front of her as if she's a slave hailing her master. The coincidence isn't lost on her as she waits for her next exquisite torment.

Her palms are forced upward, with trembling fingers and breath. In one ear, she hears a flick, then a dying whir. Like someone spinning a tiny wheel. Now in the other. She bites her lip to silence herself, her breathing carrying her burden, when she suddenly feels a prickling in her palms as if stabbed by needles. Not enough to bleed, Her Mistress is careful to not break her flesh. This time. Her Mistress knows her crimson limits. The prickling goes away, then she hears another dying whir. Then she realizes it's a pinwheel, and bites her lip for another reason entirely.

The prickling begins again in her palms, then slowly, tenderly, up her wrists. Her arms. Her shoulders. As she shivers in pain and pleasure. Her back. Her hips. Her thighs. As she moans in pangs and delectation. No weeping wounds. The pinwheel renews its trek across her flesh much quicker. As she convulses in agony and joy.

Then feathers dance along the prickled path, and she's filled with a tickling warmth. Like sipping tea after suffering the cold. Then she feels a wet tongue at the base of her spine, and she shivers as it trails to the base of her neck, vertebrae by vertebrae, with kisses both surprising and welcome.

Minutes pass until she's pulled upright again. Fingers march across her cheeks, then spread her mouth open and binds it with excess silk. Erotic terror fills her as she can only breathe through her nose.

She's shoved again, this time on her hands and knees. The ambient air feels cool on inner thighs slick with her delight. Feeling floods back to her legs. The clasps on her nipples are plucked off with a muffled yelp, then massaged by fingertips drenched by her thighs. Her Mistress always knows how to tantalize her pebbles. And how to make her regret it. Quick as a turned page, she feels something cover where fingertips played. Then a painful sucking that doesn't go away no matter how much she squirms.

Suddenly, she feels a faint tapping on the soles of her feet. A flat, leathery thing. As the thing travels up her calves, the tapping turns grotesque. More so as it explores the back of her thighs. The riding crop makes its statement clear on her ass, with a sharp slap and a sudden stop.

Again. Again. Again. Again.

She can barely stay still, but she knows she'll get worse if she falls down. All she can do is be grateful the taut scarf muffles her screams. The thrill of withstanding pain, not letting it break her, makes her head swim. Her Mistress must have noticed her swooning because she feels the whiff of the crop abruptly stopping a fateful inch before wrecking a most precious thing. Fear of the gap closing snaps her back to reality, and she welcomes the reddening of her ass.

She can sense Her Mistress admiring a job well done, then she feels a great soothing. The coolness of the ice cube on the heat of her welts makes her covered eye flutter. It's left to melt on the cleft below her Venus dimples, sending her into twitching fits.

Then they hear the clanging of the railroad crossing. Then they know they can get *much* louder.

Her Mistress shoves her head to the mattress, tapping her stomach with the crop to keep her ass up. A welted ass she rolls tauntingly, daring Her Mistress' worst instincts.

She's put in her place by reminding her of the sucking on her nipples, dull pain shatters into stinging as Her Mistress flicks them with her fingers. Knowing how much impact to hurt the most while keeping the devices fixed. She groans with each strike.

She yells with anguish and elation when Her Mistress grabs the tuft of hair twixt her legs and pulls. Seconds feel like eternities. She doesn't have time to recover when freed because Her Mistress introduces her to a new, familiar pain while slapping her aching ass with a hand. Then grabs and shakes it. She gnaws on the scarf, and growls like a carnal beast as Her Mistress continues.

Again. Again. Again. Again.

Tapping returns, with fingertips, onto her rosebud drenched with lustful juices. The solitude of tremendous pleasure gives her no choice but to cum. What is usually a wave is now an avalanche, encouraged by her sensual torture. Her stifled, orgasmic scream drones until it winds down like a choke. She shivers in threes; words eventually come to her in monosyllables. She thinks this is what it must feel like to be high.

When she, at last, comes down from her cloud of wicked delights and ends, she finds herself in Rudella's arms under the moonlight.

As important as the pain in all things S&M is comforting the sub when it's over. A bust-ass workout without a come-down sucks for the heart; a BDSM session without comfort sucks for the mind. Rudella's glad she remembered to skip "Tome-Wan" during the session since the song gets goofy and would've ruined the mood. She also delicately rubs Vitamin K cream on Piri's aches and pains before placing ice packs on them, with heat packs tomorrow. All while listening to the first, soothing disc of "Anjunadeep 07".

Being such an extreme domme doesn't bother Rudella because it's what her girlfriend wants, and she discovered she loved being a pain merchant to the willing. They built up to their plateau; only a fool starts off where they are. Piri always set the boundaries and was the one to take them down. And they only have sessions when she really needs them.

The goal of this session is achieved, and Piri's stresses are miles away. Rudella's satisfied because Piri's satisfied… she's also going to love when the Shield-Maiden returns the favor with Roman hands, Russian fingers, and a foreign tongue.

Everyone who wants a relationship has a triangle over their head. Each corner has a neon-scrawled choice (Sexy, Smart, Sane), though only two are lit. Rudella's harmless love of death is Piri's reminder that she picked Sexy and Smart. But it's a lack of sanity she could deal with. Unlike the lipstick-in-your-tit kind of crazy Linnea Quigley is in "Night of the Demons". Then the Thanatophile started joining podcasts at home. Jenkins' Death Babble took off enough that Rudella's been asked to happily talk corpses with like-minded folk, once in a while. A leitmotif of Piri's since was her whining about Rudella not being a guest on CHIRP (Chicago Independent Radio Project [107.1 on the dial, chirpradio.org online]) or do something cool and anarchic like Christian Slater in "Pump Up the Volume".

Throughout her vagabondage, death was the iron filament drawn to the magnet called Piri. Many times, violently so. For Rudella, death was a warm companion and her career. Even now. They understand and respect the other's conflicted point of view, but there are flare-ups. Like the current one, with Piri wanting Rudella to do the interview elsewhere so she won't hear morbid talk, and Rudella bringing up how she respected Piri by leaving when she had Kilhanna business to do.

Their arguments were vigorous, but they had to find quieter ways to settle things since moving to an apartment. Ways that used skill, not luck. Chance was a mortal enemy of anger. That's why they decided, after an argument that might've gotten them evicted, to settle things with "Tetris Effect" when one felt the other was close to losing their shit. Tetris is nothing but skill, and this version has calming, colorful stages already acting in their serene favor. Which is what they're doing now, on the Deserted stage, for the fate of temporary banishment.

A lifetime of casual gaming is nothing compared to a mortician's focus, and Piri grumbles her way to a nature hike. Rudella watches her from the window as she heads to the foliage across Main St., stops, then stomps with a purpose westward. Probably to try sneaking into the quarry again. Rudella pockets her phone just in case she gets a call asking to pick someone up from the police station.

The podcast that sent Piri to either kick rocks or get chased is Putridly Yours, hosted by NecroSis. It's yet another true crime podcast by a woman, but it stands out because it dares to be funny. Making a comedy out of a tragedy demands that NecroSis has a smaller reach, but those she reaches love her embrace. You'd be surprised by how many fans know victims or murderers and find catharsis in laughter she provides.

Rudella gives herself a half-hour to get ready: going over topics she wants to ramble about while eating lunch. As her Hot Pockets spin in the microwave, she checks her blog for new messages. There's one, from someone she never wants to see about something she never wants to think about.

High school sucks twas ever thus, and Rudella was a Korean, weirdo of a teen in a four-year popularity contest. There was a girl, Josie Mae, who made her fucking miserable throughout the tetrad. You've heard the stories. Rudella was never a threat to the school nor herself, so she got through the senseless pain with the Tall Man, Herbert West, the Bride of Frankenstein, Lestat de Lioncourt, and other horror icons. Teachers were useless. Her bumonim were clueless, but that was her choice.

The message from Josie Mae starts with how she found her. Rudella doesn't have a social media account, especially not after the privacy fuck-up that was the Cambridge Analytica scandal, but her name's on her blog. Josie Mae goes on to deeply apologize for everything she did in high school. She found out she had cervical cancer a few days ago, and wants to set as many things right as she can before it's too late. She doesn't know why she did what she did all those years ago, but she's a different woman now. She has a husband, two sons, and a dog, and she doesn't want to lose them. She hopes Rudella can forgive her because she could use it. She thanks Rudella and suggests they catch up soon.

Did you know Redneck Rudella can type?

After she… colorfully decimates Josie Mae for waiting 'til she was dying to make things right and denies her amnesty, Rudella realizes she has less than ten minutes to eat her cold Hot Pockets and check her notes. To get herself into a happier place, she does both while rocking out to Patti Smith's heathen cover of Them's "Gloria". The first time she heard it, she didn't realize it was a cover until the chorus, then she lost her angsty, 14-year-old mind on her bouncy bed.

Right on time, NecroSis calls to start their laptop chat. Rudella makes up a lie about a train passing by so she can finish her lunch without choking. Luckily, since both hate video calls, the lie succeeds. Rudella then tells NecroSis that she sounds like Juliette Lewis. NecroSis thinks about "Cape Fear" and "Strange Days", and approves. She tells Rudella that she sounds like Holly Hunter. Rudella thinks about "The Incredibles" and "Crash" (the good one), and approves.

On the subject of Chicagoland, NecroSis asks what it's like living there. Rudella goes on her well-honed spiel about traffic. NecroSis cuts her off with a giggle, then tells her about the molasses horrors of NYC and LA traffic. Pittsburgh is also a pain, with its narrow streets, a lack of a grid system, hills, short on-ramps, and weird intersections (oh, the weird intersections…). No wonder George Romero filled it with zombies.

Rudella asks, with more than a little excitement, what kind of crime scene she's getting. Each episode of "Putridly Yours" gets a crime scene photo as a cover image. From the La Belle Époque of Paris, "The Beautiful Age", at the turn of the 20th century. Partially because NecroSis thinks the photos are artful, but mostly because they're public domain. She tells her guest she's getting a hanging suicide in the kitchen, who golf-claps in gratitude.

Getting into the chat proper, NecroSis asks if Rudella knows about supervised consumption sites. News to her. NecroSis explains, with her brand of charm, how Norway, Germany, Australia, Spain, and many other countries have government-sponsored vehicles and buildings in areas with high drug use, and all the social decay that follows, because the war on drugs has been so fucking useless. They also exist in the US, but they're vigilantes because Uncle Sam doesn't want to deal with that shit.

Rudella's baffled, but can't help feeling it reminds her of something. NecroSis asks if she's seen "The Wire". She hasn't, but she says her girlfriend wouldn't shut up about it while she watched it. NecroSis compliments Piri's double-bout of good taste, then tells Rudella what happened in the third season. Drugs were so bad in Baltimore that the police major decided to secretly set up a shitty section of the city where drug use was legal, nicknamed "Hamsterdam".

Everything clicks for Rudella, who asks if it worked. NecroSis tells her to ask her cool girlfriend. Rudella *almost* plucks her phone out of her pocket, then accepts that it's not that important. But when Piri comes home…

On the subject of her cool girlfriend, NecroSis asks if she has more pearls of wisdom. Piri has plenty, like how Tolkien is the Kerouac of fantasy in that both were conservative authors whose road trip masterworks were loved by the counterculture. Or how Dante's Inferno is the "Watchmen" of its time, since people take "The Divine *Comedy*" too seriously and forget it's a satire, but Ludovico Ariosto's "Orlando Furioso" is better than the two. Blah, blah, book geek, blah.

NecroSis asks Rudella to tell the listeners about the gal behind Jenkins' Death Babble. The gal says that, for years, she was a mortician, her favorite job and the only one she wanted. Until she was fired thanks to a private equity vulture buying the funeral home she worked at. NecroSis says that explains a lot of the details in her blog most people don't, and shouldn't, know about death.

NecroSis asks what it was like growing up as a thanatophile since she thinks, like herself, it's like Rob Zombie's "The Hideous Exhibitions of a Dedicated Gore Whore". Rudella giggles an affirmative, then adds it was as solitary as she thinks, though she got to hang out with coroners and did fun things with her "cousin", Calantha. Like the night they found a dead cow.

It was bloated, and they got the young, dumb idea to get the tire iron out of Calantha's trunk and hit the balloon of a belly and make it fart. The iron almost knocked Calantha out because they forgot leather was typically made of cow hide, so it bounced back as hard as she swung. After learning her lesson, she kept hitting the cow without getting caught in the recoil, but nothing happened. Rudella got the idea for them to do a running dropkick, so they did. And it worked, sadly. The only thing more terrifying than the thunderous fart the cow ripped was the nightmarish funk that shot out while they were downwind. Corpse farts were already worse than egg farts or protein shake farts, but she could see a screaming skull smoking from that black and white ass. She can still taste the stink, decades later.

When NecroSis finally stops laughing, she says it's a good thing PETA isn't listening. Rudella says she'll take them seriously when they start raiding motorcycle clubs.

When NecroSis finally stops laughing again, she asks what it was like to be a mortician. Rudella ponders for so long, NecroSis thinks she lost the connection. A reason the Ex-Mortician eventually gives is that she, like police and medical pros, was paid to see the worst of humanity, and she loved the privilege.

She describes Japan's concept of omote and ura. Omote is what a person reveals to the world; ura, what they keep in private. People do anything to hide their ura from those they don't trust, but extreme situations expose them. Dealing with the death of a loved one brings out the ugliest, most tragic and confusing parts of a person's ura. For Rudella to be able to see that meant they trusted her, even temporarily.

Running with the subject of trust, NecroSis brings up the murder of Sylvia Likens. Rudella, knowing what podcast she's on while also knowing what happened, politely suggests this might be when NecroSis jumps the shark since there's nothing funny about what happened to her. To which the host states, of course, there's nothing fucking funny about what happened. That's why she's gonna focus on the fucking psychotic, selfish, jealous, clown car-having, child-destroying, backwoods, corroded asshole bitch of a shit-stained attempt of a human being, Gertrude Baniszewski, who caused her to die. Rudella sighs in relief.

Gertrude, who should've been choked by her umbilical cord and dragged up and down the Mason-Dixon, took in Sylvia and her sister, Jenny, to live with her and her seven dick cheese nuggets in Indianapolis for 20 bucks a week. July '65. She began beating the sisters for whatever reason she could think of with whatever she could find, and literally feeding them garbage. Then she focused on Sylvia.

Gertrude, who should've been the first test subject for what a nuclear reactor did to someone's intestinal tract, twisted Sylvia's descriptions of the things she did with a boy she liked in California. She warned her one-trick daughters they'll get pregnant if they did anything with boys, then turned her beatings to Sylvia's crotch. One of the deep-fried warts, Paula, joined in.

Gertrude, who should've smeared herself with ground beef before throwing herself in a wolf den during a hunger strike, let one of the neighborhood potholes, Coy Hubbard, bring his friends over so they and the Baniszewski horde could brutalize Sylvia with fists, words, and cigarettes. Then Gertrude forced Sylvia to get herself off with a bottle in front of everyone. Including her sister, Jenny.

Gertrude, who should've been a finger trap for Freddy Krueger and a rusty chainsaw with Parkinson's, forced Sylvia to live in the basement, tied up and nude and starved. Sometimes dangling from the stairs. Neighborhood goblins could, for a nickel, do what they wanted to her. Including tossing her into hot water and rubbing salt on their handiwork. Or smothering her with soiled diapers.

Gertrude, who should've starred in a snuff film with a swarm of syphilitic war criminals high on Viagra and angel dust, took a hot needle and started carving "I'M A PROSTITUTE AND PROUD OF IT" on Sylvia's stomach before making a neighborhood gnat and one of her genital scabs, Stephanie, finish. Sylvia's torment continued for days, until her heart couldn't take anymore on October 26th. The fermented shit of a matriarch beat her corpse with a book to wake her up.

Gertrude, who should've rotted in prison or fried in the chair, got paroled from her life sentence in '85. She changed her name to Nadine Van Fossan and played dumb about the fucking abhorrent, reasonless things she did and got children to do to a 16-year-old girl named Sylvia Likens. Then she died five years later from a fate too kind: lung cancer.

NecroSis adds that all of her… suggestions for Gertrude apply to anyone who hurts a child, as well as sexists, racists, tech bros, and people who hate ketchup.

Rudella politely suggests they end the podcast on a happier note, then asks if "Silence of the Lambs" did more to help or hurt serial killers in movies. She suggests storytellers learned the wrong lesson, making their killers geniuses like Hannibal Lecter when they're really (sub)average like Jame Gumb. "Summer of Sam" learned the right lesson, though.

NecroSis takes the bait and brings up two highly-visual, Brad Pitt serial killer movies with '90s-edgy titles (what a niche): "Kalifornia" and "Se7en". John Doe in the latter is definitely a bi-product of Lecter. Early Grayce in the former is definitely how many serial killers are. She thinks it's because writers are self-indulgent and can't resist a good monologue. Much more fun to craft an eloquent speech about the disease that is man than a rant about how that dumb bitch didn't put out none.

Closing out, NecroSis tells Rudella she should check out Park Chan-wook's "Lady Vengeance" and Kim Jee-woon's "I Saw the Devil" because she found out recently Korea has the best revenge flicks. Rudella almost gets offended, but there's no way NecroSis could know she's Korean since there aren't pics on her blog. She chooses gratitude, then signs off on a thanatotic high.

Piri wears out the introvert with even more talk when she gets home so, thanks to oversleeping, she almost misses the mailman with a package. Her bumonim didn't give her everything in their video store that one time; they've been sending her boxes with massive binders full of discs. Texting her the shipping number each time. She's expecting more backbreaking labor, but it surprised to instead get a bubble mailer.

On what passes for their dinner table, thanks to Piri preparing a few resell shipments, Rudella sees what's inside. Her Rewind or Die membership card (No. 003), her employee badge, and her work t-shirt. She's not surprised it still fits since her appa bought it oversized, but she *is* surprised it still smells like the store. She remembers leaving it in an office drawer and guesses it probably stayed there until there wasn't an office.

As an antisocial employee, she was glad to be a stock girl; running around the converted CVS making sure everything's tip-top while avoiding as many people as possible. Being a candy girl and a card laminator sucked since that was the people part of the job. The other, magnificent thing about her job was her appa made her watch every new thing that came in. That way, at least one of them could make recommendations or help someone remember a thing or three (both to her chagrin). Because of that, Rewind or Die didn't have porn. It's magnificent because she got to watch **a <u>lot</u>** of movies.

Studios gave the store posters, but her eomma thought she could do better. So she drew and painted posters. First as replacements, then for movies she thought needed them. Basically, anything with the screwball comedy queen, and pride of Indiana, Carole Lombard (the one for "Twentieth Century" still makes her proud).

Rudella puts her card in her wallet and her badge near the TV, then looks at the stacks of binders with awe and love. The two columns come up to her shoulders, and she knows there are still more coming. She has no problem pulling a Smaug, not parting with a ssssingle disc, but she's also aware enough that the dragon's sickness is real. It'd be a crime for the well-curated remains of Rewind or Die to end with her, so she decides to open a non-profit video archive whenever she retires. She's social enough to tolerate people now, and she'll get to say her job's watching movies all day.

She gets back to what she planned to do today after the package business. Their two-year anniversary is approaching, and this makes Piri's fifth year as a Pagan. The desire to paint something doubly celebratory is strong, so Rudella goes to her storage unit to ponder.

It took a few times for Rudella to remember Piri calls herself a Pagan because she didn't know what else to call what she made for herself, not because she thinks she's a Pagan. The last mistake involved trying to connect with her through Pagan Metal, but Piri's also too much of a clubhead for that. Rudella plucked Arkona from the pile (give "Liki Bessmertnykh Bogov" a listen, if you dare), and fell in love with the Dark Folk of Wardruna (diito "Raido"…) and Karl Sanders (…and "Slavery Unto Nitokris"). Which is a long way of saying Rudella had to think like a girlfriend, not an armchair theologian.

While "Speed Racer", the best sports movie for artists, plays, she entertains the idea of painting something encapsulatory of her love and respect. However, part of her knows if she did a painting for Piri, she'd keep it and that would put a whisper in her mind to keep all her paintings. Then try to sell them. Then get sucked into vicious, heartless art world. So she does the other thing she wanted to do today.

In an undisclosed location, Rudella unloads all of her paintings and turns them into a bonfire while listening to

Strawberry Switchblade's only album. Flames erase effort and temptation, allowing her to continue creating art carelessly and joyfully. While it burns, she returns to thoughts of what to do for Piri. It'd be simple to buy an engagement ring, but neither are the marrying type. If they stay together 'til death, it's because of love instead of duty or limerence. Then she remembers Piri wanted to go to Indiana Beach in the way someone gets *really* excited for, then forgets about soon after. Y'know, a typical nine days' wonder. Rudella, among the fire and flames, giggles at the idea of normies suffering her and her parasol.

Don't make the mistake of thinking the lack of Piri's panic attacks is good news. Rudella does. White Knights are also genderqueer: men think they can save their lover, and women think they can fix them. Piri's just gotten *real* good at bottling things in, under the artifice of love conquering all. Her agony debts fertilize the repugnant seed in her mind, her suppressed triggers water it into catastrophe. All it needs to do is wait. It loves a good train wreck... and Piri loves trains.

She's also a bit of a social media stalker, only interested in one person... although dear old Mom was never interested in her.

It started a few weeks ago on a whim. Thoughts of her mother surprised her. Then curiosity ensnared her. What she saw was worse than every shitty thing that was ever done to her.

Not only was her mother happy, Piri had a younger brother and sister.

She spent that night going through posts, seeing her siblings with perfect pairs of eyes have the mother she always wanted, until she passed out from heartbreak. She told Rudella it was because she played too much Scrabble.

Since then, Piri ends her nights with check-ins to them. The wrong kind of masochistic tendencies taking over her life. Her sister starts Girl Scouts soon. Her brother wins a spelling bee. Her sister has a sleepover. Her brother isn't allowed to join. Her sister is hiding in the dryer. Her brother plants his first garden. Her sister loves her mommy the mostest. Her brother loves her more.

What finally stops Piri is this post, while Rudella's out buying her hearse. Of her mother grateful she got being a parent right the first time. With her younger brother and sister. Piri held onto a child's hope that her mother would regret how she treated her. Not only is that not happening, she doesn't exist to her anymore.

She can't even cry, such is the depth of her disappointment, grief, and shame. All she can do is look at the door aglow that suddenly appears on the bedroom floor.

The first thing that greets her in this new realm is the sound of screeching metal. She can't see what's causing it, or anything, thanks to remnants of the door. As it fades, a terrible clamor introduces itself. Then screams, though she doesn't know why they're familiar. Her surroundings pulse into view, until she regrets that they have.

The ground of cracked asphalt and what makes her special leads her to a track of mangled steel and thoughts unwanted. The track leads her to a hopper, overturned and overprotective. The hopper leads her to mutilated versions of herself; their agent of ruin, an armored truck covered in grotesque branches and debts. Its engine still runs, resembling laughter satisfied.

One Piri besides herself breathes, barely, and she digs through the staring corpses to find her. Their singular gaze follows as she burrows deeper than the mound of bodies has space for. The more she digs, the more she finds. Except who she's bloodying herself to save.

Miles later, the tunnel of Piri parts takes her no closer to the survivor. And unblinking eyes continue to follow. Piri Proper, with sinew in her nails, can't bear the stench of her yesterdays. Everything about her is smothered by it. Whenever she pauses from exhaustion, her deep breaths make her burn with it from the inside. Whenever she wants to quit, she remembers her other self feels the same ache.

At last, she finds a hand wanting hers. Frantically, with a purpose, she carves space until the hand becomes an arm becomes a body. The Other Piri looks at her savior with a child's gratitude, then feels slimy fingers around her neck. The distant light blurs until it disappears, and she breathes no more.

The All-Deads collapse in her burrow, and she falls even deeper into a world unknown due to neglect. She knows not the worth of screams, so she plummets in silence. No light, no darkness, no time. Until they snap around her like a yearning whip.

When her senses stop oppressing her, she notices she's gloved into a gown. The amber one ribboned with lavender she dreamed of having for her quinceañera. She notices she's boxed into a ballroom. Beautifully lit and vibrantly colored like a Miles Aldridge photograph. She notices she's spotlit by attention. The girl attendants, in gowns as if sculpted by Eiko Ishioka, applaud her arrival and lead her to the marble stairway. Which lead to the queen.

Her mother, draped in pearls and pride, waits for her with a smile on her face and a hopeful heart. In her hands, a velvet pillow. On the pillow, a tiara of diamonds and destiny. Piri takes the tiara and shows it to her cheering court. Then she slices her neck with it. The severed vein becomes a fountain of blood; she's dead before her body hits the final stair. The queen brings out her son and other daughter to more cheers, and they flock to the courtyard.

A hand reaches out from the pooled, cooled blood and braces itself on the marble. Another hand does the same. Slick and sanguine, it takes effort for them to help the rest escape. When Piri is free, she stumbles through the palace until she finds a fountain of milk to bathe in. As she plunges in, the hidden depths worry her. More so because she feels herself inescapably pulled to directions here and there.

The sewage pipe spits her out. Nude and shivering, Piri shambles through a concrete jungle with vines of wire and grass of steel wool. Her pain is immense as she looks for something, anything to cover herself with. To live in. To eat. Desperation draws her to choices no sane person would consider, but they're the only ways she sees others live here. She cuts herself open and stuffs herself with found objects, then holds herself up with detritus until her death makes her a Joel Peter-Witkin art piece like the rest of her... companions.

Piri rushes past the body garden with a monstrous grin frozen on her face. She doesn't know where she's going, only that she needs to run. She can still smell the burning torches, see the gleaming pitchforks, hear the undeserving hatred. Her legs are about to give out when she's swept up by a stranger and rides off on their horse. Its hooves spark on the wool, igniting their reason for not being followed.

Terentia reveals herself to Piri, then asks for her help. A horde of thieves and other wicked folk are on their way to Onion Castle, but she can't put her armor on by herself. Without hesitation, Piri offers her services and the two hurry to her chamber. The armor is dramatic and avant-garde, as if designed by Alexander McQueen. It takes some doing, but Piri manages to get the pieces where they need to, how they need to. Under the hard light, with all the textures, the proud Terentia looks like an Ellen von Unwerth photograph.

Then the armor kills Terentia in a violent fashion, and Piri is left alone.

CHAPTER EIGHTEEN

Two Years Later

Rudella stares at the empty bedside under dawn's early light, flickering to when her heart sang an aria of shock and horror.

The day she swapped her safety cone for her hearse was supposed to end with a joyride through suburbia. Life, however, was what happened while you made other plans. She came home to Piri convulsing and foaming on their bedroom floor, then spent the night waiting in an emergency room worrying about why.

When, at last, a doctor came, it was with more questions than answers. Piri had to be committed, and was in no state to fill out the form. Rudella swam in confusion, with fear slowly tainting the water. The love of her life had a psychotic break, with no way of knowing when, or if, she would come back.

Rudella was rotting inside as she signed Piri's life away, and her abandonment issues flared up. It was another hour before she drove home, giving up on a question she asked herself and couldn't answer. She couldn't make herself go inside since the truth of yesterday's tragedy would be inescapable.

Which was why she spent most of that day in the dark of her storage unit, only leaving because she left her charger on the kitchen counter and she might get a call about Piri.

In a renovated bathroom, Rudella diligently shaves her legs; the first time in a long time for the one who'll appreciate it.

Weeks passed since Piri was confined for her safety. Weeks passed since Rudella was able to talk to or see her, as her last memory of Piri haunted her waking and dreaming. Weeks passed since Rudella abandoned everything else in life except meagerly eating and sleeping and waiting. Weeks passed since Rudella found her only comfort in the electric melancholy of Ladytron. Weeks passed since Rudella was denied the answer to a question that prickles her conscience.

Eventually, she felt she had to attempt a sense of normalcy, if only so Piri had something normal to come home to. When she came home. If she-- A routine she had since she moved to Illinois was play Lucky Day Lotto every day. Tickets were only a dollar, and she could win at least 99,999 more of them. She never did, and Piri always gave her crap for sticking with it as long as she did, but she could spare a dollar daily. Plus whatever a handful of apple and cherry Laffy Taffys cost.

Her phone, as always, was in cobra-striking distance while she boiled her lunch-dinner: one polish sausage. She also was towards the end of "The Americans", a show about Cold War spies that was *really* the best show about making a marriage work. She got a notification, when she thought any was bad news, about how her Amapon account was hacked and she needed to give her password. Scammers loved their schemes. Then she checked the news and found out she won $700,000. Lucky Day Lotto didn't usually get that high, but Powerball and MegaMillions had also grown to absurd amounts lately.

A few weeks ago, Rudella would've jumped around and joked about being so excited that she'd punch a puppy. There was an excitement brewing in her, but it was understandably overshadowed by her weltschmerz. Having mastered poverty, she knew how to stretch a dollar. Being suddenly much richer didn't make her too uppity to stop buying groceries at Aldi, but now she can buy awesome totes. Like some Piri had her eye on. Plus, she had a plan to grow her newfound wealth into more without having to show off her concha. Among other things on her checklist, she could look into surgery for her endometriosis.

The homemade cane syrup on Rudella's waffles fresh off the iron tastes particularly sweet as she watches crows through the living room window.

When she discovered charitynavigator.org, she was overwhelmed by how many groups needed help. Even if she had billions of dollars, she knew it would be maddening to try supporting everyone. So she started off with two groups: Hero Initiative and The Ocean Cleanup. The comic book world was vicious and didn't take care of its creative people, which was what the former did. As for the latter, the Great Pacific Garbage Patch was only getting bigger.

Helping others while she couldn't help Piri was nice, but she needed to find other ways to distract herself from her anxiety. You would think having neighbors fixed things, but having abandonment issues didn't stop Rudella from being antisocial. In fact, she'd rather be left alone until she could see Piri again. The Twosome talked off and on about moving to Keller. It was a small town in the cornfields that seemed perfect for the kind of solitude they wanted. No trains or semi-trucks were a massive plus.

After checking in on Keller, she found the perfect situation. The town's sole funeral home was secluded and vacant for years, with the price to prove it. The outside was gorgeously Edwardian, it even had a tree full of crows in front, but the inside looked like a surly tornado ran through. Her appa was always glad to keep his hands busy. And no one was around to tattle. And she could find a carpenter to sign off on their work so she could move in when they're done, though I wouldn't ask about the legality of that. Which was how she kept busy, and distracted, until Hallowe'en. But the vexing question lingered.

As Rudella takes a look around her new life, she grabs her keys and sets out to bring her someone special into it.

It was in the middle of January when she was told she could finally visit Piri. Not quite a year; it may as well had been a decade. She received updates from her doctor in the meantime, and was recently able to talk to Piri over the phone. Being able to hear her, even for just ten minutes a day, was a relief beyond measure. Still, being able to see her… touch her… smell her surmounted even that.

If only nervousness wasn't an ally while Rudella waited in the empty visiting area. The knots in her stomach twisted by that agonized query made her repeatedly run to the bathroom. When she returned from her latest trip, she saw a new body on the couch. She could only see their back, draped with wavy hair, but she knew whose it was.

That didn't mean it was easy to see Piri again. Rudella knew Piri needed whatever she was getting, but she didn't know how much fulfillment changed her. Part of her had a childish need to welcome ignorance, yet she approached the wavy hair. When she was close enough, she heard Piri whistle Napoleon XIV's "They're Coming to Take Me Away, Ha-Haaa!" after confusing it with Kongos' "I'm Only Joking", then made sure no one was around before she laughed.

As Rudella sat next to Piri, she asked if it was ok to hug her. Piri held out a hand and told her shaking it would be better. She's not ready for that level of intimacy yet. It hurt Rudella, but she obeyed. After Piri pulled away, Rudella told her she never saw her hair so long. Piri smirked as she told her she couldn't have scissors, then mimicked cutting her wrist like construction paper and bragged about her medical eye patch. Rudella suggested she should kiss someone's ass to at least get her ends clipped. Piri told her she's already a kiss-ass, but drew the line at being a suck-ass: the next step was a shit-eating grin.

They talked for a few more minutes. Or rather, Rudella talked about the new Keller house and how she left plenty of space for Piri to make it hers, and Piri enjoyed the break from recovery life. Speaking of space, the latter asked the former how she felt about it. She liked "Battlestar Galactica" and "Doctor Who", but she felt people were too focused on what's *out there* when there's plenty to lose their shit about *down here*. Piri admitted that she had a hankering to give "Babylon 5" a try since a leitmotif of chaos and order on a space station would be a welcome break, but she couldn't watch it because… well, you know. She smiled a smile unseen in almost a year when Rudella told her she'd watch it and keep her updated each visit. Piri also admitted she had an ulterior motive: Rudella hadn't been much of a geek for a long time although it's so obviously an essential part of her, and she shouldn't deny it. Or else they both could be in here.

A nurse placed a hand on Rudella's shoulder, and she understood what that meant. Before she left, she wanted to ask Piri a question. The Question. She couldn't look at her as her voice cracked from fear of the answer, but she persisted: Was being here her fault? She felt her abandonment issues kept her from addressing problems she saw since that could crack their foundation and create a chasm between them. Piri looked at her with the quizzical, distant gaze she had since the start of their tête-à-tête, then admitted part of why she's there was to find out why she's there. But she didn't blame anyone but herself.

From that day, it took more than a year for Piri to find the answers she sought and pay all her agony debts. Tame all her comorbidities. Leaving her was never an option, but Rudella knew she was making progress when, towards the end of the second season of "Babylon 5", Piri hugged her. It was over almost as quickly as their arms locked around each other, but it was a beacon in the blizzard of healing.

The blizzard's gone as Rudella waits in the hospital's pick-up lane for Piri to be rolled out, then carry her into their home.

Paved roads and duplexes seem ancient to Piri as they pass her by, the effect of her hard-earned regeneration into her better self.

As she goes home, Keith Raniere finds he isn't going anywhere (in a few months, he'll find out it'll be for 120 years). It's hard to know which is more upsetting: the fact that the NXIVM cult he founded was used by him to sexually and emotionally abuse, and brand, women and children, or that he's the low-fat vanilla ice cream of cult leaders. It's not victim-shaming to point out how... offensively bland he is and wonder what they saw in him. Especially after all the revelations on him and his cult. He obviously fulfilled a need in his followers that made them overlook things like branding women, but it's a need that could've been fulfilled by being a regular at a bar or finding a group on Meetup. If anything, Keith Raniere is a warning to be a better neighbor so no one you know falls for the antics of someone with the charisma of asparagus who brands women. Be the Krispy Kreme to his saltine.

Their new home isn't a surprise to Piri; Rudella kept her updated during her visits, and asked for opinions on this and that. They even named it: the Lilith Pit. A holdover of Piri's regret for missing out on the Lilith Fair, a late-90s festival reaction to misogyny in the music industry. But seeing pics and hearing tales is nothing compared to experience.

Rudella's in her eccentric art student phase. Ok, that might be redundant. When "Cruella" comes out in a few years, Piri will (constantly) remind Rudella she dresses like Estella before she loses her damn mind and becomes Cruella. Then will have to be dragged pouting from the TV after watching it four times in a row. Law of averages say Disney was bound to trap at least one of them with their live-action reimaginings.

Riding in a hearse isn't as creepy as Piri thought it'd be, but it's still weird to ride in one so casually. Living south instead of east means the Twosome are free from the billboard tyranny of Krazy Kaplans Fireworks on I-94. After saying their farewells to Lake Stop, and Round the Clock's lemon rice soup. A ways down Route 394 and its evolutions among the cornfields, past a few stoplights and stop signs, they arrive at the only house on the street.

Before they get out of the hearse, Rudella gives Piri some birdseed and tells her to stay close. The crows in the tree are quite protective of her and need a peace offering. Piri raises an eyebrow, but Rudella dismisses it and warns her they may or may not have attacked her appa. She adds that sort of thing makes them great guards, and Piri only has to feed them a few times because crows have fantastic memories. She can barely contain herself when she finishes with news that a group of crows is a murder. The eyebrow lowers. Slowly.

The Lilith Pit is a thanatophile wonderland (the things you can get cheap at estate sales and a State Treasurer's unclaimed property auction...), with gaps that can make it equally whatever Piri wants it to be. It's also interestingly bisected: to the right of the entrance, the funeral parlor and office. To the left, an archway gorgeously curtained in black velvet to hide the living room and kitchen. At the center, a stairwell leading up to the beds, baths, and attic. The basement is on the parlor side, by stair or elevator, since that's where mortician dealings, big and small, go on. Embalmings, cremations, and other preparations. Not Piri's favorite place by a country mile, which is why everything that would go in the basement, like a washer and dryer, is in the garage. In the back yard, a path for coroners to take decedents to the elevator. Most importantly, thanks to Rudella and her appa, the home looks professionally renovated and was done for a song. Plus a nightly bottle of soju.

High on Piri's list is obliterating her hospital routine so she can create a home one. Instead of replacing one thing with another, she found while she was away that it's best for her to do a whole lot of nothing 'til it feels natural, then build a new routine. Which is why she, in her mechanic jumpsuit phase, and Rudella set out to watch all 172 episodes of "Star Trek: Voyager". "Babylon 5" scratched an itch... but it also caused a new infection.

They choose the USS Voyager because it feels like the right fit (if you think it's just because it's captained by a woman,

Redneck Rudella has a few words for you). Piri's into it for the (pseudo)science, which sends her on a great etymological journey. Whenever (pseudo)science pops up, she whips out a "Science, bitch!" from Jesse Pinkman. However, there's *so* much (pseudo)science in each episode that it's shortened to "Sci-bitch!" Then Rudella gets tired of the screaming, so it becomes a whispered "sybech" and her exclamation whenever something cool and science-y happens. On screen or in life.

Rudella's into it since it's a counterpoint to "Battlestar Galactica". "Galactica" is a dystopia about spacefaring to find an old home, trapped in the conflict of two species. "Voyager" is a utopia about spacefaring to find an old home, trapped in the conflict of a galactic quadrant. That "Voyager" starts free of, at the time, 30 years of continuity due to that quadrant being unexplored doesn't hurt. She finds it fitting that the ship looks like a spade since it's space-digging its way back to Earth. She also still doesn't feel the cosmos are her thing. She *also* finds it sad she'll never see Caprica Six and Seven of Nine in the same episode; "Angry Blonde Automatons" would've been killer. At least in Keller.

Unlike with the Verve Pipe, Piri understands the message her subconscious gives her through her urge to watch "Babylon 5" and "Voyager". Watching the former, she understands that she needs to be a fixed point despite what comes her way through therapy. Watching the latter, she understands that she deserves to return to normalcy after being far from herself. Both series ran multiple seasons, back when a season had upwards of 22 episodes, so her subconscious has plenty of food for thought. Which doesn't mean her two years away didn't work; her therapist, Amanda, was and continues to be very helpful. Piri just has subconscious help instead of being her own worst enemy now. The big reason why she didn't see a psychologist until it was too late is because she wanted to be emotionally open and vulnerable only with Rudella. Everyone says revealing yourself is like peeling layers of an onion, but they always forget peeling hurts. A lot. Plus, Rudella didn't have a psychiatric degree, and Piri wasn't as willing an onion as she thought.

Around the middle of Piri's first month back, and the third season of "Voyager", Rudella asks her if she wants to talk about what she'll do once she's adjusted. Piri wants to hear what Rudella will do, instead. The Thanatophile points out they live in a renovated funeral home, and she has a mortuary degree. They have enough money to live comfortably thanks to her smart handling, but she'd like to go back to work. Keller doesn't have a funeral home besides this one, and other towns would also use her services. Despite business coming from those places, she could run the parlor by herself since they're so small. She'd have to give people a reason to come to her, so she was thinking about offering themed funerals along with regular ones. More work, but more fun (and money). She doesn't want to rush Piri through her period of adjustment, though, and doesn't mind waiting.

Piri thanks her girlfriend for being patient, then tells her she had two years to think about what she wanted to do whenever she was better. She wants to help those who society would avoid, if it could, which is why she wants to be a special needs teacher for children. Getting a GED isn't hard, and she could be teaching in as little as two years. That's how long it'd take with the online course she was looking at. Watching the misadventures of Captain Janeway wasn't the only thing she did on the couch: she found a special needs school two towns over, so she won't have to travel far for work. The pay sucks, but no one should want to get rich helping people. Besides, sex work and reselling were great for her bank account, and her insurance took care of her hospital stay.

They kiss, for the first time in a long time, then beam up a new episode while Piri's mind drifts to some of those she left behind.

The Retired

Time and opportunity bring into view the lives of the Whore and the Mender, and what they're up to now.

Holly's hanging up Cassandra Luxx. Not for fear or shame; she learned tons of ways to protect herself in her 20 years of sex work, and sex work was her gig because she loved to fuck. Still does, but fucking for a paying audience lost its thrill. And she has enough money to build a condom castle with an Astroglide moat. Even with her Champagne tastes.

Like any Star Trek captain who survives into retirement, Holly moves away from her crowded life to a cabin in the woods. People allow social media to curate their lives into an echo chamber of lies and misguided rage, and she's tired of getting caught in the noise. She doesn't even bother going to the movies anymore because the fucking idiots don't have manners, and seats don't have trap doors or ejectors.

The cabin isn't enough, though. Not with her tastes. She hasn't moved in yet, so she wanders in and around it in her Dolce&Gabanna jeans (and bear mace with Swarovski crystals) waiting for inspiration. She flashes back to that magical Winter almost twenty years ago, when she saw "Fellowship of the Ring" on the big screen with her other nerd whores. She won't build a condom castle, but she's excited to be the first porn star to own a Hobbit-hole. Her first hole she'll always be happy to stuff.

She considers piggybacking off the research of others to find the basic layout of one... but it's *her* 'hole (heh). She labels and arranges empty sex toy boxes until she figures out what works best for her. Then she takes a picture and explains to a flustered contractor what she wants. He quickly switches to excited when he realizes what she wants AND can afford it. The build will take about seven months, but he'll throw in a cobblestone path for free because it'll look cool.

Back in Chicago, the keys to Tender Revolution are changing hands. Gaspara has done everything she could for the Windy City's discarded women, and she's exhausted. After giving herself since the Towers fell, she's taking her pearls to a place that gives back. But first, the transition period.

When women come back to her, it's not always bad news. Nibs got her nickname because she had a habit of nibbling her pillow while she slept. She also needed four tries before staying clean with the least amount of effort (lest we forget, recovery is always a work in progress). She hasn't touched a drug in eight years, and she turned her life around like Vicki Sue Robinson turned the beat around. She couldn't have done that without Gaspara, and leapt at the chance to repay the unpayable.

Gaspara liked Nibs all the times she stayed at Tender Revolution. She didn't need much minding, and she helped unprompted when things needed to be done. She just couldn't help but fall back into her chemical romance after she left. Eight years is a long time to avoid a toxic ex, though, and Nibs looked better than ever when she showed up to help.

Some would say Gaspara has seen too much of how addiction wrecks women. She definitely would. Despite that, she knows there's a line of empathy she can't cross because she was never an addict. Nibs can, though. When Gaspara sees that, and the women accepting Nibs, and knowing Nibs isn't going anywhere, she asks Nibs if she wants to take over in a few months. She accepts; tearily, because someone finally looks at what she does instead of what she did.

When the day comes to give up the keys, Gaspara finds giving up responsibility harder than she thought. It's a massive pain in the ass, sure, but it's also powerful to know victims trust her enough to put their lives in her hands. Even if the pay is shit. Nibs understands that, and that she has to take the keys, instead. So she does.

Because the pay was shit, Gaspara can't go far for a vacation that took almost two decades to take. Luckily, she just wants to go to the Bahamas by boat. Doubly luckily, her previous line of work gets sympathy from a travel agent. The only reason to be kind is for its own sake. At the same time, you get what you give.

The first thing Holly does when her 'hole is finished is show it off to her nerd whores, in a fancy Cyndi Lauper tee. She's out of the life, not out of their lives. They're as awe-struck and jealous as you think. One wonders how can she hang pictures or posters on curved walls, to which Holly replies with a shrug. Another wonders what it's going to be like to mow her roof since her 'hole is underground, to which Holly replies with a dirty joke. Yet another wonders where the hooch is, to which Holly replies with a gesture to the pantry.

The Ron Zacapa rum flows heartily, though Holly makes sure no one's too drunk to drive home. She doesn't want her first night in her subterranean English cottage to be a sleepover. When she eventually makes everybody leave, one asks if she wants to break in her new place (if you know what I mean [and I think you do]). It's not a sleepover if only two people are in the queen size from Roche Bobois.

A few days of nothing in particular later, Holly sets up her life as a retired sex worker. Mainly, getting another phone line and custom laptop (the best Linux has to offer). She feels it'd be wrong for her decades of whore know-how to wither away in her 'hole (heh), so she sets up a service for sex workers to contact her for advice. She decides to call it "Cheek to Cheek", then feels like she should quit now since she'll never be that smart again. She changes her mind, then tells her friends, who tell their friends, who tell *their* friends. She also tells them to contact her with Signal, a free app that allows complete privacy with calls and texts.

Her first lesson is time management. She didn't make a closing time since she didn't think a lot of sex workers would need her help. More fool her. She almost picks 9-5, which would mean she would have to be up by 9. Fuck that shit with a stolen dick. She settles on the much more manageable 12-6. When some don't get the hint, she turns off her work phone (whatever's high-class and not diddled by the ghost of Steve Jobs).

Holly finds it's fantastic helping her fellow whores. All that time on her back, and knees, is paying off beyond her fat bank account. Strippers are her favorite to talk to; after being their shoulder, they gossip (oh, how they gossip…). News about Cheek to Cheek eventually slips into the mainstream, and she turns down interview requests left and right. Those who need her will find her; the populace treats sex workers, at best, like zoo exhibits. Her days of stabbing uppity bitches and entitled pricks with a corkscrew are over. Why a corkscrew? Because it hurts more.

Fresh off the Florida Keys, Gaspara enjoys the start of her cruise to the Bahamas. Since it's a clear day, she picks a deck chair, warm sun on her brown skin, and reads Vladimir Nabokov's "Ada or Ardor"; his incest epic. A strange choice, sure, but those who don't know it will stay away. As will most who do know it. Those who know it and bother her anyway are the people she wants to talk to. If no one does, she still has a fucked-up book to keep her company. She also makes sure to not spill her virgin margarita; it has lime juice, which can cause second-degree burns if left on skin in the sun.

No one takes the bait, which is fine since she spent almost two decades listening to people. She spends her dinner silently admiring how the grape juice in her glass moves with the ship and reading an article on her phone. A woman was arrested in a $2,000 scam for a Brazilian butt lift after stealing the money from her father, turning it in to the police, saying that she found it, and waiting 90 days to claim it. For some reason, she didn't think her father would report it missing, nor that the police would tell him she found it. Her last words while getting cuffed are something about having celebrity immunity since she's an influencer.

When she gets to an article about sand trafficking, a younger man asks why she's enjoying herself when there are others here who might be as worthwhile. She tells him she would have, but the opportunity never presented itself. He calls himself an opportunity, then asks her for a random fact. She tells Opportunity drug dogs used in shows and movies get depressed when they don't find any, so their handler has to bring some with them. Opportunity laughs, suggesting Fido wants something stronger than belly rubs on the job. Their flirting continues over swaying Welch's and conspiratorial cheese curds. Then she gets his dick wet.

Naïvete isn't a strong suit for Gaspara, so she doesn't expect her one night of Bangkok to be any more than that. Plus, sex was nigh-impossible in Tender Revolution, so she learned how to make the most of it whenever she got it. Like with Opportunity. She leaves his room in the morning, freshens up in hers, and goes back to her deck chair with Nabokov after breakfast.

After a few pages, she gets distracted by the view. Water in every direction, as far as she can see. Living in Chicago, she saw a lot of water east, and that's it. She thinks about what it'd be like to live on Lake Michigan, then she *really* thinks about it. Finding a cheap houseboat that isn't a piece of shit would be the hardest part. As long as she has food and fuel, she could be fine with anchoring in the middle of the lake. Winter would suck, but she could make port somewhere with central heating.

A wad of spit on her pearls assaults Gaspara out of her reverie. Before she can punch whoever did it into the ocean, crew members are already separating them. Amid thoughts of grievous harm, she assumes she ruined a relationship last night. However, the French assailant blames her for bombs the United States dropped in wars the assailant feels are wrong. A symptom of Modern America that infected the world is people make their opinions declarations instead of conversations.

There are almost three million stories in the Windy City; these have been two of them.

Remember "The Fine Print"

Keller welcomes its new and extraordinary daughters better than you assume Small Town America would.

Mostly because its denizens have a strict "you don't bother me, I don't bother you" policy. That doesn't mean attitudes are Antarctic; more like, you won't get an attitude if you don't give one. It's not a town with homogeneous opinions, but no one has to tap the sign. If there's a semblance of homogeny, it's that all the elderly people think Rudella dresses cool. Not that she minds. She finally achieved her ideal style: a wicked amalgam of David Lynch and Tim Burton's sensibilities. Mavis still henna's her hair, but she found a stylist to Bettie Page her hair who was around when the pin-up girl got started. She even uses honey to shape her hair, though Rudella tells her to lay off when the weather's hot and full of flies.

Keller's mayor and trustees know Piri very well. When she learns many municipal problems begin and end at town hall meetings, she makes sure to be at each one. The regulars think the Punk chick with the eye patch is weird, but they come around when she asks the board the right questions. Well... right for everyone but the board. Lots of things get fixed that were put off for months (like more library books), to the point where people ask her to be mayor. She laughs whenever they do, then tells them she's too fucked up for that kind of responsibility.

Before Summer's over, Rudella takes Piri on an oft-delayed trip to Indiana Beach. The Goth makes sure to make the normies suffer her parasol, but they make her suffer them first by way of a rope bridge. It's the only way in and out of the amusement park, dangling over a river and bobbing when jerks jump on it. She's too afraid of falling to go Redneck, so Piri pulls her along and they fun the fuck out of the place. Piri loses Rudella in the gift shop since it's like a small town shoppe, reminding her she lives in a small town with many shoppes. Then they slap each other with elephant ear pastries before eating them and figuring out which is the best worst wedding song: Ludo's "Love Me Dead" or Joy Division's "Twenty Four Hours". You decide.

Piri drives herself to her twice-weekly appointments with Amanda, who's great for her because she knows Piri prefers tough love to typical sympathy. Her Paseo gets spectacular gas mileage. Panic attacks become almost nonexistent, she learns to not bottle things inside, and she becomes Rudella's cosplaying thighhumper again. She also swings from being a light sleeper to practically comatose, such is her comfort with her life. But she knows her problems can't be fixed, only lessened and monitored.

The pain of losing Mur-Mur still pulls at Rudella, which is why the Lilith Pit is cat-less. It's balanced with thanatophilia and all the things Piri brings. Shelves and shelves upon shelves of books and CDs, promises fulfilled. Racks of video games across the decades for her night routines. She didn't bring Rudella back to her geekier days, though that didn't stop her from decorating geekily.

However, she did convince her Thanatophile to acknowledge the anime binder. And she sometimes sings "Odoru Ponpokorin", the wonderfully nonsense opening song of the long-running "Chibi Maruko-chan". A win's a win.

Rudella's given up painting in storage units, and moves onto painting in the basement. She's the only one who goes down there since it's also her mortician space, so she gets the solitude of the unit without a monthly fee. When she's done with a painting, she offers it to the cremator and spreads the ashes in the back yard.

Right now, she's in the middle of a new piece. She still has her painting robe, looking more like sheets of stucco due to all the brushes she wiped off on various places. The stereo on the stool pumps the Power Metal of Unleash the Archer's "Apex". Next to the stereo is a tiny, pink remote with a pulsing red light.

When her appa helped her build the Lilith Pit, it was the first time she noticed how old he looked. When her eomma came to get him, the geriatric realization spread to her. Rudella didn't know how to process her feelings, but knew she had to and trusted she'd find a way before it wrecked her.

She presses the button on the remote; the light pulses faster. Like her paintings up to this point, she didn't approach it with a plan outside of "purge this particular thought". The particular thought takes the time and colors it needs on its way onto canvas. This one needs to be gray. One shade, thin strokes.

Using oil-based paint allows her to create textures by layering her strokes. Two presses; the light pulses slower than it had at the start. What seemed like a dandelion when she began a few days ago is currently patches of cirrus clouds. Since that kind of cloud is usually white, the painting looks sickly. She doesn't know if that means she thinks her bumonim looked that way, but she also doesn't feel she purged anything.

She asks herself how she feels about getting old. Old, not older. Older is a daily occurrence, old is near the end. Death doesn't bother her; it's the end of the party and parties weren't meant to last. She doesn't want to be the drunk in the corner wearing a lampshade, but she wants to get a lot done before heading to the door. And there's nothing past the door. However, that's not *getting* old.

Thinking about it long after the CD ends, she realizes she doesn't know how she feels about getting old. She also realizes that's tied into the painting. Maybe she'll get an answer when she's done. Maybe she won't. Maybe she won't care what the answer is. Maybe she has to use more canvases to get an answer. That's the quirk of art for an artist. What she does know is she's done for now, so she cleans and puts away her brushes, then hangs her robe. On her way upstairs, she grabs the remote and makes the light flutter like a guitar solo.

Higher she goes, to the bedroom, and places the remote atop the Lament Configuration. Therapy doesn't stop Piri from being kinky. The strobing pink goes to the drenched, vibrating panties she's wearing, limbs bound to each bedpost with velvet rope. The name of the game is "orgasm denial"; as in, Her Mistress demands she deny herself from having an orgasm. Even as a makeup brush dances, tickling and sensuous, across her nipples. A cruel game, yes, but one she plays long after words become meaningless. She wouldn't have it any other way.

Time goes on. Rudella and Piri kiss on their fifth New Year's together. They watch "Fisher King" after their regularly scheduled "World's End" because insomnia sets in. Piri's never seen it, like a lot of movies, so she's taken by surprise by the most romantic film directed by a cynic. Terry Gilliam doesn't shy away from or look down at the love story, but he also strips away all sentimentality that could easily overwhelm it (for a Richard LaGravenese script about a '90s NYC romance with Jeff Bridges [what a niche] with sentimentality left in, see "Mirror Has Two Faces"). Piri overidentifies with Parry, the homeless eccentric in love with a working eccentric, for obvious reasons, and ends up crying through half a roll of toilet paper.

Still lousy with insomnia, Rudella pops in the most unromantic romantic film directed by a cynic: "War of the Roses". Danny DeVito takes Michael J. Leeson's adaptation of Warren Adler's novel about divorce and squeezes every satirical drop from it. You'd think it's relationship suicide, seeing it with a lover, but Piri laughs as much as Rudella. Laughs all the way to sleep.

Time goes on. The 'Rona makes its presence known, people are too selfish to listen to reason, and the world shuts down. Rudella put off buying more paint, so she ran out before buying more at the now-closed hobby shoppe. She's too loyal to buy elsewhere, so she finds other ways to occupy her time. Like keeping Jenkins' Death Babble alive. Or biking and 'blading with Piri. Or camping in the back yard with her.

You already know what happens around now, dear reader, so let's pop in on Piri the day of the census taker. She's on the pink-and-black striped couch, listening to the latest podcast from Bacon Slater. He's a liberal shock jock she found a while ago, and he's currently laying into loud, ignorant people in grocery store lines who're a kick to the back of the head away from being no one's problem. Then he segues into why "welfare queen" is racist. Rudella's in the garage, carefully separating her lavish black clothes before washing them like their tags demand, and watching "Versus" (the best yakuza-vs.-zombies flick ever). Then there's a rapping at the chamber door.

Piri wonders who the fuck is at the door, then where the fuck is her surgical mask and hand sanitizer, then who the fuck is at the door. After strapping in and rubbing down, she finds the answer to her first and last questions. The masked woman with a clipboard introduces herself as a census taker, and Piri has to remind herself who that is.

CT tells Piri this will only take a few minutes for everyone over 18 who lives here, which is much shorter than she thought it'll be. Piri tells her there's just her and Rudella, and CT is glad this'll be much shorter than she thought it'll be. They get through a few questions easy peasy... until "Nationality".

American, born and raised. CT reminds Piri she can say "Latina" or "Hispanic", which gets a raised eyebrow and a repeat of her answer. CT doesn't check the box. Instead, she looks at Piri with a growing sense of confusion and frustration. Having the lower half of her face covered makes the gaze more prominent. CT asks Piri why she's ashamed to claim our people, then something clicks in the Punk. A few somethings, actually.

Staying calm, Piri asks CT if she knows how many more of "her people" than everyone else helped her when she was homeless. Shared their food with no strings attached. Gave her change when she asked. Came to save her the times she was raped and cried for help. Acknowledged her existence. None. Every race and creed treated her like shit for over a decade, and the tone of her flesh did her no favors.

After apologizing for bringing up bad memories, CT asks Piri why she isn't angry with all Americans. Piri asks her what makes her sure she isn't. CT doesn't understand why Piri claims to be American if she's angry at them. Piri tells her it's because she was born here, but if she wants to play the hereditary game, her ancestors were on the continent first. When it was Turtle Island.

A laugh of disbelief puffs from CT's mask, then she says Indians can't be her ancestors since they didn't speak Spanish. Piri shares some facts she got from a torn cover. Native Americans lived in North and South America before the Conquistadors came with their raping, pillaging, murdering, and Spanish. Spanish is a Latin language and *that's* where Latino, Latina, and Latinx come from; it's not a suburb in Mexico.

The Conquistadors brutalized the original cultures of the Americas, to the point where even their religions were demonized. Piri says she laughs when anyone says they're proud of their Latin heritage wearing a cross since she knows Tezcatlipoca, the Aztec god of providence, is flipping a table somewhere.

Never being anything but calm, she adds that she isn't judging anyone who claims to be Latin, Hispanic, or what new titles come down the pike. She hasn't lived their lives; plus, the titles are meaningful and help people. Trying to steal their identities would make her no better than the Conquistadors.

Having eaten CT's liver with some fava beans and a nice Chianti, Piri asks what the next question is.

A Lemon-Sized Disaster

In which Rudella runs out of distractions and excuses to take care of a tenacious pain, yet must still contend with fear.

Science eventually triumphs enough over disease that the world can open again, permanently. Keller survives mostly intact because of their unofficial motto, and because they know being such a small town means they're at the bottom of the help list if a 'Rona outbreak happened.

The first thing Rudella does is rush to the hobby shoppe and beauty parlor; partially because of old habits, and partially to make sure everyone there survived. You can split that fraction. The first thing Piri does is rush to the diner for funnel cake. She knows everyone there survived because she checked in during both lockdowns. Also, the ladies are now frozen pizza snobs: Corner Booth or nothing.

Adapting to the new old normal is interesting. Rudella spent most of the lockdowns loaning her mortuary space to nearby towns, so she forgot how she handled Distant Traveler's

Funeral Home by herself, although it was open for a few weeks before the world shut down. Because of that, she decides she needs help. Someone twixt a soldier and a secretary. She doesn't expect her ad to get a reply so quickly in so remote a place, and she's right. When Abrienda does call, however, she's most welcome. The death hippie's a little older than Rudella and doesn't have the degrees to handle decedents, but she's willing to help however else she can for a little money and a place to stay. Rudella lets her move into the attic after Piri gives her the once-over, and warning about corpse cops.

While on the subject, Piri gets her online degree to teach special needs kids, and wastes no time applying to Rain or Shine Center two towns over. They gladly accept her and tell her she can start as an aid the next day. She gets all the supplies she'll need, hangs her semi-professional attire on a chair, then goes to bed early. When it's time to leave… she can't find the will to open the front door. Once she does, everything changes and a stream of children few want to help will depend on her and her understanding until they graduate. The potential responsibility is crippling. Something Amanda told her pops into her head: when she's overwhelmed by a choice she made, she should remind herself that she wanted it. She does, then she opens the door.

Time marches on. Rudella and Piri settle into their new rhythms. Abrienda starts to feel restless. Being Rudella's right hand, or as much of one as she can be without a degree, is what she needs. She doesn't mind tedious work like checking supplies and answering the phone. At the same time, she wants to do more for the funeral home. Mortuary school is out of the question since it's too expensive and too far. An idea comes to her from the Victorian Age she's excited to share.

Death was omnipresent to the Victorians. If she had a TARDIS, Rudella would kiss now farewell and spend the rest of her life time-looped in that era. A thanatotic remnant from then is the memento mori: photographs people took with their dead loved ones.

She kicks herself for not thinking of it when Abrienda suggests she do it. She could still take the idea since it'll be annoying to handle the decedents for customers only to back away for the camera… but she's a boss bitch, not a bitch boss. Abrienda is grateful, and the two geek-out while they plan.

Seeing Rudella and Abrienda connect in ways she never can gets to Piri a little. She isn't a jealous woman, but she knows who she has and how hard she worked to keep her. She knows Rudella wouldn't cheat on her, but she doesn't know if Abrienda wouldn't be a temptress. Enough bad romance novels begin that way for her to be unable to shake away the thought.

After another giggle fit about death and dying twixt the funeral staff, she asks Abrienda if she could help her in the kitchen. Piri tells her, friendly yet terse, what's on her mind. Abrienda doesn't want to fuck up what anyone has, including herself, so she puts out that spark before it turns into smoke. Satisfied, Piri asks Abrienda to get plates from the top of the cabinet.

Distant Traveler's has a peculiar schedule. It closes for three days each month, and the people of Keller believe it's for professional reasons. However, it's due to the blinding, nauseating pain Rudella suffers because of her endometriosis. For years, she threatens to get a hysterectomy but, even when she can afford it, she convinces herself that the longer she stands the pain, the less she cares. Plus, despite the science and the obvious relief, she's afraid of getting cut open.

It's never easy for Piri to see Rudella agonize during her period, but she always does what she can. Abrienda, being new, doesn't have a grasp of nature's cruelty to her boss. They may connect through death, but there's a wall of professionalism between them. Because of these things, she simply accepts her breaks and tries to stay out of Piri's way.

After one of the rougher periods, Piri brings up getting a hysterectomy. Again. She tells Rudella it's silly to keep something that wrecks her so badly when she can get rid of it so effortlessly. Rudella points out that surgery isn't effortless, and Piri tells her she knows what she means. Rudella tries to change the subject, then fails when asked a question:

"Is this what you want?"

If the tables were reversed-- The tables *were* reversed, and Rudella didn't leave Piri convulsing on their bedroom floor. Having nowhere to go, Rudella admits she's afraid of getting cut open, despite the countless times she's done it to corpses. Or, maybe it's because she's done it to corpses. For her, that's the step before putting them in a box or an oven.

She didn't realize that until now, and it's like seeing her reflection for the first time. She doesn't like what she sees, so she tries to hide from it. Piri won't let her, though. Neither does she push her. She stands by her girlfriend until she's comfortable with her reflection, and can finally get the help she needs.

If you have someone like Rudella or Piri in your life, as a lover or as a friend, appreciate the lucky fact of their existence. A lot can go wrong in life to keep you from them, and you can always fuck them up and out of your life. Your connection can also be finite, ending in a day, in a year, or in death. But having them in your life, for however long they stay, is a rare gift.

Don't ruin it.

If you don't have someone like them, the world is massive and you are small. To think no one out there understands nor wants you is foolish. They're there, and they want to know you. The annoying catch is they find you when you're not looking. The best you can do is remind yourself of two things. No one likes a piece of shit, so try to be a decent human being. The other?

You are worthy.

Rathan Krueger is a mythmaker, heathen, and ginger-enthusiast. His father took him to see "Alien^3" when he was six, and hasn't been right since. Token hetero.

Thought my novel was cool? I'm glad it was able to do something for you. It'll be swell if you tell people who'll also get a kick out of it, and give it a good rating where you bought it.

Thought it sucked? No hard feelings, everything isn't for everyone. Maybe I'll get you with the next one.